RAVES FOR *REAPING REDEMPTION*

Reaping Redemption's pacing is spot on with the right mix of intense action and hard-hitting emotional moments. The mystery reveals twists that are surprising but earned. Noyes writes action scenes that feel immediate and real, almost cinematic, but she never loses sight of the emotional stakes. *Reaping Redemption* is an intense, thought-provoking read with meaningful character growth, and I strongly recommend it to readers who love smart, character-driven thrillers.

- K.C. Finn
Reader's Favorite 5 Star

Sure to be embraced by fans of the genre, *Reaping Redemption* is a gripping crime/conspiracy thriller jam-packed with twists and turns. Using a fast-paced narrative, Christine Noyes spins a captivating tale of murder, crime, and mayhem centered around a gifted FBI analyst struggling to come to terms with his past. Not a dull moment in the book! Fans of thrillers should not miss out on this series.

- Pikasho Deka
Reader's Favorite 5 Star

Christine Noyes has a captivating writing style that had me engrossed from beginning to end. With fast-paced action and *Reaping Redemption's* genuine and relatable characters, I struggled to put the book down. I found great enjoyment in reading this novel.

- Alma Boucher
Reader's Favorite 5 Star

REAPING REDEMPTION

also by Christine Noyes

Close Enough to Perfect
a memoir

A Picture of Pretense
a Bradley Whitman novel

Shadow in the Sandpit
a Bradley Whitman novel

Meet Your Maker
a Bradley Whitman novel

Pathside Predator
a Bradley Whitman novel

Winter Meets Summer
a romantic comedy

for children
A Big Al Bear Hug
Big Al Helps Clean the Park
Big Al's Treasure
The Case of the Missing Cooler
Big Al Coloring Book

coming in 2025
Maestro's Move
a Bradley Whitman novel

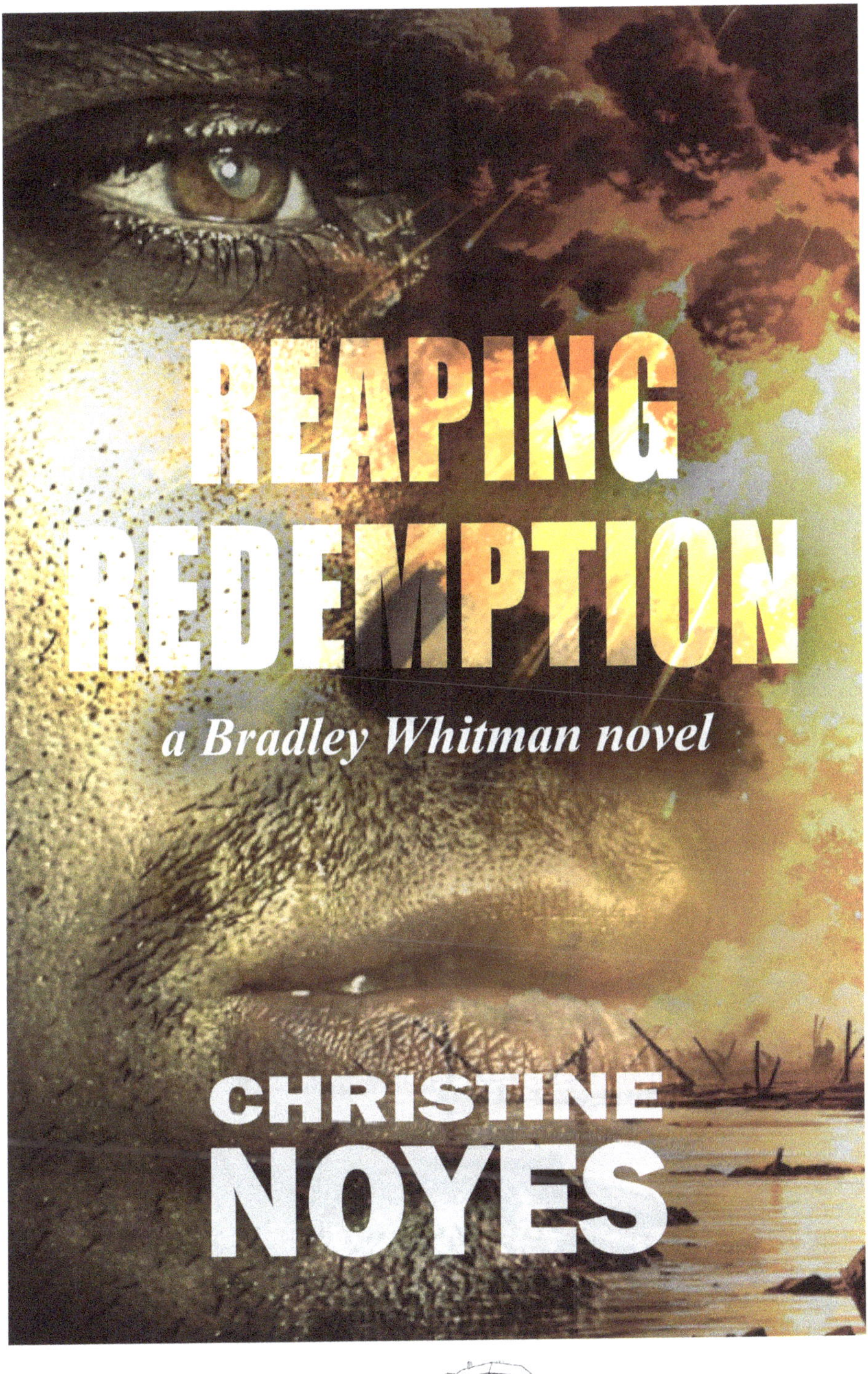

REAPING REDEMPTION

a Bradley Whitman novel

CHRISTINE NOYES

Haley's

Athol, Massachusetts

Haley's
488 South Main Street
Athol, MA 01331
marcia2gagliardi@gmail.com • 978.249.9400

Copy edited by Debra Ellis.

Cover designed by Christine Noyes. Cover photos courtesy of Pixabay.

International Standard Book Number, trade paperback: 978-1-956055-27-6

International Standard Book Number, eBook, Kindle: 978-1-956055-24-5

Library of Congress Cataloging-in-Publication Data pending

For everyone who has been knocked down and gotten back up.
And for Al, forever in my heart.

CONTENTS

NO SAYING NO

Although the man didn't reveal a weapon, his warrior disposition could not be questioned. He stood with arms crossed upon his puffed-out chest and shoulders drawn back to accentuate his thickly corded neck. A square chin thrust toward the camera, and he held his head high. What first appeared to be fog showed tiny fragments of structural debris swirling around him in the light breeze. Bloodied body parts lay at his feet.

Drawing attention to his surroundings with the wave of his hand he spoke in perfect deep-throated English. "This is your destiny. You cannot escape it, for it has already begun."

Derek studied the man in the latest of several videos. Each of Ali al Haqani's communications played more ominous than the previous. As FBI executive assistant director of criminal, cyber, response, and services, Derek had viewed every reel with disquietude.

Derek turned to his FBI National Security Branch counterpart. "The messages you intercepted. Has your team been able to decode them?"

Sam Houghton shook his head, "No. That's why I'm here. That guy you told me about. Whitman. Can you get him here?"

Derek paused. He didn't know how receptive Bradley would be to his call.

It had been a year since, hoping to disappear, Bradley took leave of absence from the FBI. Derek responded, "I'll do my best."

Watching the sun rise over the peaks of the Himalayan mountains may have been the most spiritual experience of Bradley Whitman's thirty-five years. For all the trouble it took to get him there— waking at 2:30 that morning, packing his wheelchair into the jeep, and bouncing in the passenger seat while his driver navigated the narrow, cratered road through the darkened pine forest—it was worth it.

"Rajesh, you were right," Bradley spoke softly.

His driver responded, "There is nothing more beautiful on this earth."

The orange glow awakened the deep blue sky and cast a golden hue on the valley below. Bradley could detect no beginning nor end to the panoramic masterpiece.

Darjeeling in the state of West Bengal, India, is known for both growing tea and the sunrise view from its highest point atop Tiger Hill. Among snow-capped mountains basking in the early morning rays stood Mounts Kanchenjunga, Makalu, and Everest.

Bradley couldn't think of a time when he felt more serene. He had been searching for exactly that feeling, and it seemed he had found where he needed to be.

He reached for his traveling companion, a black and rust colored Doberman Pinscher named Rusty, and stroked his head.

"What do you think, boy?" he asked the dog.

Rusty gazed at the sun, cast a quick glance toward Bradley, then back at the sun. Much like Bradley, Rusty apparently did not wish to interrupt the harmony of the moment.

A stillness overtook Bradley. He could discern no time or weight of his own presence—only being. He no longer felt foreign to his surroundings as he had since an enterovirus doomed him to a wheelchair at the age of six. At that moment, he felt part of them. For an hour, they sat quietly before Rajesh reminded Bradley of their next destination.

Bradley stirred from his tranquility. "Ah, yes. Batasia Loop and the n-gauge train." Bradley engaged the throttle of his PW-4x4Q all-terrain power wheelchair. The electric motor lightly whirred as Rusty walked alongside toward Rajesh's jeep.

Bradley had hired Rajesh and his vehicle for the duration of his visit to India. Due to his previous difficulty maneuvering through Bhutan, for the present leg of his journey, Bradley planned ahead. By hiring Rajesh, he'd hoped to avoid similar disappointment.

"Jump in, boy," Bradley said to Rusty when they reached the Jeep.

Rusty, wearing his red service dog vest, leapt into the passenger seat then continued into the back seat. Rajesh lifted Bradley from his chair and into the Jeep's front passenger seat. He used a ramp to load Bradley's chair into the vehicles short truck bed then strapped it down.

"He's in India," Derek said to his executive assistant, Madelyn Cross.

"I thought he disappeared. Your wife told me you didn't know where he was," Madelyn exclaimed.

"Cate doesn't know that I know," Derek explained. "But I've been keeping tabs on his travels."

"Ah. It's best you keep that to yourself. Cate will be furious with you if she finds out."

"She's not the only one who's going to be furious," he said, thinking of Bradley's request that no one try to find him. "I'm going to need a plane. Gather every piece of information we have on Ali al-Haqani. I have a classified folder that will have to make it onto the jet before it leaves. I want it up in the air in an hour. I'll have the go-ahead of the director by then."

"Classified?" Madelyn raised a brow.

"Officially, Bradley's been away on medical leave," Derek said. "The director and I decided to leave the door open for his return—another reason I've been keeping an eye on him. He's still got clearance. I just need to re-activate him before he looks at any classified documents. So, I need to talk to him as soon as possible. Even if someone needs to track him down. We can't wait for a messenger."

"Do you know where in India he is?" she asked.

"The Sterling Darjeeling hotel, Ghoom, West Bengal."

Madelyn peered over her notepad. "Keeping very close tabs, I'd say."

"I just wanted to make sure he was okay," Derek said, feeling her questioning gaze.

"I'll get right on it," she replied.

In the daylight after his magical morning experience, Bradley enjoyed the bumpy ride back through the pine forest. "I've been looking forward to this train ride. I hear the views are spectacular. Have you ever been on the train, Rajesh?"

"No, I never found the time."

"Come with us today. No sense in you just waiting around for me."

"I've made plans to meet my son while I wait," Rajesh explained.

Bradley smiled. "That's nice. Family is important." A stitch of guilt slipped through Bradley's happiness armor.

4

Rajesh's cellphone rang.

"Yes, . . . who? . . . when? . . . okay, give him the number." Rajesh hung up the phone and handed it to Bradley.

"Someone is trying to get in touch with you. They said it was important," Rajesh said as he drove.

Ten minutes later, the phone rang, and Bradley answered.

"Bradley, it's Derek."

Bradley paused, "How did you . . . what's wrong? Is everyone alright?"

"Yes, everyone is fine. But we do have a . . . situation."

"What kind of situation?" Bradley asked.

"A classified one. I need you, Bradley."

"Derek, I don't think . . . "

"I know, but I need you," Derek stated emphatically.

Bradley closed his eyes and sighed. After a short pause he replied, "Alright. I'll catch the next flight home."

"I've got a plane on its way. It'll arrive tomorrow at Bagdogra International Airport at 3:30 p.m., your time. I'll send you what I can now. The classified material will be on the plane with Agent Noor. She can answer any questions you have. Bradley."

"Yeah."

"I'll have to reinstate you," Derek said, tentatively.

Another pause. "I understand."

The line went dead. And just like that, Bradley was back in and there was nothing he could do about it. He couldn't say no. Derek was like a brother to him. And Bradley knew Derek would not have called if it weren't of the utmost importance. It didn't surprise him that Derek knew exactly where to find him.

"Rajesh, I'm afraid we have a change of plans."

A NUMBERS GAME

Back at the hotel, Bradley booted his laptop and connected to the secure FBI site. Along with what little history they knew about Ali al-Haqani, Derek had posted al-Haqani's Massachusetts' Hopkinton Engineering Institute's chemical engineering thesis, HEI transcripts, and four videos from Al Jazeera television for him to view.

He read and reread the documents and watched the videos multiple times. He didn't know exactly what situation the FBI faced, but he was certain it was deadly.

Standing tall and rigid in the videos, Ali al-Haqani projected body language providing Bradley all he needed to see to know the man posed a threat. The Afghani didn't rant and rave like some extremists. He spoke slowly and methodically, enunciating each word to impress its importance. If he had a speechwriter, Bradley thought, that person did a very good job. But Bradley didn't get the impression that al-Haqani would speak anyone else's words. Along with al-Haqani's imposing posture, his manner indicated that he could most likely recite his dissertation with authority and without the text.

Although that's not the typical garb for a graduate of the prestigious Hopkinton Engineering Institute, Bradley thought. This looks more like a CIA problem than FBI. Unless he's on American soil.

Bradley felt the familiar sensation of darkness within—a heaviness seeping through his chest like thick black sludge enveloping the sun and snuffing out the light.

Rusty instinctively came to his side and placed a paw on Bradley's leg. Although Bradley's paralysis prevented him from feeling the weight of Rusty's limb, he could sense the sentiment behind it, and it made him smile.

"I'm okay, buddy. Thanks," he said as he stroked Rusty's head.

Bradley put the laptop aside and began to meditate, a practice he had recently instituted in Tibet. With his eyes closed and his arms resting palms up on his chair, he focused on his breathing.

Rusty silently lay beside him.

After a brief period of silence, Bradley imagined himself alone on a beach at sunset. He summoned the feeling of heat from the sand on the bottom of his bare feet as he stood and looked to the sea. Just as the sun dipped below the horizon, she appeared from the ocean and walked toward him. She looked beautiful in a white, flowing gown that somehow remained dry. It blew in the breeze with her long brunette hair.

They outstretched their arms to each other.

As always, the vision ended there. He never gets to hold the hands of the woman he loves, the woman he was supposed to marry nearly ten months before. She fades before his eyes and eases him back to reality.

His eyes still closed, he sighed, "Laney." Then he smiled. The heaviness in his chest faded with her, and Bradley picked up his laptop and continued.

The following afternoon, Bradley and Rusty boarded the Cessna Citation jet that Derek had sent and, within minutes, were on their way to DC. As promised, Agent Noor, tall and slender with caramel skin and long black hair tied in a ponytail, greeted Bradley on board and provided him with a file folder containing classified documents.

After introductions, Bradley asked, "What can you tell me about the case, Agent Noor?"

"We have confirmed intelligence reports that an attack on American soil is imminent. Our information points to two bombs."

"Dirty bombs?" Bradley asked.

"Only speculation at this point."

"And what do we know about Ali al Haqani?"

Agent Noor read from her own file. "He's a relative newcomer but is quickly building his extremist network. He's an Afghan citizen, grew up in Asadabad, but went to college in the states at Hopkinton Engineering Institute in Massachusetts. He graduated nine years ago with a master's degree in chemical engineering. After graduation, his passport shows him traveling to Saudi Arabia, Pakistan, and then back to Afghanistan.

"We nearly intercepted a couple of his men at the Port of Houston, but they managed to slip away. We missed them by minutes." Agent Noor gritted her teeth and shook her head.

"You were there?" Bradley asked.

"Yes. We found the abandoned warehouse where they built the bombs. The building scanned positive for radioactive substances. You'll find pictures of the remnants in the folder. It's just a matter of time before they detonate them."

"Do you know who these people are?" Bradley asked.

"Just that they're followers of Ali al-Haqani. They received coded messages from al-Haqani himself. When I said we just missed them, I meant it. They left in a hurry. We found these." Agent Noor pulled two pieces of paper from the folder and handed them to Bradley.

Seeing Arabic writing, Bradley asked, "Have these been translated?"

"Yes." Once again Agent Noor pulled a sheet from the folder. "It's just a list of numbers. Our people haven't been able to find any pattern, sequence, or key to unlock the code."

"How certain are you that Ali al-Haqani is behind the attack?" Bradley asked.

"He's using homegrown terrorists directed by the two guys who managed to get away. We captured and interrogated one of the Americans at the warehouse. Trust me. He told us everything he knew, which wasn't much. Just that he heard the others talking about getting the information about the targets from al-Haqani. We're still trying to identify his two men and the other Americans. They were careful not to share their own names or personal information but didn't seem worried about using al-Haqani's name."

"I might need to talk to the American in custody," Bradley said.

"That's way above my pay grade. You'll need to speak with my boss."

"Derek won't be a problem."

"Who's Derek?"

Bradley sat up straight and peered at Agent Noor. "Who exactly is your boss, Agent Noor?"

"Executive Assistant Director Houghton."

"Director of what division?"

"National Security Branch."

"Why am I here then?" Bradley asked.

"I don't know, sir."

"My name is Bradley, Agent."

"Call me Naila. You must be pretty important for them to send Cessy for you."

"Cessy?" Bradley eyed Naila.

She chuckled. "That's just our nickname for the jet. What's your dog's name?"

"That's Rusty," Bradley replied. Rusty lifted his head when he heard his name. "He definitely appreciates Cessy. The trip over on the commercial airline was much less comfortable for him."

Bradley flipped through documents from the file folder and pulled a picture of Ali al-Haqani from the stack. He recognized the photo as a still from the latest video dated July 25.

"Naila, what's the date today?" Bradley asked.

"Back home it's August 7."

"How long have you had this information? The codes, specifically."

"This is day thirteen."

"I'm a last resort," Bradley sighed.

"Excuse me?"

"They're running out of time, and for some reason Derek thinks I may be able to help," Bradley explained.

"Are you talking about Executive Assistant Director Derek Richards?" Naila asked.

"The one and only."

"Yes, sir—I mean Bradley. It was his office that sent me the file folder. Can you?"

"Can I what?"

"Can you crack it?"

"I guess we'll find out. Have you got a laptop?"

"I do."

"Boot it up. Let's get to work," Bradley said as he turned on his own computer.

They had another eighteen hours before landing in Washington. Bradley hoped to have something to contribute by the time they arrived.

He browsed information from the folder, including details on attempts to break the code. The national security team had tried replacing letters for numbers in ascending, descending, and many variations of order. They still attempted a theory having to do with book chapters, pages, and words using the Quran, Bible, and Talmud among other possible texts, a long, tedious process even when using computers.

Bradley decided not to rule anything out. He needed to start fresh. Naila had handed him two separate messages which, Bradley thought, likely meant two different targets. And, with the amount of time that had already passed, he knew they didn't have much left.

He examined the format of numbers in one of the messages: 16:14;9-14:18;19-1:18;21-14:12;20-14:11;19-5:10;2-2:17;28

"The consistently spaced hyphens makes it pretty clear that it's a three-digit code—seven words or characters. What would our terrorists need to know?" Bradley considered the information the message might contain. "Where, when, and how?"

"Well, we know how," Naila said. "With a bomb."

"Yes, but I'm sure there are multiple plans in place— contingency plans. The smart ones always have them. And al-Haqani is smart—and very precise."

"What makes you say that?"

"The details in his thesis are extreme, almost over-the-top," Bradley explained. A thought occurred to him as the words came from his mouth. They were looking for a key, a document or book that he may have used to create the code. "Maybe the thesis is the key. Let's start with that."

Both opened the file containing al-Haqani's college thesis.

"Alright, Naila, how many pages is it?"

"Ninety-two."

"An over-achiever. How many chapters?"

"Eight."

"So, chapters wouldn't figure into it," Bradley stated.

"Why not?"

"If you look at all the first numbers, then second numbers and third, they each contain a number higher than eight. It wouldn't work."

"Of course. Okay. I see what you're getting at now. What about page, paragraph, and word . . . or letter?" Naila asked.

"Let's see. Page two only has six paragraphs. No. I think our best bet is to try page, line, and letter. Let's see if it spells out a word. I'll take the first four sets of numbers. You take the last three."

Bradley and Naila went to work. Their first attempt produced garble. They continued to test different formats on the thesis without success. An hour later, Bradley suggested they abandon the prospect that the key to the code involved al-Haqani's thesis.

"Al-Haqani will use something personal. Something important to him. He's arrogant and egocentric with a messiah complex, the trilogy of terrorists," Bradley said. "As he sees it, it's all about him saving the world for his people. Someone with that kind of complex will risk everything to succeed."

Bradley suddenly flashed back to a memory of himself lying on the floor in his Revere, Massachusetts, home, blood leaking from his leg and shoulder and deep gashes in his head. A dead man lay beside him.

He shook the memory away and reminded himself that he had become a different person.

"How do you know all this about him?" Naila asked.

"The truth is, I don't know, exactly. But I profiled him from his writings, videos, and body language."

"So, you're a profiler?"

"I'm a problem solver. I'm happiest when I'm knee-deep in data, whether it's words or numbers. I'm a fact geek, a profiler, and miner of information."

"You might be just what we need," Naila said.

"I hope you're right. But I know one thing. We don't have enough time to guess what he used as a key to this code. I need to do a deep dive on Ali al-Haqani. While I'm doing that, I've got some other ideas. You don't happen to read Arabic, do you?"

"Who do you think translated those two messages."

"Perfect. Nine out of ten times these things come back to religion. I think the next key we should try is the Quran, but in Arabic print. The word and letter placements are different in the English translation. So using the same method, why don't you see what you come up with?"

"Got it," Naila said and immediately went to work.

Bradley then began researching the history of Asadabad during the time of al-Haqani's childhood.

CONFESSIONS

When Derek took the job as executive assistant director, he did so with the stipulation that he could work from the Chelsea, Massachusetts, FBI headquarters and make monthly trips to DC. But the trips became more frequent and unbearable.

Tired of traveling back and forth from their home in Medford, Massachusetts and staying in DC hotels, Derek and Cate purchased a townhome on S Street NW only twelve minutes from Derek's office in the J. Edgar Hoover building.

Originally, Cate stayed in Massachusetts while Derek traveled and accompanied him only occasionally. But, as Cate soon learned, crises in the country seemed to be nonstop, and her time with Derek dwindled. Cate gave up her volunteer work at Revere Enhancement and Community Housing, otherwise known as REACH, to move to DC with Derek. They kept their home in Medford and returned as often as they could.

She missed working at the tiny home community that housed and fed the homeless. REACH was the idea of Bradley's friend Zayt, a three-tour veteran of the war in Afghanistan. When Cate originally heard his proposal, she didn't hesitate to lend expertise from her former career in hospitality management. She was instrumental in designing and setting up the kitchen, dining hall, and order and delivery systems.

Since moving to Washington, she had yet to find something to fill the void. The problem was never knowing on any given day if she would be in the Commonwealth or the District of Columbia. It wasn't like she could do such volunteering via Zoom.

Cate decided to talk to Derek about selling their house in Massachusetts and making DC their permanent home. Derek had only made the original arrangement so she could keep her job at REACH. Now she wondered if Derek ever thought about cutting ties.

It was nearly 8 p.m. by the time Derek walked through the door. Cate waited until they sat at the dinner table before she broached the subject.

"Derek."

"Cate."

They spoke simultaneously, then shared a laugh.

Derek said, "Go ahead. You first."

Cate began, "Well, I've been thinking. I'm not working anymore and, with Bradley gone, there's really nothing keeping us in Massachusetts. What do you think about making this our permanent home?"

Derek sat back in his chair. "You mean give up the house?"

"Yes. Your work is here. And my job with REACH and Bradley were the major reasons we didn't make the move in the first place. I'm done with the job and Bradley is God knows where. There's really no reason not to move," Cate reasoned.

"How long have you been thinking about this?"

"Oh, the last couple of months, I guess."

"What about Lynn and Doug?"

"We haven't seen Bradley's parents since he left. How different would things be?" Cate said.

"And Holly, John, Mike, and Olivia?"

"Old friends will always be old friends, honey. We could still see them on occasion. We'd just have to travel a little further."

Derek grew quiet. Cate could see he struggled with something.

"What is it, Derek?" she asked.

"Cate, I think you should go home."

Cate's perfectly trimmed brows raised. "What?"

"I want you to go back to Massachusetts for a little while. You could give Zayt a hand at the REACH community. And this could be the perfect time to decide whether you really want to sell the house." Derek tried to maintain a neutral expression.

"What are you talking about?"

"It's just that I'm going to be working 24/7 for the foreseeable future. and I'll feel terrible if you're sitting here alone in this place. If you go home, you could volunteer. You could see Lynn and Doug, maybe even get together with Holly."

Cate sensed something more behind Derek's comment, though he tried hard not to show it. She slouched in her chair with her head tilted and eyes squinched. "What's going on, Derek?"

"Nothing. I just think you will be more comfortable at home while I'm working."

"You may be able to keep secrets, but you're a lousy liar. There's a reason you want me to leave, but you can't tell me. Which means it's work related and you're probably trying to protect me."

Derek lowered his eyes.

Cate continued. "Remember the limousine? When that maniac planted the bomb that nearly killed us both? We promised to always stay together because when we are together, nothing can hurt us. I'm not going home."

Derek leaned forward and concentrated his gaze on Cate's emerald-green eyes. "This could be much bigger than a pipe bomb in a tailpipe, Cate."

"I don't care. If you're staying, so am I. And that's the end of it."

"I really want you to . . ."

"Give it a rest, Derek. I'm not going."

Derek stared at his plate and pushed the food around before he spoke again. "In that case, you may want to get the guest room ready."

"Guest room? For who?"

"Bradley will be here tomorrow night. With Rusty." Derek peered at Cate without lifting his head.

Cate's voice raised two octaves. "Bradley? He's home?"

"Not quite yet, but he's on his way."

Excitedly, Cate asked, "When did he call you? Why didn't you tell me?" Then she realized Derek wasn't going to tell her. He wanted her to leave.

"He didn't call . . . " Derek started to say.

Cate's demeanor turned cold. "You weren't going to tell me. You were going to send me home and not tell me Bradley was here? Derek? Is that what you were going to do?"

"No. Yes. No. I was going to wait to see if Bradley wanted people to know he was here before I said anything."

"People? I'm just one of the people?" Cate's eyes pinched and her nose flared. She jumped from her chair and stormed into the kitchen.

His chin resting on his chest, his eyes closed, and with a heavy sigh, Derek pondered his next move. He could get it all out in the open now and produce one major argument, or he could dribble it out a little at a time and fight many small ones.

He slowly stood and walked into the kitchen.

Cate stood by the counter. With excessive force, she threw pots and containers into the sink.

Derek said, "He didn't call me. I called him."

Her hand in midair about to chuck a plastic storage container into the sink, Cate froze. She slowly lowered her arm and placed the container on the counter. She turned. Her cheeks burned the color of an heirloom tomato ripe for picking.

"And how was it that you called him when neither one of us knew where he was?" Cate asked, knowing she would not like the answer.

"I've been tracking him."

"Tracking him? All this time? You've known where he was this whole year and didn't bother to share that with me?"

"Yes."

Cate's eyes began to well. Hurt replaced her anger.

Derek could deal with Cate being angry, but it killed him to see how much he hurt her. "Cate, I'm sorry. I was trying to do right by Bradley while still making sure he was okay. And, because of his clearance, I had to keep an eye on . . ."

With a sense of disbelief, Cate seethed, "Don't you dare, Derek! Don't use your work to . . . I'm tired of it. All those times I wondered if Bradley was okay, and you never said a word. I've been scared to death something might have happened to him. I'd ask myself how we would know if he got hurt—or sick?" Cate's body lost rigidity, as if all her energy drained. "But I guess it didn't matter how worried I was because you knew he was alright." She shuffled toward the stairs.

"Cate, I'm sorry."

Cate never looked back. She slowly ascended the stairs to their bedroom.

Feeling deflated, Derek returned to the dining room to clear the dinner table. But nothing could cleanse his palpable feeling of guilt.

LANDING ON HIS FEET

They would land at Ronald Reagan Washington National Airport in less than two hours. Although Bradley believed they were on the right track to find the key, they had made little progress breaking the code. They needed more time.

Bradley and Naila worked their way through several documents and books including the Quran, Talmud, and Bible. Because each of the writings existed in different print and language versions, the task proved extremely cumbersome.

Neither Bradley nor Naila had slept since they left India seventeen hours earlier.

"Why don't you get some rest, Naila. We'll be landing soon, and I have a feeling that things are going to get more hectic once we do."

"I think I will take a quick nap. You should, too," Naila replied.

"I will. Soon."

But Bradley knew he wouldn't. Bradley possessed a tenacious personality. Once he sunk his teeth into something, he refused to give in, which oftentimes led him to make poor choices with his physical health and safety. And that, along with the unexpected death of his fiancée, is what prompted him to take a leave of absence from the FBI.

"I'm missing something. I can feel it. It's here. Somewhere in all this information is the key to the key," he whispered so as not to disturb Naila.

Bradley knew he needed to get inside al-Haqani's head. He opened the first of four videos. Al-Haqani's manner was calm and inclusive while still menacing. He made direct eye contact with the camera. Bradley got the odd feeling Ali al-Haqani spoke directly to him. This is an introduction, Bradley thought.

What Bradley originally saw as arrogance he later interpreted as pure confidence. Not that Al-Haqani wasn't arrogant as well, but the man in the video seemed to have an agenda that he was certain he could enforce. Bradley watched the second and third videos. Each time Al-Haqani focused on the same subjects—corrupt governments, Allah's greatness, and death to all infidels. He ranted about World War II and the United States' use of the atomic bomb. He detested the role women played in the United States and spoke about how vain the American people are. The fourth and latest video ran the shortest at only twenty-seven seconds and two sentences. Bradley replayed the footage.

And the strong shall be as tow, and the maker of it as a spark, and they shall both burn together, and none shall quench them. I am the fourth beast, and I shall devour the infidels, and they shall not be remembered nor come to mind.

No introduction. No preamble. Al-Haqani went straight to his point. That was different from the other videos. It was a message, but for whom? Western infidels? His followers? His rivals? His . . . warriors?

Bradley typed the words "And the strong shall be as tow" into a search engine.

"Isaiah, King James Bible, Chapter 1, Verse 31," Bradley whispered.

He clicked the link. There it was. The last verse of chapter one in the Book of Isaiah. Word for word he read:

And the strong shall be as tow, and the maker of it as
a spark, and they shall both burn together, and none shall
quench them.

Bradley read the rest of the chapter.

"Nothing about the fourth beast," Bradley once again spoke
aloud. The longtime habit helped him to think clearly.

Bradley typed, "I am the fourth beast and I shall devour" into
the laptop.

When the results appeared, Bradley sat up straight, wiped
his tired eyes, and looked again. Daniel 7:23, King James Bible,
English version. He read the passage.

Thus he said, The fourth beast shall be the fourth kingdom
upon earth, which shall be diverse from all kingdoms, and
shall devour the whole earth, and shall tread it down, and
break it in pieces.

Bradley poured water from his bottle, splashed his face, then
watched the video again.

It's not a direct quote, he thought.

The website Bradley referred to contained the standard
version of the King James Bible. The two passages Al-Haqani
referenced came from the book of Isaiah and Daniel. Al-Haqani
used the verse from the book of Daniel out of context, but had
made his point.

"Please, God. Let this be it." Okay, Bradley, he thought. The
first two letters must mean chapter and verse. The third number
is either a letter or a word.

Bradley used the navigation premise on the website to
bring him to the first two numbers listed in Al-Haqani's coded
message, 16:14. He scrolled to Chapter 16, Verse 14. The third
number in the sequence was 9. He counted until he got to the
ninth letter in the sentence. It was an I. He wrote it down.

What about the spaces? Do I count them? he asked himself.

He counted again, including spaces. He stopped on the letter T and wrote it down on a separate line. Then he counted the words as he intended to put the ninth word on the paper. THREE.

Bradley felt hopeful. He proceeded to the next set of numbers, 14:18;19.

Bradley's excitement turned to disappointment when the next set of numbers produced an I, a space, and no word at all, considering that the sentence did not possess nineteen words. Then, through his exhaustion, he remembered that there were two coded messages. It's possible I tried the wrong one, he thought.

With the second coded message in hand, Bradley repeated the process and again produced a jumble of nonsense. Frustrated, Bradley sat back in his chair and took a deep, cleansing breath.

I'm close, I can feel it, he thought. What am I missing?

He closed his eyes and conjured a vision of Al-Haqani sitting at a table, pen in hand. Bradley then imagined Haqani running his finger over a passage in the open bible. He pictured Haqani's imposing posture, the bold expression on his face, and the fire in his eyes. As Ali al-Haqani put pen to paper, the imagined scene revealed what Bradley may have been missing.

Adrenaline kicked in as Bradley picked up a notepad and pen. Referencing the coded message, he reversed the set of numbers to read from right to left, just as any Afghan would have written them.

Using the book of Isaiah as the key and considering all three options again—letter without counting spaces, letter with spaces, and word number—he wrote, B, A, DAY. Next he wrote, E, E, TEN, followed by W, T, UNDER.

The fourth set of numbers did it. Bradley realized he could stop looking for letters and began to concentrate on words. When he finished, his chin dropped.

Before he woke Naila, he wanted to make sure. He switched back to the Book of Daniel and, with the set of numbers from the second message, went through the same process. But that time, the process went quicker because he knew he needn't count letters.

"Shit," he exclaimed, and wheeled over to Naila napping in one of the jet's reclining chairs.

"Naila, wake up," Bradley said.

Naila slowly opened her groggy eyes. The look on Bradley's face told her that her nap was over.

"What happened?" she asked.

The pilot's voice came over the speaker. "We are making our final descent. We'll be on the ground in twenty minutes."

"I need you to double check something for me," Bradley said, wearily and hurriedly.

Bradley explained to Naila what he wanted her to do. He sat beside her and didn't take his eyes off the paper as she wrote.

She worked on the Book of Isaiah first. Bradley knew by the second word that he had been correct. When she finished, Naila's eyes were wide with alarm. She looked at the date displayed on her watch. August 8.

"I have to call Director Houghton," she said as she reached for her phone.

"Wait, no. It's not secure. Besides, it's almost midnight."

"He said he'd be waiting for us in his office," Naila replied.

"Is there a car waiting for us at the airport?" Bradley asked.

"Yes, there's supposed to be."

"Okay, then. It's only about a fifteen-minute drive to the Hoover building. I think it's best to deliver the message in person."

Bradley placed the decoded messages in his shirt pocket. They gathered the documents, closed their laptops, and readied for landing. The twenty-minute descent seemed to take an hour.

Once the plane had rolled to a stop in its hanger, things moved quickly. Before the pilot opened it, the ground crew had positioned a lift to the jet's door. Bradley, Rusty, and Naila boarded the platform, and it lowered them to the concrete floor of the hangar. A van with a mechanical handicap platform waited with his luggage already inside. Within minutes, they were headed to the J. Edgar Hoover building.

"Leave the luggage in the van," Naila told the driver once they arrived.

Director Houghton's assistant waited with credentials for Bradley and Rusty in the near empty main lobby. Then, the four rushed to Houghton's fifth-floor office. When Bradley, Rusty, and Naila entered, Director Houghton stood from behind his desk. But it was Derek, sitting on a couch, that Bradley's eyes veered to.

Bradley hadn't prepared himself to see him. Derek stood. Multiple competing facial expressions surfaced, but he settled for an easy smile.

"He did it," Naila exclaimed as they entered the room. "He broke the code."

"Are you sure?" Director Houghton asked as he came from behind his desk.

"Bradley?" With that one vocalization, Bradley understood that Derek also asked, Are you sure?

"I'm as sure as I can be," Bradley said as he handed Houghton the slip of paper from his pocket.

Houghton read the first message aloud. "Day ten furnace governors three."

Then he read the second, "Day ten under ground white house three."

"Less than two days," Houghton mumbled as he read. He showed Derek the note, then walked behind his desk. He buzzed his assistant.

"Yes, sir," came the female voice from his speaker.

"Is the team assembled?" Houghton asked.

"They're waiting for you," the voice said.

"Thank you for staying, Laura. You can go home now." Houghton turned to Bradley and Naila and said, "Let's go."

"I'll be in my office when you're finished," Derek said.

"You're not coming?" Bradley asked.

"It's not my team. Besides, I've got work to do."

Bradley asked Derek, "Can Rusty stay with you?"

Derek nodded.

"Rusty, you go with Derek," Bradley said to the dog.

Rusty went and stood by Derek's side. He leaned into Derek's leg as if to reconnect after their long separation. Derek reached down and pet him on the head.

"I'll see you when you're done," Derek said.

Derek returned to his office with Rusty. He found a bowl in the break room, filled it with water, and set it on the floor by his desk.

"I bet you've had quite the adventure," Derek said to the dog.

Rusty looked up at Derek and tilted his head. Then he took a drink of water and lay on the floor.

The text of the note replayed in his head. The White House note was obvious. In two days, al-Haqani arranged for a bomb to be placed underground in the White House and to explode at either 3 a.m. or 3 p.m. Exactly where and how he intended to accomplish it, Derek could not figure.

The second target seemed to be the Capitol building. He concluded that the use of the word furnace might refer to one of the maintenance rooms or it could be literal. Derek had no knowledge of the heating system in the Capitol.

Well, Derek thought, I'll have to trust that the national security branch will figure it out.

"If anyone can help, it's Bradley," Derek said to Rusty.

Being in the room with Bradley had felt awkward—an unfamiliar feeling when it came to their relationship. Even during their most contentious moments, the two were comfortable in each other's presence. Derek wasn't sure what to make of it.

Coupled with having to leave Cate when she was so angry with him, Derek was not having the best of days.

Derek dialed Cate's cellphone number.

"Yes?" Cate spoke sharply.

Derek felt the dagger, then said, "I had a feeling you wouldn't be asleep. I wanted to let you know that Bradley is here. He looks good."

"Well, it's nice of you to let me know," Cate said, oozing sarcasm.

"Cate, please. I'm sorry. I should have told you. I know that now. But sometimes it's a fine line between what I can say and what I can't—what I should and what I shouldn't. I won't always make the right decision."

Cate sighed. "I will get over this, Derek. But right now, I'm hurt." She paused. "When are you coming home?"

"I don't know. I'm watching Rusty while Bradley is . . . busy. I don't know how long he'll be. Should I wake you when we get there?"

"Call me when you leave the office."

"I will. I love you, Cate."

"I love you, too. But we're not done with this, Derek."

Cate hung up.

It was 2:35 am when Rusty heard the whir of Bradley's chair and jumped from the floor. Derek lay sleeping on the couch.

"Hey, buddy. How're you doing?" Bradley stroked Rusty's head.

Derek stirred, then opened his tired eyes, "Hey."

"Hey," Bradley replied.

Derek sat up and wiped his eyes.

"How did it go?" Derek asked.

"I've done as much as I can. It's up to the national security branch now," Bradley said. "You look like shit, Derek," he added.

Derek grinned. "Yeah, I know. You look great. And so does Rusty. How is that? I can't imagine you got much sleep since we last talked."

"Rusty had plenty on the plane. It's good to see you," Bradley smiled.

"You, too. What do you say we get out of here?"

"Yeah."

Derek dialed his cellphone and spoke only four words, "We're on our way."

Derek lifted Bradley into the passenger seat of his Suburban. In the twenty-three years they'd known each other, it was the first time he had ever done that. Bradley had always been self-sufficient and drove his own custom truck. Derek wondered where the truck was but decided not to ask.

Rusty didn't need any help. He jumped into the back seat.

Earlier that day, Derek had appropriated a ramp to enable him to put Bradley's wheelchair in the back of his SUV. As they drove the short distance to the house, Derek brushed his hand across his stubbled face. "This could be a little awkward. Cate is a bit angry with me."

"What did you do?"

"If I tell you, you're going to be mad at me, too."

"I'm too tired to be mad. Give it up. What did you do?"

"I've been tracking you since you left. I know you said you didn't want us to look for you, I just wanted to make sure you were alright. But I never told Cate, and she found out yesterday."

Bradley chuckled. "You don't think I knew you would keep tabs on me?"

"You knew?"

"Of course I did. If it were you who took off, I would have done the same. What I really needed was to be alone. Look, Derek . . ." Bradley took a short pause, ". . . a year ago, I was at a crossroad, a potentially dangerous crossroad. I needed to get away to figure things out on my own. I needed to recalibrate and find some balance."

"And did you?"

"I think so, yeah," Bradley smiled. "Why didn't you tell Cate?"

Derek shook his head. "I don't know. I guess I wanted to try to honor your wishes, at least a little. Have you been in touch with your parents?"

"Twice over the course of the year. I sent a couple text messages to Dad just so they didn't worry. They don't know I'm here, though."

"Well, here we are," Derek said as he parked his SUV on the side of the street.

"Wow! Nice place. And it's so close to your office. When did you buy it?"

"About five months ago. Cate looked at a few places before we found this one. We got lucky. The Realtor called us as soon as it went on the market. One look, and Cate was sold."

A handicap ramp leading to the front door could be seen with help from the scant light of the moon.

"You have a ramp," Bradley stated.

"It was the first thing we added when we bought the house."

Bradley's heart warmed with appreciation. Until that moment, he hadn't realized how much he missed Derek and Cate.

Rusty jumped from the car and waited for Bradley. Derek removed Bradley's chair from the back and helped him into it.

Derek asked, "Are you ready for this?"

"More than ready."

Bradley made his way up the ramp to the front door. As Derek opened it, Cate stood in the foyer.

Bradley inched his way inside and stopped, staring at his friend. "Hello, Cate. You look more beautiful than the day we met."

"Bradley, I missed you so . . ." Cate choked on her words. Instead of trying to finish her sentence, she stepped forward, sat on Bradley's lap, and wrapped him in a hug.

Bradley held her tight. He could feel her tears settling on his cheeks. Neither said a word. They just sat, clinging to one another. Rusty waited his turn next to Bradley's chair and watched the lengthy embrace.

When they let go, Cate wiped tears from her face, kneeled beside Rusty, held his head in her hands, and kissed his snout. When she stood, she said, "Come into the kitchen. I've got breakfast for you."

He followed Cate through the open concept living room/ kitchen. Cate had placed two bowls on the kitchen floor near the end of the counter—one filled with water, one with dog food. When Rusty noticed them, he glanced at Bradley.

Bradley smiled and encouraged, "Go ahead, boy."

Rusty practically hopped to the dishes and launched himself into the food.

The three chuckled at his enthusiasm.

"Sit right there, Bradley." Cate pointed to a spot without a chair. The place setting included a glass of orange juice and toast. "You sit, too, Derek," Cate added coolly.

Derek looked at Bradley and lifted his brows.

Bradley said to Cate, "How is it I can go away for a year, and you look even younger than when I left?"

Irritably, Cate turned to Bradley and replied, "How is it you could disappear for a year?"

Cate's tone caught Bradley off guard. He could only stare at her with his mouth agape.

"Shit." Cate slapped the kitchen counter. "I'm sorry, Bradley." She went to him and hugged him from behind. "I swore I wouldn't do that."

"No, it's alright, Cate. It's a reasonable question," Bradley said. "Is it alright if I explain everything tomorrow, though? I'm kind of exhausted."

Cate placed plates of bacon and eggs in front of both Bradley and Derek. She put her hand on Bradley's shoulder and replied, "You never have to explain yourself with me."

Bradley touched Cate's hand.

Derek lightly huffed.

Cate shot him a glare.

After eating, Derek took Rusty outside to relieve himself while Cate showed Bradley to his bedroom. His luggage sat on a bench at the end of the bed. He had forgotten all about it. A brand-new dog bed lay on the floor.

"You have your own bathroom right through that door," Cate pointed. "Is there anything I can get for you?"

Bradley reached for Cate's hands and held them. "I'm sorry I worried you, Cate."

She leaned down and kissed him on the cheek. "Get some sleep."

"Goodnight," Bradley said.

Cate left the room.

Bradley rummaged through his suitcase for his gym shorts. He heard Rusty's nails clicking on the floor in rapid succession. When he turned, he watched Rusty run into the room and go directly to the dog bed. Rusty circled it five times before fluffing it up with his paws and settling in.

Derek stood in the doorway. "Have you got everything you need?"

"And more," Bradley said. "Hey, don't worry about Cate. She will always forgive you."

"I know. But sometimes it's a painful process." Derek chuckled. "Goodnight, Bradley. I'm glad you're back."

"Goodnight, Derek," Bradley said. But Bradley wasn't sure if he was truly back.

BLUE SHIRT DAY

When Bradley woke, morning had just transitioned to afternoon. He glanced at the floor and saw Rusty's empty bed.

Bradley desperately needed a shower. Having seen the fully handicap accessible bathroom, he knew that Derek and Cate had gone to great lengths to purchase and renovate their house with him in mind—without knowing for sure if he would ever see it. He wondered if he could be as good a friend to anyone as they were to him.

Trying not to think about what went on a few blocks away, he lingered under the hot water. But he couldn't help himself. He calculated that the national security branch had either fifteen or twenty-seven hours to stop Ali al-Haqani's soldiers from potentially obliterating two of the nation's most iconic and essential buildings. And there was nothing more he could do.

The same type of situation used to get Bradley into trouble. The old Bradley would find a way to insert himself into the field instead of keeping to his analyst status. And as much as he would like to be out there right now, he knew he shouldn't. He breathed deeply as steam relaxed his upper body.

Cate sat on the living room couch reading a book. Rusty lay beside her.

"How did you sleep?" she asked as Bradley wheeled into the room.

"Soundly," Bradley replied. "When did Derek leave?"

"He was gone by seven." Cate put the book on the end table and stood.

"He must be running on pure adrenaline."

"He usually is these days. How about some coffee?"

"I haven't had a decent cup of coffee since I left. I'd love one. I found Indian coffee to be bitter. I think it's the chicory." Bradley followed Cate to the kitchen where they sat at the table.

"Bradley, I know you can't tell me what's going on, but is Derek in any direct danger? Is that why you're here?" Cate asked.

Bradley reached for Cate's hand. "No, Cate. Derek will be fine."

"He asked me to leave," Cate said. "Things can't be fine."

"I just meant that Derek is not a target or at the center of anything explicitly dangerous to him."

"God, you two are so alike. Do they teach the art of evasion at Quantico?" she asked.

Bradley smiled. "I missed you so much. Tell me what's happening in your life."

"With me? Absolutely nothing. We spend most of our time in Washington now, so I had to give up my job at REACH. I really miss it."

"Zayt must really miss you. Have you talked to him lately?" Bradley asked.

"Not for a few weeks." Then Cate grinned. "He's got a girl."

"Really? Is it serious?"

"It seems to be. They've been together for about eight months. Her name is Tasha, Tasha Williams. She's a Boston police officer."

"Leave it to Zayt to find a girl with a gun." Bradley shook his head. "What is she like?"

"She's the sweetest, scariest woman I ever met. Honestly, when she puts on her cop face, watch out."

Bradley laughed. "So why haven't you found something here in Washington to fill your time?"

"It's complicated. We still travel back and forth from Medford to Washington, so I can't do anything that requires a strict schedule."

"Derek still works out of the Chelsea headquarters?" Bradley asked.

"Uh huh. But not as much anymore. It seems like there is one major crisis after another these days that brings us to Washington."

"Is Nick still in charge of the Chelsea division?"

"Nick Gaston? Yes, as far as I know."

Bradley sat quiet for several moments. Then he said, "Cate, I've got to make a call."

"Do you need privacy?"

"No, it's not that kind of call. I've got to make arrangements to get my truck delivered."

"Where is it?"

"Quebec City."

"Canada?" Cate's voice nearly squeaked.

Bradley chuckled. "Yes. Shit, wait. Do I still have a house?"

It was Cate's turn to chuckle. "Yes. Your parents didn't want to sell it because they hoped you would be back. Zayt keeps an eye on it. He stays there sometimes."

"Great. I'll have it delivered there."

At that moment, Bradley knew for certain he was a different person than the one who disappeared the year before. He was making plans for the future instead of obsessing about the fact that two bombs might soon explode within blocks of where he sat.

He dialed a number on his cellphone.

While Bradley was on the phone, Cate got a call. He could tell Derek was on the other end. Bradley finished arranging for his truck to be delivered to his home in Revere, Massachusetts, then disconnected the call.

"That was Derek," Cate said. "He wants you to call him. He still doesn't have your new phone number. Neither do I, by the way."

Bradley dialed Cate's phone, then hung up. "Now you do, and he doesn't." He winked, and Cate sported a satisfied smile.

Bradley called Derek.

"Hey, Bradley. Houghton wants to know if you can come in. You impressed the hell out of him with your insight into al-Haqani. He asked me if I could loan you to him. I'm leaving it up to you."

"Hang on a minute, Derek." Bradley turned to Cate and asked, "Can I leave Rusty with you for the afternoon?"

"Of course." They both looked over to the couch where Rusty had stretched out. "It seems he needs a little more rest," Cate said.

Bradley returned to the phone and said to Derek, "Yeah, I can come in. I just need a ride."

"I'll send the van. Your permanent credentials will be waiting for you in the lobby. Head directly to Houghton's office. He'll be waiting for you."

"Alright. I'll be ready."

Bradley spent the day with the national security branch behind closed doors. It was close to 8 p.m. when he finished and decided to see if Derek was still in his office. He found him sitting behind his desk, looking harried and exhausted.

"Jesus, Derek," Bradley said as he went through the door.

Startled, Derek flinched in his chair. "Christ, put a bell on that thing, will you?"

Bradley was seriously concerned about Derek. He looked pale and agitated, and Bradley watched as Derek unconsciously rubbed his chest multiple times.

"What are you still doing here?" Bradley asked. "You're killing yourself with this job."

"And you're just walking through a field of daisies?"

"Actually, no, it was tea fields. You should try it sometime. I'm serious, Derek. You don't look good. I understand now why Cate feels the need to be here in Washington."

Derek dropped his pen onto his desk, leaned back in his chair, and with a deadpan gaze asked, "What are you talking about?"

"Nothing. Come on. Let's go. We both could use some sleep."

"Did Cate say something to you? Is that why she wants to sell the house in Medford? Because she's worried about me?" Derek asked.

Surprised, Bradley said, "I didn't know she wanted to sell the house."

Derek sighed. "She mentioned it the other day right out of the blue. What did she say to you?"

"She didn't say anything, Derek. It was just me being stupid, talking about things I know nothing about."

Derek shook his head. "You read people better than anyone. Shit! She told me she loved being here in Washington, that she wanted to try something new. That's why she left her job with REACH, she said."

"You're reading too much into my thoughtless statement." Bradley scolded himself, although he was pretty sure he had read Cate accurately. "We're both tired, let's get out of here. Tomorrow could be a tough day."

Later at Cate and Derek's home, just as they sat down to dinner, Derek excused himself. "I'm sorry. I can't keep my eyes open."

Once Derek went upstairs, Bradley turned to Cate. Worry darkened her emerald eyes.

"Cate, why don't you go with him. I can take care of myself down here. Rusty and I will be fine. Go be with Derek."

"Are you sure? I hate to leave you . . ."

"He needs you, Cate," Bradley said.

Cate rose from the table, kissed Bradley on the cheek, and said, "Goodnight, Bradley."

"Goodnight, Cate."

With Rusty already fed, Bradley dished himself a bowl of salad and a plate of pot roast. He sat at the table with the dog by his feet. Having stayed in hotels and hostels while traveling, Bradley hadn't had the opportunity to cook. He missed his kitchen. It had always been one of his greatest joys, yet he hadn't cooked an entire meal in well over a year.

He made the decision. "No matter what happens tomorrow, Rusty, I think we should go home."

Bradley swore he saw Rusty smile.

After dinner, Bradley cleared the table, put the leftovers away, and cleaned the kitchen. He took Rusty outside. It was a warm night for that time of year. Stars shone plentifully in the mostly clear sky. Gazing at the heavens and thinking how grateful he felt to have Cate and Derek in his life, Bradley sat on the ramp and waited for the dog.

At 2:45 a.m., unable to sleep and followed by Rusty, Bradley left the guest bedroom. Though confident that Ali al-Haqani would not strike in the middle of the night, Bradley needed to see for himself. As he rolled down the hallway past the kitchen, he noticed the outside light shining. Derek's shadow loomed large through the front window.

"I had a feeling you'd be up," Bradley said as he moved his wheelchair onto the front porch.

Derek handed him a bottle of water. "I expected you, too."

"He won't strike tonight. He wants the world to watch."

"I think we all assume that. But a long time ago, I learned not to assume."

"Yeah."

For several moments, they sipped their water in silence.

Hesitantly, Bradley said, "It had nothing to do with all of you, you know. Me leaving like I did."

Choked up, Derek responded, "We thought you were dead. We got the note and started reading and thought you . . . " He couldn't finish the sentence.

"It nearly came to that. That's why I had to leave." Bradley dropped his chin and shook his head. "Jesus, Derek. I'm sorry."

"I should have been there for you."

"You were! All of you. There's nothing more any of you could have done for me. I had to get through it on my own. And I did. I've learned a lot about myself this past year. I'm not the same person I was when I left. Well, not entirely." Bradley chuckled.

"Yeah, I can see that. It's great to have you here. We really missed you."

"Same here." Bradley paused, then continued, "Listen, no matter what happens today, I've got some things to take care of back home."

"I know. I wish we could go with you, but . . . "

"Yeah."

When 3 a.m. came and went without incident, both were relieved.

Bradley and Derek left for the office at 7:15. Derek looked slightly better than he had the previous day, but Bradley noticed he wore a blue shirt.

"It's a blue shirt day, huh?" Bradley frowned.

Derek glanced down at his shirt. Seeming confused, he asked, "What do you mean?"

"You always wear a blue shirt when you're worried," Bradley said, matter-of-factly.

"No, I don't."

"Come on, Derek. It's common knowledge that you do. Everyone knows it."

"Everyone? Who's everyone?"

"All of us in the Chelsea office, Cate, all our friends, your parents, my parents. Everyone!"

"That's ridiculous."

"Are you telling me you're not aware of your . . . tell?" Bradley chuckled. "For a detailed guy, you sure miss a lot of them when it comes to yourself."

"It's ridiculous. I don't choose my clothing based on how I . . . " Derek paused. "Do I?"

"Your mother says it started in college. She said she could always tell what kind of week you were having by doing your laundry," Bradley replied.

"So, my friends and family sit around and talk about how I dress myself? Tell me. Do I have a tell before I kick someone out of my car?"

Bradley smirked. "I guess we could find out."

Derek looked over at Bradley with a set face, saw Bradley's smirk, and started to chuckle.

"Son of a bitch. Blue shirt day," Derek said.

They parted at the elevator. Before Bradley got off at the fifth floor, Derek said, "Keep me posted as much as you can."

"You got it."

NOW WHAT?

Derek's morning included a call from Nick Gaston in the Chelsea, Massachusetts office. Nick updated Derek on a medical fraud case they'd been working on for months that was about to result in four high-profile arrests.

They finished their business, and Derek asked Nick, "How is Mara doing?"

"She's great. The morning sickness has eased up, but her crazy cravings haven't. Last night it was sour cream and onion potato chips dipped in chocolate ice cream."

Derek chuckled at the thought. "Give her my best. And let me know when you make the arrests."

"Will do," Nick replied.

Derek hadn't told Bradley that Mara, Nick's wife and fellow FBI agent, was pregnant. He didn't think it his news to tell. And he certainly didn't want to tell Nick that Bradley was back. Not that soon, even though Nick was Bradley's boss. They hadn't discussed Bradley's future, and he wanted to make sure Bradley was back for good before making any plans.

For Derek, the rest of the morning moved slowly. He prioritized making sure the critical incident response group, CIRG, was ready if needed. He also had multiple online meetings, phone calls, and reports to sift through that kept him busy but did not help the time pass.

He thought of Cate. They had talked the previous night before Derek initially fell asleep. He apologized to her again, and she forgave him. He wondered if she did so because he was just too tired to argue. Either way, he was happy the disagreement was behind them.

He had asked her that morning about her plans for the day. She told him she had none and that she would stay home with Rusty. He was relieved to hear it.

Noon passed. Then so did one o'clock. Derek hadn't heard a word from Bradley, but he imagined them all quite busy in the national security branch situation room.

He felt a tightening in his chest, the variety of discomfort that came with knowing people may lose their lives if the FBI couldn't stop the bad guys. Derek found himself rubbing his chest, then looked down at his blue shirt and frowned.

By 2:45 p.m., Derek found it difficult to concentrate on work, so he turned on the television in his office and set it to a local news station. Ten minutes later, Derek's assistant buzzed him to tell him Bradley wished to see him.

Derek jumped up. "Send him in," he nearly yelled.

Bradley immediately noticed the TV on and said, "You can shut that off now. Nothing is going to happen today." He revealed a wide smile.

"In custody or dead?" Derek asked.

"In custody. Quietly, quickly, and efficiently," Bradley replied.

"Al Haqani?"

Bradley shook his head.

Derek flopped down in his chair. "Jesus, I'm getting too old for this. How close was it?"

"They had an hour to spare. Knowing what to look for made it much easier. But had they not intercepted those messages, it's likely al-Haqani could have succeeded. We found some holes in the security systems."

"What kind of bomb did they plan to use?"

"They found no evidence of radioactive material."

"I'll have to give Sam a call and congratulate him. How are you doing?" Derek asked Bradley.

"I feel great. I forgot how good a win feels," Bradley said.

"Well, enjoy it now because Ali al-Haqani is still out there, and I doubt we've heard the last of him."

"No, I'm sure we haven't," Bradley sighed.

Derek paused, then said, "Let's go get a coffee."

Bradley wheeled out of the office behind Derek and waited while Derek told Madelyn that he would be using the break room for a little while.

Derek closed the door behind him. "Coffee or orange juice?"

"Coffee. I've missed Colombian coffee," Bradley chuckled.

Derek brought two cups of coffee to the table and sat.

"I guess we need to figure out where to go from here," Derek said.

"In regard to what?" Bradley asked.

"You. I pulled you back in, and I'm beyond grateful that you came, but now I need to know if this is what you want."

Bradley sighed, looked at his feet on the wheelchair rests, then out the window. "Honestly, I haven't had much time to think about it. And for better or worse, I'm not the same person I was a year ago. I don't know how effective I'll be."

"That's not a concern. Maybe you have changed, as you say, but I've seen the same incredible FBI analyst these last two days that I've always seen. It's a matter of what you want, Bradley. And it's okay if you need to think about it. I don't want you to rush it."

"Yeah. I'd like to think about it," Bradley replied.

"Look, I don't mean to pry, and this has nothing to do with the job." Derek paused. "How are you dealing with the loss of Laney?"

Bradley stared at the coffee swirling in his cup. Then he said, "It's difficult to explain. It's like when Laney was alive I was this shiny metallic mirror. And when she died, I shattered into a thousand pieces, but all the pieces stayed hovering around me and, over time, most of the fragments found their way back to the mirror, but not all. And you can still see the cracks." Bradley shook his head. "I don't know if that makes any sense to you."

Derek sat astounded by the picture Bradley had painted. At first speechless, Derek replied, "I think I understand."

"I'm having my truck delivered to Revere, and I should go see my parents. Also, I hear Zayt has a girlfriend." Bradley chuckled. "If you could give me a few days to think about this, I would appreciate it."

"Take whatever time you need. I haven't told anyone you're back. I've no idea if Cate has."

"Why did you want to have this conversation in here, Derek? Why not in your office?" Bradley asked.

"I guess I just wanted this to be an informal conversation, you know? Just between friends instead of Director Richards and Agent Whitman."

Bradley smiled. "Thanks."

"I've got to get back to work. Are you going back to the house?"

"Yeah. There's nothing left here for me to do. Hey, don't work too late tonight. I want to take you and Cate out to dinner."

"I'll do my best."

Bradley said goodbye to Madelyn and headed for the elevator.

"Bradley? Is that you?" he heard a woman's voice call from behind.

Bradley stopped and turned his chair.

"It is you," Agent Christine Woods declared. "How are you?"

"Christine, I'm doing great. How are you?"

With a questioning expression, Christine said, "I'm doing well, thank you. I was told you disappeared."

Bradley had never considered what his fellow agents thought about his sudden departure. It had been some years since he worked with Christine and then never too closely. They collaborated on the Vincent Vega case back in Boston when the white-collar crime division she worked with helped with the limousine bombing that almost killed Derek, Cate, and the rest of Bradley's friends. Then again, later, after she transferred to Washington and joined the child exploitation division, she helped him navigate through the Pathside Predator serial killer case. She was a very good agent, and Bradley suddenly remembered the price he was supposed to pay for her help in the Predator case.

"Disappeared isn't quite accurate. I took a leave of absence. In fact, I just got back yesterday," Bradley said.

"Are you going to be here long?" Christine asked.

"I think I'm leaving tomorrow, heading back to Massachusetts."

"Oh, that's too bad. I was hoping we could get together for a drink or something," Christine's lips formed a small pout.

"As I recall, I owe you dinner," Bradley said.

Christine laughed and replied, "That is true. I did make that stipulation, didn't I. But I won't hold you to it."

"I'm hoping to take Derek and Cate to dinner tonight. Would you like to join us? Unless you're busy or have a date."

"No, I'm not busy, and I certainly don't have a date. Dinner sounds great. Call me here in the office later with the details. I've got to run. I'm late for a meeting. It's great to see you, Bradley."

"Yes, you too, Christine."

If Bradley needed more evidence that he had changed, that was it. He remembered agreeing to take Christine to dinner but not having any intention of doing so. He had made it a habit to do that with people—brush them off, including his close friends. He saw clearly what he hadn't seen before. Little by little, he had allowed his darker side to dominate his actions. Bradley was adamant that he would not let that happen again.

Back at the house, Bradley, Cate, and Rusty sat in the living room in front of the gas fireplace.

"You pick the restaurant," Bradley said to Cate, "but it must be upscale food done really well."

"How does Italian sound?" she asked.

"Perfect. Do you and Derek have a favorite?"

Cate giggled. "Several, but it might be a good night for Florentina's. Would you like me to make the reservation?"

"Let's do it. Whatever time works best for you. I'll call Christine and see if she can meet us there," Bradley said.

"You know, Bradley, you've changed," Cate said with a smile. "You seem much more relaxed than you ever have. What's your secret? Derek could sure use some of what you've got."

"You would have to tear him away from Washington first." Bradley lightly shook his head knowing that would be an uphill battle, then continued. "Do you know there are whole societies that make government decisions based on how happy their citizens are? Not how much money they have or how much stuff, but how happy. Isn't that something? And in Italy, they shut down most businesses midday so they can go home and eat, rest, or just be with their families."

"What a wonderful thought. I can't imagine Derek popping home for lunch."

Bradley saw a flicker of sadness in her eyes.

"It's time for me to make a decision, and I have no idea what I'm going to do," Bradley confessed.

"A decision about work?" she asked.

"Yes. I'm going home tomorrow to do some thinking. I'll go see my Mom and Dad and talk things through with them. I know they won't be able to tell me what to do, but I think it will help me to talk with them. Speaking of Mom and Dad, I should call them," Bradley said.

"You haven't called them since you've been back?"

"No, I wasn't sure if I was going to leave again. But I've decided it is time to go home."

"You need to call them. Now!" Cate demanded. "Your poor mother must be worried to death about you."

Bradley pulled his phone from his chair's pocket and began to dial. Cate removed herself from the room.

"Hello?" Doug answered tentatively.

"Hi, Dad."

"Bradley, is that really you?"

"Yeah, it's me."

"I almost didn't answer the phone because I didn't recognize the number. Jesus, son, how are you? Where are you?" Bradley could hear Doug's smile.

"I'm in DC with Derek and Cate. I got in yesterday."

"Got in? From where? Never mind, never mind. God, it's good to hear your voice. I've got to get your mother. She's in the kitchen. She's been so worried. Hang on." Bradley could hear his father walking from outside, through the garage, and into the kitchen. "Lynn, honey, you have a phone call."

Bradley heard Lynn whisper something to Doug, and finally he heard Doug say, "Just take the phone."

"Hello?" Lynn said quietly.

Bradley smiled. "Hi, Mom. It's me," and that's all it took for Bradley to start weeping like a child.

"Bradley!" Lynn began to cry. Neither one could speak until they cleared the tears away.

"I'm coming home," Bradley said.

"Are you alright, sweetheart?"

"Yes, I'm great. I'm in DC with Cate and Derek, but I'm going to fly to Boston tomorrow. It will be a day or two before my truck makes it home, but I'll come and see you as soon as it does."

"The hell with a day or two. We're going to pick you up at Logan. What time are you coming in?"

"I don't know. I haven't bought a ticket yet. You don't have to pick me up, Mom. I can take . . ."

"I haven't seen you for a year, Bradley. I'm not waiting another day. We're picking you up from the airport. Just let us know when you're arriving, and we'll be there."

"Alright. Thanks, Mom. How have you been?"

Lynn started crying again. "I . . . I . . ."

"Bradley," Doug said, taking the phone, "your mother is a little emotional right now. How are you?"

"I'm great, Dad. I'll tell you all about my trip when I see you. I've really missed you," Bradley said.

Doug cleared his throat. Bradley could tell he was choked up. "We've missed you, too."

Bradley went on, "Listen. I've got a lot of arrangements to make, so I'd better go. I just wanted to let you know that everything is good and I'm coming home. I'll text you later with my flight information."

"Alright. Bradley, I love you, son."

"I love you, too, Dad. Give Mom a kiss for me. I'll see you tomorrow."

Rusty sidled up to Bradley to comfort him. "I'm alright, boy. Everything is good," he said as he wiped away his tears.

"Are you alright, Bradley?" Cate asked as she came into the room.

"What is it about talking to my mother that turns me into a blithering idiot?" he asked, still wiping his tears.

Cate placed herself on Bradley's lap and put her arm around his neck. "That just speaks to the wonderful relationship you have with your parents. And the fact that you haven't seen them in a year." Cate hugged Bradley tightly, then got up.

"You know, I could go with you and help you get settled. God knows what kind of shape your house is in," Cate said.

"No, you've done plenty already, thanks. Besides, you know my mother is already putting together a care package with cleaning supplies."

Cate chuckled. "I'm sure you're right."

"Derek needs you here. He's working too hard, Cate. I don't like it. He looks worn out."

"I know. He won't listen to me," Cate said.

"I'll talk to him before I leave. But you're going to need to be more relentless, too. Get mad. He hates it when you're mad or sad or hurt——or if you have a stubbed toe." Bradley laughed.

Cate smiled and gave Bradley a playful slap on the arm.

"You're right, though, Bradley. I may have to use my womanly ways on him. Speaking of womanly ways, I made the reservation for eight o'clock tonight. You'd better call your friend."

Bradley rolled his eyes. "You know it's not like that, right?"

"I'm just teasing you, Bradley. I have to make up for lost time."

"Right. I've got a plane to book." He grinned.

Bradley bought two seats, one for him and one for Rusty, on the 7:30 a.m. shuttle from Ronald Reagan airport to Logan airport in Boston. He would arrive at Logan by 9 a.m. He sent the flight information to his father. Next, he called the child exploitation division of the FBI and asked to speak with Christine Woods.

"Hi, Christine. This is Bradley. Are we still on for tonight?"

"That's my plan. How do you want to do this?" she asked.

"Well, I don't have a vehicle here, so would you mind meeting us at Florentina's at eight o'clock?" Bradley asked.

"Ooh, I've been meaning to try that place. Yes, I will meet you there. I'm looking forward to it," Christine said.

"Me, too. I'll see you then." Bradley hung up.

"Look at you getting things done," Cate teased. "But what about the others?"

"Others?" Bradley eyebrows pinched.

"Yes. All the others that received that God awful note you mailed to us last year. You know, the one that took the place of goodbye?"

"Cate, when I said you needed to be more relentless, I meant with Derek, not me." Bradley paused as Cate stared him down.

Then he thought about how he would handle the others. "I'll get in touch with them when I get home. I promise."

Cate replaced her glare with a smile.

With Cate's nudging, Derek got home in time to pick up Cate and Bradley and got to the restaurant a few minutes early. As they waited to be seated, Christine arrived.

"Hello, Christine," Bradley smiled. He noticed she had changed from her work clothes. She looked both comfortable and elegant in loose fitting pale pink slacks and a multicolored pink top that finished below her hips. A strand of pearls graced her neck. Her thick and wavy dirty-blonde hair reached her shoulders. Bradley had never seen her with her hair down. "You look very nice."

"Thank you, as do you."

Bradley said, "You remember Derek Richards, and this is his wife, Cate."

"Yes, Derek. It's good to see you again." They shook hands. "It's very nice to finally meet you, Cate."

"Likewise, Christine. How is it we haven't met before?" Cate asked.

"You know how it is. You can run in the same circles, but if you're a step behind or ahead you never connect," Christine replied.

"Nicely put." Bradley grinned.

The maître d' showed them to a table along the far side of the room and removed one of the chairs to make room for Bradley's wheelchair. Christine and Cate sat next to each other in the upholstered chairs against the wall. A white linen cloth covered the table, and fresh flowers bathed in a simple white vase in the center with a tealight on either side.

"I've been wanting to get here since I moved to Washington, but it never seemed to happen," Christine said with a smile.

"I'm glad. I owed you something special," Bradley said.

"You don't owe me anything. I only said that back then so you might ask me out to dinner," Christine said. "I didn't know you were in a relationship until just recently." She placed her hand on Bradley's and said, "I was sorry to hear about your fiancée."

Bradley placed his hand on top of hers and replied, "Thank you."

"So," Christine said, removing her hand from Bradley's, "I take it you've all been here before?"

"Not me. This is my first time, too." Bradley said.

Cate replied, "This is one of Derek's and my favorites. Of course, there are so many wonderful restaurants here in the city."

"And Cate is determined to try them all," Derek laughed.

Cate playfully swatted Derek with a backhand and said, "I just love watching the precision and professionalism of the staff. If I had ever had a chance to open my own restaurant, it would be very much like this place."

"Are you in the business?" Christine asked.

"I used to be. But it's been a long time," Cate said as she lightly pursed her lips.

"That's because you've been doing all that volunteer work for the REACH program," Bradley piped in. "Cate was instrumental in setting up the kitchen, dining room, and much more at the homeless community back in Massachusetts that my friend built."

"Really?" Christine asked. "I have a friend who could use your expertise."

The waiter appeared and asked if anyone would like a beverage.

"Shall I order wine for the table?" Bradley asked.

Bradley had studied the wine list and chosen a 2018 Sangiovese from Napa Valley. The waiter presented each with a menu, then recited the dinner specials including lobster ravioli, veal chops, and pan-seared branzino. He waved for the busboy to fill their water glasses, then backed away from the table to get the wine.

"I won't be happy until I've tried everything on this menu," Cate giggled.

"This is just too hard to choose," Christine sighed.

"It's easy for me," Bradley said as he put his menu down.

"Me, too," Derek added and did the same.

Cate and Christine looked at each other with surprise.

"How could you possibly make a decision that quickly," Cate asked the two.

"Because," Bradley replied, "they have Osso Bucco on the menu."

Derek chuckled. "Exactly," he replied.

"You're both going to order Osso Bucco? Isn't there a law against two people ordering the same meal at one table?" Christine laughed.

"There should be," Cate said, giving Christine an approving nod.

Bradley grinned. "It's the dish that made me fall in love with food—and cooking. It's also the meal I had twenty-three years ago on the first night we were all together. And, if I recall correctly, so did you, Derek."

Derek nodded and smiled. "It is. It's still one of the best meals I've ever had. Or maybe it was the company." He reached for Cate's hand, then leaned over and kissed her on the cheek.

"Look at these two, Christine. After all these years, Derek can still get Cate to blush," Bradley said.

Cate put her hands to her cheeks. "Am I?"

The wine arrived, and the waiter poured a small amount in Bradley's glass. Bradley swirled the liquid, moved the glass to his nose, then took a sip. He nodded to the waiter who then poured the wine.

When the waiter left, they lifted their glasses and Bradley toasted, "To old friends," then looked each in the eye and tapped their glass one-by-one.

"Mmm, that's very good," Christine said after tasting the red wine. "I've never heard of this before."

"It's best if you can get it from an Italian vineyard, but this will do," Bradley said.

"Have you been to Italy?" Christine asked.

"I was there a couple months ago," Bradley replied.

"When are we going to hear about your travels, Bradley?" Cate asked.

Bradley shrugged his shoulders as the waiter returned to take their dinner order.

Christine ordered veal marsala while Cate chose lasagna Bolognese. As previously determined, both Derek and Bradley ordered Osso Bucco.

Lively conversation moved quickly and easily until the food arrived. With each bite, one of the four diners moaned with delight at the dish before them, and they spoke sparingly. When the waiter came back to check on them, Bradley ordered another bottle of wine.

Cate and Christine gave up on their meals at the halfway point. Derek and Bradley ate every bit of the veal shank, vegetables, and polenta and used the crusty bread to sop up the remaining red wine and veal stock.

"They could be twins," Christine said, watching Bradley and Derek soak up the sauce.

Bradley swallowed the last of his bread and smiled.

Conversation picked up over coffee.

Bradley asked Christine, "What did you mean earlier when you said that you had a friend who could use Cate's expertise?"

"Oh, right. My friend Justin works in a homeless shelter, and he's been so frustrated trying to make improvements. He says they don't have enough beds, aren't getting enough donations, and there're twice as many homeless to serve."

Bradley shifted his gaze to Cate.

Cate asked, "Where is the shelter?"

"It's just off New York Avenue, not far from here," Christine replied.

"Maybe you should make a visit, Cate," Derek said.

"Maybe I will," she smiled.

A little while later after he paid the bill, Bradley turned to Christine and said, "Thank you for coming tonight."

"Thank you for inviting me. I hope we can do it again sometime when you're back in town," Christine replied.

"I hope so, too."

Outside the restaurant, Derek and Cate said their goodbyes to Christine. Bradley accompanied her to her car and kissed her on the cheek.

When he met Cate and Derek at the Suburban, Cate said, "She's wonderful. How long have you known her, Bradley?"

"Oh, I don't know, seven or eight years or so," Bradley guessed.

"Huh," Cate uttered.

After getting Bradley settled in the SUV, Cate asked Bradley, "Out of curiosity, why didn't you ever ask Christine out on a date?"

"I guess I wasn't looking to have a relationship back then," Bradley said. "I wasn't looking when I met Laney, either. It just kind of happened. To be totally honest, Cate, I never really thought I would be good at relationships. I suppose that's why I never pursued one."

"Well, that's certainly not the case, is it?" Cate smiled.

"No, maybe not. But I think I've got a lot more healing to do before I could even think about it again, if ever," Bradley revealed.

Cate reached over the front seat and put her hand on Bradley's shoulder. "That's the beauty of meaningful relationships. They usually happen when you are open to them and you least expect them."

Bradley burst into a laugh, startling both Derek and Cate.

"That wasn't supposed to be funny, Bradley. It was supposed to be sweet—and poignant," Cate objected to his reaction.

"I'm just remembering the circumstances when the two of you met. It was hardly unexpected, Cate." Bradley chuckled. "But you were definitely open to it."

"What are you talking about?" Cate asked.

"You never gave Derek a chance. You hooked him that night on the cruise ship the minute he sat at our dinner table," Bradley snickered.

Derek said, "Actually, it was earlier in the day, on deck. She sat next to me at the swimming pool bar."

Bradley smirked, as he lowered his voice and rhythmically spoke. "Really? And was she shy and reserved, Derek?"

Derek spoke in the manner of a television game show host. "On the contrary, Bradley. She was chatty and flirty. And she looked amazing in her bathing suit."

"And tell us, Derek. What prize did she win just for playing the game?" Bradley continued to play along.

"Why, me, of course," Derek announced.

Cate screeched. "Oh, my God. I can't believe you two. Stop it. It was not like that at all."

Bradley and Derek chuckled at their wit.

Then Bradley said, "It was exactly like that, Cate. You knew what you wanted, and you went after him. There's nothing wrong with that. And to be fair, Derek was an easy mark. He didn't put up too much of a fight."

It was Derek's turn to object. "What the hell do you know? You were twelve years old, for chrissake."

"You were both doomed from the beginning," Bradley replied. I was just glad you turned out to be one of the good guys, Derek."

"Me, too," Cate agreed.

Derek just shook his head.

EXPLAIN YOURSELF!

The shuttle from Washington landed at Logan right on time. When all the other passengers had deboarded, an airline attendant brought Bradley's wheelchair onto the plane and helped him in. Then the attendant gathered Bradley's bags and followed him and Rusty outside to the pickup area.

Through the glass doors, Bradley saw them standing next to a blue van. He could feel emotions welling but tried hard not to let them take hold. When Lynn saw him, she ran and threw her arms around him. Doug was right behind her.

Doug instructed the attendant to put the bags in the back of the van and then handed him some money.

"Bradley, you look wonderful. So healthy," Lynn said.

Balancing on his hind legs, Rusty lifted his front paws off the ground and waited for his hug.

Lynn giggled and gave him a hug. "You look wonderful, too, Rusty."

"Hello, Bradley," Doug said as he shook Bradley's hand, then, still holding his hand, leaned down for a hug. "Your mother's right. You look good."

"Thanks, Dad. I feel good. Who does the van belong to?" Bradley asked.

"It's ours. We bought it second-hand. Got a great deal on it, too," Doug said before sliding the side door open. He pressed a button, and a platform slid out and lowered to the ground.

"Dad, you didn't have to do this. You shouldn't waste your money like that." Bradley shook his head, then steered onto the platform.

Doug pushed a button to raise Bradley, then turned to Lynn and said, "Didn't I tell you he would say that?"

Lynn nodded.

"We didn't buy it because of you, Bradley. Well, maybe partly, but we have more and more friends from the church that require rides to their doctors' appointments, and those ride-share companies aren't always reliable. So, your mother and I have been doing our part to help."

"Oh. That's great." Bradley couldn't help but feel a bit self-centered at that moment.

"Why didn't you tell us you were coming back, Bradley? I could have gotten the house ready for you," Lynn asked.

"It wasn't planned, Mom. I got called back for an emergency at work. But that's done now," Bradley replied.

"Are you telling me that the FBI knew where to find you this whole time, and we didn't?" Lynn asked.

"I didn't tell anyone where I was, Mom. But Derek apparently had been tracking me. Don't give him a hard time about it. It's my fault, not his."

"Where have you been, son?" Doug asked.

Bradley smiled. "To the beginning of the earth and back."

"Isn't the saying 'to the ends of the earth and back'?" Lynn asked.

"Usually, but not this time," Bradley said. "We've been to Italy, Spain, Tibet, Bhutan, India, and, oh, Canada," he said, adding, "and a few others."

"I just don't understand why you had to leave the way you did, Bradley," Lynn said.

"I know, I'm sorry. I'll try to explain it but let's hold off on that conversation until later, alright? I'm just really happy to see you."

Obviously excited about getting back home, Rusty panted heavily and danced in the back of the van for the final mile of the ride.

Bradley's house, or rather the old industrial laundry building in the abandoned industrial park that he transformed into his home, looked the same as when he left, although he noticed the firewood pile under the lean-to stacked high.

Doug parked the van and opened the sliding door with the push of a button. Rusty bounded out and ran wide circles in the driveway, then sat and waited for Bradley. Doug grabbed Bradley's luggage from the back while Bradley lowered himself to the driveway.

"Wow, this feels weird," Bradley said.

"It feels right," Lynn added.

Doug unlocked the door, and Rusty ran inside, sniffing and checking every inch of the place. Bradley's home consisted of an open living space with the only walls around the bathroom in the back corner by his bed. He gazed to the right into his kitchen. It seemed nothing had moved. The stone fireplace in the middle of the room was well stocked with wood. His couch to the left of the fireplace felt inviting. He looked forward to relaxing and reading a good book.

He had created office space at the far end of the front side of the building. He never had imagined that his computer and monitors would sit untouched for more than a year.

"I guess Zayt hasn't been using my workout equipment," Bradley said, noting that it sat covered in dust next to the back patio sliding doors.

"Will Zayt be coming up?" Lynn asked Bradley.

"Did you tell him I was coming home?"

"No," Doug said. "Didn't you?"

"No. I didn't tell anyone but you. But," Bradley smiled, "I know how to get him here."

Bradley wrote the word Hey on a piece of paper and attached it to Rusty's collar. Then he opened the back sliders, and Rusty bounded out the door, down the embankment, and into the sandpit where the REACH community made its home. If Zayt was down there, Rusty would find him. And in just a matter of minutes, Bradley expected to see his friend at his door.

Lynn started a pot of coffee, then began to sanitize the kitchen while Bradley wiped down office equipment. Doug sat on the couch and watched.

"Douglas, get up and do something," Lynn scolded.

Doug slid across the couch. "I am. I'm dusting the couch."

Bradley laughed at his father. "Good one, Dad."

Lynn huffed and continued cleaning.

Then the front door opened, and Rusty trotted inside. Zayt stood in the doorway.

They met each other halfway, and without speaking a word, embraced. When they did, Bradley could swear he saw Zayt wipe a tear from his wet, brown cheek. "Hey," Zayt said.

"You're looking good, dude," Bradley said.

"You, too, Maestro."

Bradley chuckled at the use of his former college professor's nickname for him. Zayt was the only person he ever told about it.

"I hear you've got a girl," Bradley smiled.

"Now how the hell would you know that?" Zayt asked.

"I'm FBI. I know everything," Bradley replied as the two fell into an easy laugh.

"Hey, Doug, Lynn. I didn't think I'd see you again until Thursday," Zayt said.

"What's happens on Thursday?" Bradley asked.

"That's our day to work breakfast in the kitchen," Lynn said.

"The kitchen? Down there? I didn't know you were working at REACH!" Bradley exclaimed.

"Of course, you didn't, dear. You haven't been around, have you," Lynn taunted.

Bradley took the verbal slap with a raising of his brows.

Zayt grinned, admiring Lynn's audible reprimand. "You deserved that one, Bradley. And a few more."

"Alright," Bradley said, smiling. "I know I owe you an explanation, but do we have to do this right now?"

Doug, who had been quietly sitting on the couch, shouted, "Yes."

All eyes turned toward him.

Doug wasn't smiling. He sat up straight, rigid, and unyielding. Bradley saw pain in his eyes.

"Dad?"

Lynn stopped cleaning, Zayt stopped grinning, and Bradley stopped breathing.

Doug said, "I need to know why my son felt the need to leave without warning and without explanation."

Lynn said, "Doug, please."

"No, Mom," Bradley said, letting out the breath he'd been holding. "It's alright. He's right."

"I'll let you talk," Zayt said as he began to leave.

"No, Zayt, stay. I owe you an explanation, too. I just hope I can."

Lynn got four coffee mugs from the cabinet, and they sat around the kitchen table.

Bradley took a deep breath and began. "From the time I was a kid, I found ways to fool myself into thinking I could do everything I wanted to do and be anything I wanted to be. And I did. I wired my brain to believe that. But it just wasn't true. My physical limitations kept getting in the way. After realizing I could never be a marine like Dad, all I wanted was to be an FBI field agent. I wanted to help the good people and take down the bad guys."

Bradley stopped and took a sip of coffee.

"But I couldn't do that. The best I could do was become an analyst. So I threw myself into that, and it worked for a while. Now and then, I would get a taste of the life I had really wanted, and it was great, but it would also remind me of the dreams I would never fulfill."

Bradley shook his head. "Look, I don't know if you can understand what I'm trying to tell you, but there was always this dark side to me—the side of the couldn'ts, wouldn'ts, and never wills—the side I wouldn't let people see. And that's the side that kept creeping into my head, growing year by year, influencing my decisions. Well, the bad decisions anyway."

Bradley looked at Zayt. "Like the Joshua thing. I'm sorry, Zayt. I could have gotten you killed. I never should have involved you in that case. But, more so, I shouldn't have taken matters into my own hands. And, because of my bad decisions, I put you in danger, and Derek was forced to kill Joshua. I can't go back and fix that."

Zayt replied, "Dude, you didn't force me into anything."

"The point is, I never should have asked. After that experience, I thought I had things under control, and other than a few minor digressions, I did. Then I met Laney. She made it easy. She made me feel whole. Things were good. I was good. And then, the perfect storm."

Bradley stopped and took a deep breath. Doug put his hand on Bradley's shoulder.

"Then came Laney's brain aneurysm and Amanda Lessing, the Pathside Predator. If Laney's death wasn't enough to do it, Lessing was. She showed me my true self, the one no one else saw, not even me. But she saw it, right from the beginning."

"I don't understand, Bradley," Lynn said. "What could a serial killer possibly see in you that no one else could?"

"Herself. She saw herself in me," Bradley explained.

Lynn raised her voice. "That's absurd, Bradley. She was a crazy person. She . . ."

"Lynn," Doug insisted, "let him finish."

"No, I'm afraid she was right," Bradley said. "I was just a different face in the same mirror. Before I killed her, she told me that we both knew better than others how to protect those in need, and we knew how to punish those who deserved it."

Bradley lifted his chin and stretched his neck as he tried to quell the cramp forming in his throat. He closed his eyes and pictured himself standing on a beach at sunset.

Lynn was about to speak when Doug held up his hand and stopped her. Tears formed in the corners of her eyes.

Bradley opened his eyes and continued. "You see, everything I had done up to that point in my life was for me—and only me. I wasn't being altruistic or noble. I knew best, I played God, and three people are dead. I wasn't much different from her." Bradley shook his head slowly. "But at least she gave me the answer I was looking for. She gave me the means to an end. I finally understood why I did the things I did, why I made bad decisions and put myself and sometimes others in harm's way."

A single tear formed in Bradley's eye. Doug watched it stream down his face and drip onto his chest.

"Because, as Lessing said, 'Death is peace, and we wish upon ourselves what we do to punish others.' So, this is me, was me. I understand that it's not what you expected. Neither did I." Bradley paused. "Look, I know I'm not a bad person, but I'm not the person you—or I—thought I was, either. And I've made my peace with it."

Bradley scanned the faces at the table. He could tell his father and Zayt understood. Maybe being in the military and having faced horrors of their own helped them to. But his mother would never understand. He would always be the perfect little boy, man, and son to her.

"So, to answer your original question, Dad, I was at a crossroad. I was grieving the loss of the only woman I ever loved, the one person who made me feel whole. I learned that I had been lying to myself and others most of my life, and I was at my lowest point of self-esteem. When I found myself writing letters, permanent goodbye letters, I had a choice to make."

Lynn put her hands to her face and gasped.

"Thank the Lord you made the right choice, son." Doug teared.

"I'm sorry if I've disappointed you," Bradley said.

Doug replied, "You could never disappoint us, Bradley. There's darkness within each of us. You're not the first person in the world to be challenged by it. In fact, you're not the first person at this table."

Bradley noticed Zayt nodding his head.

"Mom? Are you alright?" Bradley asked, laying his hand on her lap.

"I just can't bare thinking about the pain you were in. Promise me you will talk to us, or someone, if you ever find yourself feeling that way again."

Bradley smiled at his mom, "I promise. I love you, Mom."

"Oh, Bradley, I love you so much." Lynn swarmed him with hugs and kisses.

"Alright," Doug said, "that's enough of that. It seems this is a time for celebration, not sadness. We move forward, and we never look back. What are your plans now that you're home?"

"Well, I wanted to talk to you about that. I'm not sure. I can use all the advice I can get," Bradley said.

"If it's one thing your mother's got plenty of, Bradley, it's advice," Doug teased.

Zayt and Bradley chuckled as Lynn began to bicker with Doug.

"What are your options?" Zayt asked Bradley when the commotion died down.

"It's funny. Five days ago, I watched the most spectacular sunrise over the Himalayas, and I wouldn't have guessed I'd be back here in Revere so soon, if ever. I really thought I was done with the FBI. But people are alive today because I came back. Don't ask me any questions about that, because I can't answer them," Bradley admonished. "And it felt really good. And I know I did it the right way for the right reason. So, now I'm not sure what I want."

"Did you enjoy doing whatever it was you did in DC?" Doug asked.

Zayt's eyes furrowed when he heard Bradley had been in Washington.

"Yes, I did. It got my juices flowing again," Bradley said.

"Here's the thing, Bradley. Whatever decision you make doesn't have to define the rest of your life. You can change your mind—and your life—at any time, as you now well know," Doug said.

"Yeah, I guess so. I could go back, and if I don't like it or if I find myself making bad decisions again, I can make a change," Bradley said.

"Son, I have a feeling your darkest days are behind you. I'm proud of you."

"Thanks, Dad."

"Well, let's go. This place isn't going to clean itself," Lynn exclaimed.

"Yup, I'll get back to cleaning that couch," Doug said with a wink and went and sat down.

"When do I get to meet Tasha?" Bradley asked Zayt.

"I'm FBI, I know everything . . . my ass! You were in DC. Cate told you about Tasha."

"She told me of Tasha. She didn't tell me anything about her except that she has a scary cop face." Bradley chuckled.

"Damn right she does." Zayt grinned.

Lynn said, "She's just the sweetest little thing, Bradley. You're going to love her."

"Well, set it up, dude. I have to meet the woman who has tamed the beast," Bradley said.

"Have you got a phone? Or are you going to stay incognito for the rest of your life?" Zayt asked.

Bradley gave Zayt his cellphone number and said, "Hey, it's great to see you. I missed you. And thanks for keeping an eye on the place."

"I'll call you tomorrow," Zayt said. "Hey, Rusty."

Rusty jumped from his bed beside the fireplace and ran to Zayt, who knelt and pet the dog. "It's nice to have you home, too, buddy. Later."

Zayt left, and Bradley sighed. He hadn't realized how exhausting it was to bare his soul. But he wasn't finished. He had promised Cate that he would let everyone know he was back and was alright.

He dialed Holly's phone. He recalled meeting Holly and her father, Mike, along with other friends on the cruise ship years before with Cate and Derek when he was a pre-teen. Holly, since married to John, lived in Amherst, Massachusetts, and owned a publishing company. She and Bradley shared a love of books. Mike lived in Worcester not far from Holly, and last Bradley knew, had a girlfriend named Olivia.

"Hello?" Holly answered.

"Hello, darlin'," Bradley said.

"Who is this?" Holly asked.

"Has it really been that long?" Bradley asked.

"Bradley? Oh, my God, Bradley! How are you? Where are you?" Holly screeched.

"I'm home. I just got in today," he said.

"Where the hell have you been? I've been worried sick about you," Holly cried.

"I know, and I'm sorry. I'm really sorry I made you worry. Someday I'll explain everything to you, but I wanted you to know that I'm alright and everything is good. I'd love to see you and John and your Dad, if possible. Maybe we could meet somewhere? Sometime soon?" Bradley asked.

"Of course. I'll talk to Dad. Bradley, does everyone know you're back?" Holly asked.

"I've got to call Sheila and David. And I haven't told anyone at the office yet. But I want to know how you are, Holly. What's going on in your life? How is Grace?"

"She's going to the University of Massachusetts, of course. With John being a professor there, the tuition benefits are a no brainer."

"That's terrific. How's the publishing business?"

"Booming. Are you looking for work? I could use another editor," Holly laughed.

"I'll keep that in mind," Bradley chuckled.

"Wait, are you serious? Have you left the FBI?"

"No, I'm still in decision mode. I'm trying to figure out what I want to do with my life."

"That's simple," Holly said. "Do what makes you happy. Do what you love."

"Yeah, maybe it is that simple. Thanks, Holly. How is it you can take a major issue and bring it down to its simplest form?"

"It's something my dad always told me," Holly said. "It's so good to talk to you, Bradley. We've missed you so much."

"Me, too. Talk to your dad. This is my new cellphone number. I think I'm getting my truck delivered tomorrow, so I can meet you any time after. Call me after you talk to Mike and John. Give them both my best."

"I will. I love you, Bradley," Holly said.

"I love you, too, darlin'."

Bradley smiled as he remembered the first time he met Holly on the first night on the cruise just before dinner. Lynn and Bradley sat on deck watching the sunset. When they turned to leave, Lynn accidentally pushed Bradley's wheelchair over Holly's foot. They'd been friends ever since.

Bradley called Sheila, Cate's sister. Considered one of the best fashion consultants in Hollywood, Sheila owned multiple clothing boutiques. Her husband, David, was a successful

Hollywood movie producer distinguished for holding the record for the largest grossing film in history to date.

Sheila cried the whole time they talked. They made plans to get together and promised to plan a reunion of some sort for the whole gang. Bradley just knew that as soon as they hung up, Sheila would call Cate.

That counted for everybody except for Mara and Nick, his friends and co-workers. He wondered how married life was working out for them. The last thing he had done before he left was attend their wedding. They must be celebrating their first anniversary soon, or did they already? Bradley wondered. He couldn't remember the date of the wedding. He was in a difficult place back then. He decided to wait until the next day when he got his truck back. He would go to the office to see them in person. Hopefully, I will have made a decision about my future by then, he thought.

Bradley spent the remainder of the day with his parents. Doug brought him to the grocery store to stock up on food. Lynn moved on auto pilot cleaning Bradley's house. Bradley had to practically tie her down to get her to stop and relax. And despite a warm evening, the three and Rusty gathered by the fireplace and sipped wine. Bradley told them about his travels, including visiting Potala Palace in Tibet and feeling disappointed that he could not go inside as it was not accessible with a wheelchair. He talked of the giant Buddha Dordenma Statue in Thimphu, Bhutan, and the fabulous food of Italy. He spoke of the sunrise view from Darjeeling's Tiger Hill and the feeling of complete serenity it evoked.

Hours passed. When they realized how late it had gotten, Bradley suggested his parents stay the night rather than travel back to New Hampshire. He helped his mother put sheets and a

69

blanket on the sleep sofa, all the while wondering how he could have stayed away so long when only days earlier he wondered how he could ever leave the beauty and peacefulness of India and go home.

Life is fluid, he thought, and I hope to never take it for granted again.

OLD ADVERSARIES

The next morning, they sat sipping coffee at the kitchen table when Bradley's truck showed up on the back of a flatbed.

Bradley found odd the emotional response he felt on seeing his custom Chevy Silverado. Throughout his travels abroad, he needed to depend on others to get him where he wanted to go. But he learned to appreciate the help instead of resenting the need for it as he had in the past. It was an important lesson learned.

But back in the States, he would take back his independence, vowing never to forget that everyone needs help sometimes, especially those who shy away from it.

The driver unloaded the truck into Bradley's driveway and drove away. Keys in hand, Bradley pressed a button on the fob, and the driver's side panel pulled straight out. Another button lowered the driver's platform to the ground. Rusty bounded passed Bradley and jumped into the truck and onto the passenger seat.

"Sorry, pal. We aren't going anywhere just yet." Bradley chuckled. "Come on out."

Rusty begrudgingly jumped down from the truck.

After making plans for dinner on Sunday and saying goodbye to his parents, Bradley readied himself to go to the office. Before he left, he called Derek.

"Bradley, hey. How are things going back home?" Derek asked.

"Good. I spent yesterday with my parents, and you can tell Cate that I talked to both Holly and Sheila."

"She already knows. Sheila called yesterday."

"Of course she did. How are things in Washington?"

"Quiet. Not a peep out of our friend. I imagine he's regrouping," Derek said.

"So, I've been thinking. I want to get back to work, but I wondered if I could have the rest of the week to get settled before I do?"

"You have no idea how happy I am to hear that!" Derek sighed. "Absolutely. Take the rest of the week. I'll call Nick and give him the good news."

"Actually, I'm going to head over there shortly. I thought I might surprise them."

"You might get a little surprise yourself," Derek said.

"What do you mean?"

"Nothing, forget it. Have Nick get in touch with me so we can enact the transfer. Right now, you are still working for the DC office."

"Alright. Give Cate a hug for me."

"You bet."

Not long after, Bradley parked his truck in the Chelsea FBI headquarters parking lot, and he and Rusty entered the lobby.

"Agent Whitman! You're back!" Carl, the security guard, jumped from his chair to greet them.

"Carl, how the heck are you?" Bradley asked. "How many kids have you got now?"

"The sixth one made it here while you were away. He came out kicking and screaming and hasn't stopped since. You're looking good, Agent Whitman, and you, too, Agent Rusty. It's nice to have you back."

"It's nice to be back, Carl." Bradley showed Carl his official badge as required, and Carl logged him in. "Give my best to your wife."

Bradley and Rusty rode the elevator to the eighth floor. When the doors opened, Bradley found himself face to face with Sahani Kumar, a psychologist Derek had brought in to work the Pathside Predator case and with whom Bradley had had some unpleasant dealings. This must have been the surprise Derek referred to, Bradley thought.

"Bradley. Hello," Sahani said, obviously startled to see him.

Equally startled, Bradley replied, "Hello. I . . . I didn't know you were still working here."

"Derek asked me to stay on and help fill the position after you . . . " she stuttered, " . . . after the job opened up."

"Ah, I see," Bradley said. "Sahani, I need to speak with Nick, but can I come and see you when I'm finished?"

"Of course. I'll be in my office for most of the day," Sahani replied. "It's good to see you. You look well."

"Thank you. You, too," Bradley said, feeling short on words.

The two had a contentious relationship after Sahani used misinformation and deceit to convince Bradley to do something he didn't wish to do. As it turned out, Sahani had been right. Bradley knew he owed her an apology.

They swapped positions, Sahani entered the elevator, and Bradley moved off. The doors closed behind him.

For a moment, he sat in the foyer and absorbed intense emotion brought on by being back in the office. He scanned the bullpen to the left where the agents sat. He felt at once disappointed that Mara was not at her desk. Tony and Jim, among others, gathered in animated discussion. None of them looked his way.

Bradley wheeled by the bullpen partition and passed the interrogation rooms, conference room, and briefing room until he reached Hazel Hadley's desk at the end of the hall. Hazel had been the assistant to the supervisory special agent since before Derek held the position. She currently worked for Nick.

"Agent Whitman? My goodness, it's good to see you. How have you been?" she asked with a bright smile.

"I've been great, Hazel. You look terrific. How are you doing?"

"I'm still on the right side of the grass," she replied. "I don't see you on the schedule, so I'm guessing this is an unexpected visit?"

"It is—and a surprise. Is it a bad time?"

"It's never a bad time for you. Shall I announce you?" she asked.

"Yes, but could you be vague? I want to see his reaction when he sees me."

"I can manage that," she said with a grin.

Hazel buzzed Nick's intercom.

"Yes, Hazel?" Nick's voice came over the speaker.

"Sir, there's a gentleman here to see you."

"Who is it?"

"He is reluctant to give me his name?" she replied.

"I'll be right there," Nick said, sounding annoyed.

Bradley placed himself and Rusty directly in front of Nick's door. When it opened, Nick was so dumbfounded, he forgot they were in Hazel's presence and swore.

"Bradley! What the fuck are you doing here? Where have you been? Son-of-a-bitch, it's been a long time. Come in. Come in," Nick said excitedly, then apologized to Hazel for his indiscretion.

Before Nick closed the door, he asked Hazel to call Mara and tell her to come to his office but not to tell her why.

"I see you've still got the mutt," Nick chuckled.

Rusty tilted his head.

"It's good to see you, Nick. How's married life treating you?"

"It's great, Bradley. Jesus, where the hell have you been?"

"Here and there. It's kind of a long story."

"Are you back? I mean for good?"

"I worked it out with Derek this morning. Starting Monday, I'm back in the fold," Bradley said.

"Thank God," Nick said. "We've really missed you. Sahani is good but . . ." Nick's happy expression faltered when he realized Sahani's presence might make for a sticky situation.

"It's alright, Nick. I just saw Sahani in the foyer."

"Then you know she took your place? Or tried to, anyway."

"Yeah. It was a smart move. She's good at her job," Bradley said.

Hazel buzzed the intercom and said, "Agent Gaston is here to see you, sir."

"Send her in, please."

Bradley turned his chair to face the door. When the two saw each other, both wore the same stunned expression.

"Bradley!"

"Mara? Are you? Holy cow, you're pregnant!" Bradley said, "How did? I mean, when did that happen?"

Mara went to Bradley and wrapped him in a hug. Bradley swung his arms around her bulging belly.

"And Rusty!" Mara swooned as she awkwardly bent down to stroke his head.

"I can't believe this," Bradley said, looking back and forth from Mara to Nick. "Congratulations."

Nick's grin lit the room.

"You look stunning, Mara!" Bradley smiled.

"I feel like a bloated cow," she replied, placing her hand on her stomach.

"It's the potato chips and ice cream at three o'clock in the morning," Nick said.

"He's so supportive, isn't he?" Mara chuckled.

"I can't believe this. Nick is going to be a father," Bradley stated.

"What about me being a mother?" Mara asked.

"Well, that's easy for me to imagine. You're going to be a fantastic mother. But Nick?" Bradley said, jokingly.

"And that is why I've missed you so much." Mara smiled at Bradley. Then she grew serious. "Where have you been? We've all been so worried about you."

"I know. I'm sorry. It's just something I had to do."

"And now? What now?"

Bradley nodded to Nick.

Nick said, "He's coming back to work on Monday."

"Now that's the best news I've heard in seven months," Mara said, patting her belly. "But what about Sa . . ." She stopped herself.

"It's alright. He knows about Sahani," Nick said. "I guess we'll have to see how that plays out."

"Speaking of Sahani, I told her I would stop in and see her on my way out. I'll let you get back to work. Nick, Derek wants you to contact him about my transfer."

"Transfer? From where?"

"Washington. Just a formality," Bradley added, to head off any questions. "I know I don't start until Monday, but if you need anything, give me a call. And congratulations, again."

"Thank you, Bradley," Mara replied.

Bradley said goodbye to Hazel and wheeled his way back past the elevator to the other end of the building, to Sahani Kumar's office. Her door lay open, and she sat behind her desk.

Bradley lightly knocked on the door jamb, and she smiled when she saw him.

"Come in, Bradley," she said as she stood and moved to a chair in front of her desk. "I must say, I was surprised to see you. I didn't know you were back."

Bradley placed his chair to face her. Rusty lay at his feet.

"Nobody did," he replied. He glanced down toward Rusty. "We just got back in town yesterday."

Bradley cleared his throat before going on. He continued, "Sahani, I wanted to see you so I could apologize. I acted horribly toward you before I left, and it was inexcusable. You were just doing your job and trying to help me through a tough time, and I behaved like a . . . well, like the self-centered asshole that I was. I'm sorry."

"Wow. That's quite an apology," Sahani said as she got up and closed her office door. "But it's a bit over-the-top, don't you think?"

"No, I really don't. I've learned a lot about myself this last year, most of it not very pleasant. I was in a bad place before I left, and you were the perfect landing point for all my anger."

"You've never been a self-centered asshole, Bradley. You've done too much good for too many people to ever be one," Sahani said.

"But I did those things for the wrong reasons," he explained.

"No, I don't believe that. You may have made some bad decisions, and maybe you had underlying motives, but in the end, you always want to do what's right. Not what's best for you, but what's right. That's not self-centered, that's being human."

"I think you're being too easy on me," Bradley said.

"And I think you're being too hard on yourself," Sahani replied. "So, let's see which one of us is right, shall we? Tell me what you think you learned about yourself."

Nearly three hours passed before Bradley left Sahani's office. He felt both exhausted and rejuvenated. They discussed his experience with Amanda Lessing and how it affected him. They discussed Laney and meditation and self-deception. Bradley spoke of the spiritual nature of his travels and how he wished to incorporate that balance and peace into his everyday life. He talked about the day as a six-year-old he played catch with his dog Roscoe and flopped to the ground, never regaining the use of his legs and the denial that ensued. No subject was left untouched, not even the subject of suicide.

The answers that he thought he had gotten from Amanda Lessing, he got from within himself with Sahani's help. And he felt much better about where he stood.

Sahani and Bradley made an appointment to talk again the following week, but she conveyed that he could stop in to see her anytime.

"Thank you," Bradley said.

"No, thank you. I've been wishing for this for a long time. I'm glad we were finally able to sit and talk," Sahani replied.

Bradley pushed the button on the elevator before he heard a man's voice yell, "Bradley?"

Bradley turned and saw Tony, Jim, and several other agents streaming toward him, all smiling, all asking where the hell he had been. The elevator came and went without Bradley aboard.

When Bradley and Rusty finally made it home, Bradley opened the slider doors for the dog to go outside. He followed. It was too late to stop Rusty from bounding down the ledge when Bradley noticed two police vehicles with flashing lights in the sandpit below. The cruisers were parked by the REACH community dining hall.

He dialed Zayt's phone number and got his voicemail. Bradley left a message asking if everything was alright and told Zayt to call him when he could.

Unable to discern what might be happening, Bradley watched from his back patio. He didn't see Rusty running around as he normally would. He thought about getting into the truck and driving down to the pit, but then he saw the two police cruisers leave. Not long after, he spied Rusty outside of Zayt's cabin.

His cellphone rang.

"Zayt, what the heck is going on down there?" Bradley asked.

"Nothing major. Just some whack-job causing trouble," Zayt mumbled.

"What's the matter? You sound funny," Bradley said.

"My lip is swollen and split. The guy sucker punched me."

"Are you alright?" Bradley asked, concerned.

"Better than he is." Zayt tried to chuckle, then said, "Ow."

"Was it one of your residents?"

"No. I never saw this guy before. He came for lunch and just kind of hung around and bothered people. When I tried to get him to leave, he walloped me."

"It must have been your gracious personality," Bradley said, laughing.

"Yeah, well, I graciously sent him to the hospital escorted by the Revere Police Department."

"As long as you're alright. Hey, send Rusty home, will you?"

"I'll try. He's making the rounds."

"Later."

"Later."

OLD FRIENDS

Thursday morning, Bradley and Rusty woke with nothing to do. Even during his travels, Bradley always had a train to catch or somewhere to be. The unfamiliar circumstance caused him anxiety.

He realized how completely backwards his thinking was. He surmised that the average person would love to have a day with nothing to do—a day with all possibilities open. But Bradley had no idea what to do with himself.

As he lay in bed, he glanced at his workout equipment. In the past, his routine included rising early, spending forty to sixty minutes working out, showering, eating breakfast, and beginning work.

"Come on, lazy ass. Get out of bed," Bradley said to convince himself. Rusty immediately jumped from the bed to the floor. Bradley made himself a deal. If you do at least a thirty-minute workout, you can have French toast for breakfast.

Bradley let Rusty out, then began with some light stretches. Before long, he was into his normal workout rotation, which proved much harder since the last time he ran through it.

Sixty minutes later, sweaty and sore, Bradley transferred from his workout bench to his wheelchair. Rusty had not yet returned, so he went to take a shower. When he came back out to the living area, Rusty waited for him by the glass slider.

After feeding Rusty, he fed himself. Although he'd worked out more than promised to meet the requirements of his deal, he opted for instant oatmeal and a banana for breakfast.

While sitting at his kitchen table sipping coffee, Bradley stared at his darkened computer and monitors in the far corner. I suppose I should see if all that stuff still works, he thought.

He refilled his coffee and rolled to his desk. The computer and monitors sprang to life without a hitch. It occurred to him that other than retrieving information from Derek about al-Haqani, he hadn't checked either his personal or work emails in a year.

"This is going to be a mess," he said.

Your inbox is full, read the message. Hundreds of messages displayed as unread. He noticed many of them came from Cate. He clicked on the latest and read.

Please, Bradley. I'm worried sick. Just let me know that you are alright.

He opened another from Cate dated two months before that.

Bradley, I can't take this. I need to know that you are okay.

There were more, but he just couldn't bear to read them. He felt sick. He tried to imagine how he would feel if Cate disappeared without any real explanation. His dread increased.

Bradley decided to ask for Sahani's advice as to how to repair relationships he had damaged.

He cleared his personal emails and scanned the full folder of work messages before he deleted them.

Bradley then tried to login to the FBI database but was denied access.

"Of course, you idiot," he muttered.

He sent a text message to Derek asking him to have the tech team unblock his access. Minutes later, he received a reply from Derek.

They said it will take about an hour.

It didn't take Bradley long to revert to his overzealous work ethic. With his free time, Bradley decided to see what he could find out about Ali al-Haqani.

Al-Haqani grew up in the northeastern region of Afghanistan's Kunar Province outside the provincial capital of Asadabad. Bradley concentrated on the US war with Afghanistan during the time of al-Haqani's childhood. All of Afghanistan had been in turmoil before, during, and after al-Haqani left to attend Hopkinton Engineering Institute. His own boyhood school had been destroyed along with the local hospital, marketplace, and artillery compound. Turmoil dominated the region.

After drowning himself in the darkness of the Afghanistan war for two and a half hours, Bradley made a conscious decision to get away from the computer. He turned his equipment off.

"And that's how easy it is to get sucked back in," Bradley said aloud. But he grinned when he acknowledged he then made the decision to shut it down.

He and Rusty went out to the back patio, and Rusty, as always, bounded down the embankment and into the tiny home community to visit with its residents.

Bradley began to meditate. He found it more difficult to concentrate with city noises in the background but determined to try. He closed his eyes and thought of the beach at sunset, the hot sand, and Laney. Soon he was there.

He wasn't sure how much time had passed, but when he opened his eyes, Bradley noticed a Revere police cruiser parked outside Zayt's cabin. Must be a follow-up, he thought.

Bradley returned to his kitchen and whipped together a marinade of soy sauce, rice vinegar, ginger, garlic, and honey. He placed two chicken breasts into the mixture, covered the bowl, and stored it in the refrigerator. He then cooked and diced crisp bacon and set it aside. He tossed fresh bite-sized broccoli florets, minced red onion, shredded carrot, and diced sharp cheddar cheese into a bowl and added raisins. For the broccoli slaw sauce, he blended mayonnaise, apple cider vinegar, fresh lemon juice, sugar, and a scant amount of salt. Finally, he combined the broccoli mixture, sauce, and bacon. Bradley covered the bowl and placed it in the refrigerator next to the marinating chicken. He looked forward to dinner.

It felt good to be in the kitchen again, but Bradley knew he needed to control his cooking urges. He tended to make too much food and, quite often, too many extravagant desserts that expanded his waistline. He decided to forgo the sweets until he got back to a daily exercise routine.

Okay, now what? he thought.

He heard a knock on his door.

"Thank, God," Bradley said aloud, thankful for something to do.

When Bradley opened the door, Rusty ran inside. But it wasn't Zayt who accompanied him per usual. A woman with short black hair, silky smooth caramel skin, and deep brown eyes who reached at most five feet, five inches tall stood at the door.

"Bradley Whitman?" she asked.

"Yes, that's me. Are you Tasha?" Bradley asked.

"I am," she replied.

Bradley smiled. "Come in, please. It's nice to meet you."

They shook hands, and Tasha stepped inside.

"I wish this was just a social call and we could get to know one another better, but we have a problem," Tasha said.

Bradley paused, not sure how that could be possible since they had just met.

"What kind of problem?" he asked.

"Zayt's been arrested."

"What?" Bradley questioned. "What for?"

Tasha paused before she responded, "Murder."

Bradley's eyebrows reached for his hairline. "What the hell? Are you serious?" He had hoped it was some sort of joke, maybe a way to get back at him for leaving without a word.

"I wish I could say I wasn't. The Revere police just left. They took Zayt, in handcuffs, to jail."

"Who is he supposed to have murdered?"

"He had a run-in with some guy yesterday in the dining hall. They found the man dead this morning. They came to question Zayt. When they asked if they could search his place, he said yes. Before I knew it, they had him in handcuffs and in the back seat of the cruiser."

That's just crazy, Bradley thought, then asked, "Do you know who the arresting officer was?"

"He was a sergeant. Zayt seemed to know him, but it didn't do him any good."

"Doyle? Was his name Doyle?" Bradley asked.

"Yes. That's it, Doyle. A big Irish guy," Tasha grimaced.

"Son of a . . . ," Bradley sighed.

Bradley had met Sergeant Doyle seven years before during an investigation of a murder of a homeless woman in the same sandpit where Zayt had been arrested. Bradley had met Zayt then. Bradley had since worked with Doyle on several occasions and considered him a friend. Zayt did, also.

"This doesn't make sense," Bradley said. "Doyle knows Zayt. He's got to know Zayt would never murder someone."

"All I know is, when one of the officers came out of Zayt's cabin holding a bag, the Irish guy told Zayt he didn't have a choice. He cuffed him and put him in the car."

"You're a police officer, right?" Bradley asked.

"Yes."

"What do you think was in the bag?" Bradley asked.

Tasha shook her head. "I can tell you that the officer holding the bag had a wide grin on his face. He believed he had the proverbial smoking gun."

"But that would be impossible," Bradley said. "I'm going to the precinct to see Doyle. Zayt's going to need a lawyer. Do you know anyone?"

"I know several," she replied, "but none that I would stake my life on—or Zayt's."

Bradley picked up his phone and dialed. It took minutes before he was able to get Derek on the line.

"Hey, Bradley."

"Derek, we've got a problem. Zayt's been arrested by the Revere Police Department for murder. I don't have details yet, but he's going to need a lawyer. Who should I call?"

"Jesus. Ah, let me think. Sullivan. Call Damien Sullivan at Park Plaza. Tell him I referred you. Bradley, what the hell happened?" Derek asked.

"I don't know. I'll call you later when I have more information. Thanks, Derek." Bradley hung up.

Bradley found and dialed the number for Damien Sullivan. He asked to speak to the man and was stonewalled until he mentioned Derek's name. The next voice he heard was Sullivan's. Bradley told him everything he knew before he hung up.

"Well?" Tasha asked.

"He's going to look into it," Bradley said. "I'm going to see Doyle."

"Can I come with you?" Tasha asked.

"Yes, of course," he replied.

Revere Beach Parkway was home to the Revere Police Department. Bradley parked his truck and lowered himself to the tarmac.

Inside, when he asked to see Sergeant Doyle, the officer at the desk gave him a sideways glance.

"He's busy," the officer replied.

"So am I," Bradley said as he flashed his FBI badge.

The officer's eyes widened, and he got Doyle on the phone.

"There's an FBI agent here to see you," the officer said.

A moment later, Sergeant Doyle walked into the lobby.

"Jesus, Mary, and Joseph. I thought you were dead," Doyle said.

"Hardly," Bradley replied. "What the hell is going on, Doyle?"

Doyle held up his hand to stop Bradley from continuing and said, "Wait, follow me."

Bradley and Tasha followed Doyle into his office. Doyle shut the door behind him. He eyed Tasha, then Bradley, then back to Tasha.

"I don't know you," Doyle said to Tasha.

Bradley said, "This is Officer Tasha Williams, Zayt's girlfriend." Bradley emphasized the word officer.

"Huh, okay," Doyle responded. "Before you go off half-cocked, Bradley, I didn't have any choice. And you know I can't discuss this with you."

"We always have a choice, Doyle. What the hell were you thinking?"

"Hey!" Doyle yelled. "You can't just rise from the dead, flash your badge, and expect everyone to jump, Whitman. I'm doing my job. What the hell have you been doing?"

He has a point, Bradley thought. He took a few deep breaths and continued.

"You're right, Doyle. I'm sorry. I had no right to jump on you like that. I'm just upset. Forgive me."

Doyle stood with his mouth open. He hadn't expected Bradley to back down. Then he said, "Alright, then."

"What can you tell me?" Bradley asked.

"I can tell you we have a guy who recently had a nasty encounter with Zayt and who turned up dead."

"And?" Bradley urged.

"And we found damaging evidence in Zayt's cabin."

"What kind of evidence?"

Doyle huffed. "I can't tell you that."

Someone knocked on Doyle's office door.

"Come in," Doyle yelled.

Through the door came a tall man with white hair, pink skin, and black-framed glasses. He wore an expensive suit and carried a briefcase.

"My name is Damien Sullivan. I'm here to see my client, Warrick Gaines," the man said, using Zayt's real name.

Doyle glanced at Bradley and said, "Well, that was quick."

Bradley shrugged.

Bradley introduced himself and Tasha to Damien Sullivan.

"Would you mind excusing us?" Sullivan nodded to Bradley and Tasha.

"Not at all." Bradley turned to Doyle. "We'll talk later."

They waited in the lobby. Twenty-five minutes later, Sullivan walked in from the door that led to the jail cells. He approached Bradley and Tasha and said, "Is there somewhere we can talk?"

Bradley suggested the coffee shop across the street. He left his truck in the police department parking lot and wheeled to the crosswalk.

The three ordered coffee.

"Warrick has asked me to share information about his case with both of you," Sullivan began. "I will do this with the following stipulation. You will do nothing without my knowledge. That means you won't talk to anyone or investigate anything without me knowing it. If you agree to those terms, I'll continue."

"I agree," Bradley said.

"Me, too," Tasha replied.

"Alright. The victim was Ronald Crayton, twenty-seven years old, from Dorchester," Sullivan read from his notes. "They found him stabbed to death on Howland Street, which borders the property of the Revere Enhancement and Community Housing development. The police found what they think is the murder weapon in a drawer in Warrick's home. And they found a bloodstained shirt in his trash bucket."

"That's impossible," Bradley said.

"Maybe so," Sullivan replied. "Blood test results are not available yet. This whole thing could be a big mistake. But Mr. Gaines says he doesn't know anything about a bloody shirt or knife and has no idea how either would have gotten into his home."

"A frame-up?" Bradley asked.

"Let's wait and see what the test results say. Meanwhile, we do absolutely nothing," Sullivan demanded. "His arraignment is set for tomorrow morning at nine. We will argue he be granted release on bail, but for now, he'll be spending the night right where he is."

They exchanged contact information. Then Damien Sullivan got up to leave.

"Thank you, Mr. Sullivan. We appreciate you coming so quickly," Bradley said.

Sullivan nodded. "Give Derek my best," he said before he left.

On the drive back to Bradley's, Tasha said, "We have to do something. If someone is framing Zayt, we need to find out who and why."

Normally, that would have been Bradley's first reaction. He surprised himself when he replied, "No, Tasha, we don't. We need to let Sullivan handle this. Besides, Zayt may be out of there as soon as they get the test results. But if he has been set up, someone went to great lengths to do it. It's not in Zayt's best interest for us to muck around in this without any facts. This guy Sullivan is one of the best defense attorneys in the state. We need to trust him. We need to be patient."

"I thought Zayt was your friend." Tasha looked at Bradley as if she had been betrayed.

"He is. That's why I refuse to screw this up. We know he's innocent. We have to do this by the book. Zayt would say the same. Besides, you're a cop. You can't just go rogue like that. What police department do you work for, anyway?"

Tasha scowled. "Boston. But what good is being a cop in the BPD if I can't use it to save the good guys?"

Bradley grinned. "Zayt doesn't need saving. I'm sure he's having himself a nice nap right about now, probably dreaming about you. I'm guessing tonight will be much harder on you than it is him."

Tasha thought about Zayt's easy nature. "Yeah, I'm sure you're right about that."

Bradley dropped Tasha at Zayt's. "Call me if you need or hear anything."

"I will. Thank you for arranging the lawyer," Tasha added.

"Don't worry. This could all be over tomorrow."

"I hope so," she replied.

Back home, Bradley let Rusty outside. He felt a twinge of sorrow knowing Rusty would immediately go look for Zayt and wouldn't find him.

Then he called Derek and filled him in.

"Damien Sullivan sends his best. How do you know the guy?" Bradley asked. "I've never heard you mention him."

Derek chuckled. "Do you remember Duke Montalvo?"

"Montalvo, from the cruise? Of course. I ran him over with my wheelchair. I was a twelve-year-old invincible kid back then, wasn't I?" Bradley snickered.

"You thought so. Anyway, Sullivan was Montalvo's attorney when Montalvo was tried as an accessory in the jewel theft. That's how we met. During Montalvo's trial, he cross-examined me," Derek said.

"But, wait. Montalvo went to prison, didn't he?" Bradley asked.

"Yes, but Sullivan came damn close to swaying the jury."

"And you became friends with the guy?" Bradley asked.

"We've stayed in touch. He needs a favor, I need a favor. You know how it is. He's a good guy and an excellent defense lawyer."

Bradley sighed, "Well if the blood matches the victim, Zayt's going to need the best."

"Keep me updated and let me know if there's anything I can do," Derek said.

Bradley booted his computer and logged into the FBI database. With Ali al-Haqani on the back burner, Bradley entered the name Ronald Crayton—not an entirely ethical use of his credentials, considering it wasn't an FBI investigation. He filtered the search by adding Dorchester, Massachusetts, and the age twenty-seven.

"Bingo," Bradley said.

Ronald Crayton's adult criminal record began at age eighteen when he was arrested for breaking and entering a drug store. From then, his file listed multiple infractions including assault and battery, robbery, another B and E, several muggings, and three separate arrests for possession of a Class A substance with intent to distribute. He also possessed a juvenile record.

It's no surprise Crayton would be hanging around a homeless community for food, Bradley thought.

Earlier, Bradley had asked Tasha about the altercation that happened the day before between Zayt and Ronald Crayton.

"I didn't see it," she had told him, "but Zayt told me Crayton had been harassing the residents in the dining hall while they cleaned up and restocked. When Zayt asked him to leave, he said the guy just went crazy and sucker punched him. Zayt tried to hold him off, but he kept coming at him, so Zayt put him down."

After reading his record, Bradley assumed Crayton had been influenced by drugs during the incident.

Bradley had an enormous urge to call the coroner's office to get preliminary information on the deceased, but he had promised Damien Sullivan he wouldn't do anything unless he spoke with him first. Besides, he figured Dr. Maria Reyes's office would not have the autopsy report for days.

He smiled when he thought of Maria. Bradley had known her professionally for years. She was the most competent and thorough coroner he had ever met. She was also a sweet and kind person unless she were crossed. Then, watch out. The last Bradley knew, Sergeant Doyle had finally convinced Maria to date him. Bradley wondered if they were still a couple.

Before grilling his chicken for dinner, Bradley called his parents to let them know what had happened. Luckily, Bradley thought, Zayt's arrest had come after his parents left the REACH kitchen Thursday.

"That's absurd," Doug reacted.

"I know, Dad. I'm sure it will all work out," Bradley said while not feeling convinced himself.

"What are you going to do about it, Bradley?" his father asked.

"Me? I'm not his lawyer, Dad."

"You know what I mean. You're going to investigate this, right?"

"I'll do whatever his lawyer needs me to do," Bradley said.

"His lawyer? Bradley, there's nobody better than you to find out what's going on!" Then Doug paused. "Oh, I get it. Sorry. You can't talk about it. Alright, son. Get to it. Get Zayt out of there."

"No, Dad. That's not it. That's not the way this works." Bradley felt conflicted. Every bone in his body wanted to do exactly what his father suggested—take the matter into his own hands and solve the problem. That's what he would have done in the past. But it wasn't right. It wasn't even the best course of action. He had come to understand that. "We need to let his lawyer do his job. I told him I would help any way I could."

"Uh. Okay," Doug sounded concerned. "Are you alright, Bradley?"

Bradley shook his head affirmatively. "Yes, Dad, I'm alright. Give Mom a kiss for me." Bradley hung up.

He couldn't fault his father for being confused by his own non action. Bradley had blurred that line so often that even those around him began to see fuzzy. He knew he was making the right decision, but that didn't make him feel any better.

Bradley felt jittery and anxious the rest of the evening. He came close several times to getting in his truck and going to inspect the crime scene. He also desperately wanted to talk to Zayt. And he knew if he wanted to, he would be able to weasel his way in to see him. But he had promised Sullivan he wouldn't. Much like a drug addict who craved a fix, Bradley detoxed from his savior complex—the need for him, and only him, to save the world.

He meditated. He exercised. He tried reading a book. None of it took his mind off Zayt's predicament. As a last resort to distract himself, Bradley turned on the news.

. . . on the scene. The fire is still burning, but authorities say they are confident they have it under control. The number of casualties is climbing. The last count brings the total of injured or dead to over two hundred. Once again, an explosion has occurred in New York City's Times Square. Hundreds have been injured or killed. We will report updates as they are learned.

In other news, we are getting reports of a fire at the Mall of America in Minnesota. Let's send it over to our affiliate FOX 9 news station. Casey Long, what can you tell us about the fire?

Thank you, Sarah. We've learned that the fire is a result of an explosion within the mall. As you can see behind me, the east end of the complex is still in flames. I'm told the fire is in an area where construction has been taking place. We have yet to get an injury update, but I can tell you that I've seen twelve ambulances come and go since I've been on scene, and there are more ambulances arriving every minute. We expect to get a briefing from the fire chief shortly. This is Casey Long reporting for FOX 9 news. Back to you Sarah.

Thank you, Casey. Next up, a shooting in Dorchester . . .

Bradley turned off the television, sorry he had turned it on in the first place. He closed his eyes and tried to picture himself sitting atop Tiger Hill with the golden glow of the sun lighting his face. Instead, he saw flames.

He rested his arms on his chair, palms up, index fingers touching his thumbs, and tried to concentrate on his breathing. He tried to feel the hot sandy beach beneath his feet, but all he saw was the police cruiser parked in the sandpit with lights flashing.

Bradley opened his eyes. I don't know if I can do this. How can I just sit here and do nothing? The thought consumed him like a blanket covering his entire body that cast him into darkness.

He sighed deeply, then thought of his conversation with Sahani. Taking him by surprise, she had asked him if he liked sports. He conveyed his childhood disappointment at not being able to participate in team sports and his admiration of athletes' dedication to their craft.

"What is it you admire most?" Sahani had asked.

"Their commitment, I guess," he had replied.

"Anything else?"

"Well, yes. Their focus, coachability, and especially their short-term memory," he explained.

"What do you mean, short-term memory?" she questioned.

"Their ability to move on from a bad play, or performance," he said.

It was at that point Bradley felt like a horse led to water.

She had then said, "Exactly. It doesn't matter what's already happened. There's nothing any of us can do about the past. It's done, over. We can only control what's ahead of us. Tell me, Bradley, what happens to an athlete if they dwell on the last poor play instead of focusing on making the next play a good one?"

"They will most likely turn in another poor performance." Bradley spoke what he knew she expected to hear.

Sahani had then sat back in her chair and smiled. "That's really all any of us can do. Focus on making our next choice a good one. And, if I may take this metaphor a little further, greatness is never achieved alone."

"But what about the guilt that comes with being unable to protect—," Bradley then decided to stay within the parameters of the metaphor, "—protect the quarterback?"

"There are ten other players on the field, Bradley. They, we, all need to take responsibility. No one person will ever be able to stop the pass rush," she answered.

"You're a football fan?" Bradley asked.

"I am." She had then smiled.

Bradley could do nothing about Zayt's arrest. It had already happened. But it was his responsibility to make the best choice of how or if he would involve himself. Zayt had a team to protect him, and Bradley needed to be a team player.

A calmness washed over Bradley. He decided he could wait until the morning arraignment. Once Zayt was released on bail, they could discuss their options.

Derek Richards and Sam Houghton walked out of the early morning meeting together. Their boss, FBI Deputy Director Michael Mendez, had laid out every detail the department failed to detect, thus allowing Ali al-Haqani to bomb two highly trafficked targets, Times Square in New York and the Mall of America in Minnesota. The death count for the combined attacks stood at five-hundred-seventy-two. And the count continued to rise.

"I missed it," Houghton said, clearly angry with himself. "I was so busy watching the southern ports, I should have had my guys watching the Canadian border more closely."

Derek replied, "Sam, you told me yourself that you had heightened alerts at every crossing. You did what you could with what you had."

"Well, it wasn't enough, dammit," Sam grunted as they walked down the hall. "I should have insisted on more help." Then Sam paused. When he turned back to Derek, he said, "Something's been bothering me. The DC targets were ambitious. And, once we knew the intended targets, they were relatively easy to capture. Do you think they were meant as a diversion?"

Derek processed the idea, then responded, "I suppose they could have been. It's a win-win scenario for al-Haqani. If the Washington bombings were somehow successful, he's a hero to his people. If not, he still hits us hard and gains status at home. Run it by your analysts and see what they think. It could be a pattern with him."

"What about Agent Whitman? Is he still in town?" Sam asked.

"Sorry, Sam. He's starting back in the Chelsea office on Monday. I'm lucky to have him back."

"Yeah, for now."

Derek stopped and turned toward Sam. "What does that mean?"

Sam paused to look back at Derek. "It means a mind like Bradley's might be better suited to protecting the whole country instead of a small portion of it."

"Are you going to try to pinch Bradley from me, Sam?" Derek asked, slightly annoyed.

"I'm not sure yet, but I've been reading his file, Derek. He's a perfect fit for national security. Think about it, will you?" Leaving that last statement hanging, Sam headed to his office.

Derek stood motionless in the hallway for several seconds before he walked to the elevator and pushed the button.

FIRST DEGREE

Escorted in handcuffs, Zayt scanned the courtroom. He spotted Bradley sitting at the end of the front row behind the defense table, next to the windows. Tasha sat on the bench next to him. Zayt smiled.

"Hey, Maestro," Zayt whispered. "I see you met my girl. Hey, Bunny," he flashed a sweet smile.

Bradley nearly snickered at hearing Zayt's use of a pet name for Tasha, but instead said, "Dude, we could have all just had dinner. This is a little much, don't you think?"

"No talking," the guard reprimanded.

With his hands cuffed in front of him, Zayt shrugged. The escorting guard removed the handcuffs and instructed Zayt to take his seat at the table. Damien Sullivan arrived alone, carrying a briefcase and an immense amount of confidence.

He shook hands with the prosecuting attorney and the associate who accompanied her, spoke briefly, then approached Zayt, shook his hand, and sat down.

Bradley heard Sullivan tell Zayt, "This won't take long."

All who could, rose when the bailiff intoned "Please rise" as the judge entered the courtroom.

Sullivan had been correct. The entire procedure took less than ten minutes. The prosecutor asked the judge to deny bail based on evidence of first-degree murder. Sullivan argued that Zayt had no prior criminal record, was a respected veteran, and served the public with his job at the REACH community.

The severity of the crime typically warranted a million-dollar bail, but Sullivan succeeded in advocating for Zayt's bail to be set at the minimum amount of half a million dollars with the stipulation that Zayt be held under house arrest—meaning he would need to wear an ankle monitor and not be allowed to leave the REACH community while his case was pending.

Bradley discreetly flashed Zayt a thumbs up before he was escorted out of the courtroom and back to jail.

In the courthouse hallway, Sullivan asked to speak with Bradley alone.

"My investigator will be getting in touch with you," Sullivan said. "Her name is Cassie Papadakis. She's the best private investigator in the state. Everything goes through her, do you understand?

"The prosecutor told me that the blood tests proved conclusive," Sullivan continued. "It was the victims' blood on Zayt's shirt and knife. We've got our work cut out for us. I normally would not allow a friend of a client to be involved in a case, but Zayt insisted you would be an asset. But Cassie takes the lead, understood?"

"I understand. What about Tasha? She will want to help."

"No. I drew the line with you. Warrick will take care of Miss Williams. I pre-arranged bail like you asked. You can pick him up within the hour, but you must bring him directly home.

"I've got to go. I've got another arraignment in five minutes." Sullivan seemed to recite the entirety of information effortlessly and in one breath before he walked away.

"What did he tell you?" Tasha asked when Bradley returned.

Bradley knew she would not be happy about Sullivan's decision and thought about avoiding the conflict but quickly decided against it.

"He told me his investigator would be in touch with me and that Zayt's bail has already been arranged. We can pick him up within the hour. But, Tasha, you're not going to like this."

"What?"

"He doesn't want you to be involved with the investigation," Bradley said.

"The hell I won't. Someone is railroading Zayt. I'm not going to stand by and watch him eat a murder rap," she yelled. Others in the courthouse took note of her outburst.

"Let's get out of here. We'll talk about it on the way to pick up Zayt," Bradley said.

"There's nothing to talk about. I'm going to find out who's framing Zayt, and there's nothing Mr. Uptight Lawyer can do about it," Tasha replied.

Zayt will have his hands full trying to convince Tasha to stand down, Bradley thought.

"Let's just go and get Zayt. What do you say?" Bradley asked in a calming manner.

Half an hour later, Tasha stood outside Bradley's truck waiting for Zayt to walk out of the Revere precinct door. Bradley waited behind the wheel.

With deep emotion, Bradley watched as Tasha ran to Zayt. In one smooth motion, he picked her up, twirled her around, and kissed her. The scene could have played in a movie. Bradley began to realize that Tasha might be the real deal for Zayt, and it warmed him.

Tasha jumped in the back seat to give Zayt the front.

"So, this has been a nice homecoming for you, hasn't it, Maestro?" Zayt asked with a grin.

"You don't seem too damaged by your current predicament, Zayt," Bradley remarked.

"I'll be honest, Bradley, at first it shook me. And if you hadn't come home when you did, maybe it still would. But I've got Boy Wonder on my side," Zayt said with a grin. Then he grimaced and asked, "You are sticking around, right?"

"Like a fly to a shit pile."

"Then, there's nothing to worry about." Zayt turned to gaze at Tasha.

"Oh, there's plenty to worry about, Dude," Bradley said. "They found the murder weapon in your house and the victim's blood on your shirt."

Tasha spat back at Bradley, "All planted by someone. We just need to find out who."

"Easy, Tash. Bradley knows I didn't do it. Doyle knows it, too."

"Shit," Bradley said. "I jumped all over him. I should've known better."

"That's what you call jumping all over someone? You apologized to him . . . twice!" Tasha said, indignantly.

Bradley glanced at Zayt and shrugged. Unsure why Tasha seemed to be attacking Bradley, Zayt said, "Bunny, what is it? Why are you so upset?"

Bradley quietly chuckled, but it didn't escape Zayt or Tasha's notice, and they glared at him. Then, turning back to Tasha, Zayt asked again, "What's going on?"

"That goddamn lawyer won't tell me anything. But he'll talk to Mr. Giggles over here," Tasha said, waving her arm toward Bradley.

Bradley spurted a laugh. "I'm sorry. But—Bunny?"

"Goddamnit, Bradley. It's not the best time for that," Zayt said firmly.

Bradley choked back his laugh, "Right. You're right . . . Snookums."

Bradley faced two stern glares before Zayt continued. "Tash, this guy Sullivan knows his shit. We need to trust him. Doyle told me he's the best defense attorney in Boston. By the way, how did he become my lawyer?" Zayt asked.

Bradley simply replied, "Derek."

"Looks like I owe him," Zayt said.

"I don't trust him," Tasha said.

"Bun . . . ," Zayt started to say, then glanced at Bradley and began again, "Tash, you don't trust anybody."

"I trust you," Tasha replied.

Zayt smiled and reached his hand over the seat to hold hers.

Bradley drove the access road to the sandpit that housed the REACH community. He parked next to the extended wooden walkway that Zayt had built to accommodate Bradley's truck and wheelchair.

Shea Powers, who managed the community housing portion of the operation, came running when she saw Zayt.

"What the hell is going on, Zayt? And, where the hell have you been, Bradley?" Shea was flummoxed.

"Hello, Shea. It's nice to see you, too," Bradley uttered.

"Damn, Bradley, you're looking hot!" Shea smiled and Bradley nearly blushed. "What happened, Zayt?"

"It's all a mistake, Shea," Zayt replied. "Nothing for you to worry about." He glanced at Bradley to indicate he wanted to downplay the arrest. "Just a misunderstanding."

"Thank God. Someone told me you'd been charged with murder," she replied.

"He has, goddammit," Tasha spouted, "and it's not just a misunderstanding."

Knowing he would have to tell Shea the whole truth and how much it would upset her, Zayt rolled his eyes.

"Tash, please," Zayt said.

"I don't know how you can be so calm, Zayt," Tasha said.

"Sometimes you just have to have faith, Tash," Zayt replied.

"Yeah, well, we'll see how that works out for you. But right now, I have to get ready for my shift." She reached and he bent down to meet for a kiss. "I'll call you later," she said before she got into her car, and drove away.

Bradley watched Zayt watch Tasha. He could feel the strength of their connection.

"She's a little intense," Bradley stated.

"She's a lot intense," Zayt replied.

"She's the best thing that ever happened to him," Shea chimed in, then to Bradley, "I've got a conference call right now, but you're going to tell me later what's going on."

Bradley and Zayt entered Zayt's small cabin. Because of the police search, nothing was where it ought to be.

Zayt thought about tidying but didn't have the energy. Bradley could tell things weighed on him more than he let on. Bradley guessed that he hadn't wanted to worry Tasha any more than she already was.

"Tasha's been through a lot, Bradley," Zayt said. "I don't want her mixed up in this. I might need your help with her."

"How so?" Bradley asked.

"She reminds me of you." Zayt chuckled. "She's angry, ambitious, and smart."

"I'm not sure if that was meant as a compliment. It sounded ominous."

"I suppose it was. Those three attributes tend to get you into trouble sometimes. She's had enough trouble in her life. I don't want her to have to deal with any more because of me."

"What kind of trouble?" Bradley asked.

"The kind many women face when controlled by a manipulative, self-absorbed, heavy-handed man who happens to be protected by a badge. It took a long time for her to finally get away from him. Even longer for her to trust someone, let alone me."

"What about the guy? I assume you're saying he's a cop."

Zayt nodded and said, "I guess he's still around. She won't tell me who it was. I think she's worried I might go after him." Zayt thought for a moment. "She might be right."

"You're crazy about her, aren't you?"

Zayt just smiled.

"Then we'll just have to keep her out of trouble," Bradley said.

"I don't know how this happened," Zayt said, sitting down at his table.

"It's not hard to figure, Zayt. You never lock your door, and you have strangers walking around here all day, every day. Anyone could have planted that stuff in here. Our best bet is to figure out why."

"To save their own ass, I assume," Zayt said. "If one of the residents or people who come here to eat killed this guy, they found an easy patsy in me."

"It's one thing to plant the murder weapon in a drawer, but to go as far as to put the victim's blood on one of your shirts? That doesn't seem like it was done for convenience. Sullivan has an investigator. Her name is Cassic something. She's supposed to be getting in touch with me."

Zayt's phone rang. "Yeah, Shea. Alright, I'll be right there." Zayt hung up and looked at Bradley. "A disturbance in the dining hall."

Bradley followed Zayt to the common room where a woman with scraggly black hair and filthy ripped clothes clutched a brown paper shopping bag. Several people swarmed her, barking orders. If one approached, she kicked and screamed like a mad woman.

Zayt let out a loud, sharp, whistle as he walked through the double doors.

"Hey," he yelled. "Back away from her." Recognizing all of them as residents of the community, he glanced at the small gathering surrounding the unknown woman. "What's going on here?" he asked.

"She's stealing our food," one of the men, Justin, said. "I just restocked the cereal, and she shoved it all in that bag."

"Yeah," another resident said. "She took some bread, too."

"Alright, everyone out," Zayt commanded. "I'll take care of this."

Slowly the group receded as individuals left the building. Zayt looked down at the woman. She showed more defiance than fear. Disheveled hair covered her face, making it difficult to place an age. She wore layers of dirty clothes, and her shoes looked to be a size or two too big.

"It's alright, ma'am. Nobody's going to hurt you. And you can keep the food. I just want to talk to you. Is that alright?" Zayt asked.

The woman hesitantly nodded.

"Why don't we go sit down," Zayt said.

He reached his hand down to help her up. She eyed him skeptically, then held out her hand while keeping the bag out of his reach. He assisted her with ease, and they walked over to a table.

Bradley decided it was time to go. "Zayt, I've got some things to do. I'll call you later." Before Bradley left, he swung his chair up to the dark-haired woman with the large cheerless eyes and smiled, "He's a good man. He can help you."

Bradley drove the short distance to his home. He thought about Tasha. He couldn't imagine such a strong woman controlled by a man. But I guess that's the way things are, Bradley thought. We never know what others are going through. I'm living proof of that.

Rusty waited by the door. Bradley felt bad. He never liked leaving the dog home alone. He opened the sliders to let Rusty run, and as always, Rusty went straight to Zayt's place. Bradley warmed, knowing that Rusty would find Zayt as soon as Zayt finished taking care of that poor woman. Rusty didn't return for two hours.

Bradley had been ignoring his incoming messages all morning, something he never would have done in the past. Sahani had suggested he try not to be so connected to what others are doing or what others want but to focus on what he is doing and what he wants. And right then, he wanted to make a cup of coffee and check his email.

The first message came from Derek wanting Bradley to call him after Zayt's arraignment. Holly sent a message that read, *Dinner tonight? Leah's in Worcester, 6pm?*

Perfect, Bradley thought. The timing was just right. Once he heard from Sullivan's private investigator, he might not have time to get together with Holly, John, and Mike. Besides, he loved the third-generation Italian family restaurant. He emailed back, *I'll be there!*

Minutes later Bradley received a text from Holly that read,
I'll make reservations.

Bradley replied with thumbs up and smile emojis.

In another message, Nick wanted to reach him regarding his transfer. The rest he judged as spam or nothing he needed to respond to immediately.

He called Derek.

"Bradley, how did it go?" Derek asked.

"Sullivan got Zayt released on bail. But the blood tests came back. The victims' blood matches the blood on the shirt, Zayt's shirt, and the knife they found in his cabin. They're charging him with first degree murder," Bradley sighed.

"A setup?" Derek asked.

Bradley affirmed. "It has to be. If it was someone just ditching the knife, they wouldn't go to the trouble of putting blood on Zayt's shirt and throwing it in his trash."

"Jesus. Any ideas yet?" Derek asked.

"No. I can't do anything without Sullivan's investigator's approval. I promised."

"Good. Damien knows what he's doing, Bradley. You'll just have to trust him," Derek said.

Bradley chuckled. "That's never been my strong suit, has it?"

Derek didn't laugh. His voice sounded cautious when he asked, "So, what are you saying?"

Bradley assured him. "I'm saying I'm not that person anymore. I'm good, Derek. You don't have to worry about me."

As Bradley's boss for so many years, Derek had taken the hit when Bradley went rogue or overstepped his authority usually while cracking a difficult case. But Derek always had Bradley's back even when he once had to suspend him from the bureau. Derek had also saved Bradley from being fired.

Derek sighed. "For a second, you had me worried."

"Sorry, I didn't mean to. It's just that I'm seeing myself much clearer these days, and it's a little strange."

Derek was silent.

Bradley thought he lost the phone connection. "Derek? Are you still there?"

Derek expelled a light cough, then said, "Yeah, yeah, I'm here. I was just thinking. I wish we were having this conversation sitting together somewhere with a nice cold beer."

Bradley smiled. "Yeah, me too. Hey, I'm getting together with Holly and John tonight. Mike, too, I think."

"Tell them Cate and I miss them and we'll plan something soon."

"Will do. I'll keep you informed about Zayt. Give Cate a hug for me," Bradley said, then hung up.

He dialed the office number next, electing to go through official channels instead of trying to reach Nick on his cellphone.

"Hi, Hazel. This is Bradley Whitman. How are you?"

"Hello, Agent Whitman. I'm fine, thank you. Would you like me to put you through to Supervisor Gaston?"

"If he isn't too busy, yes, please," Bradley said. Something about Hazel demanded politeness. Even as a foul-mouthed agent before he held his current position, Nick used his best manners in Hazel's company.

"Hey, Bradley? What the heck is going on?" Nick asked.

"With what, Nick?"

"With the transfer? Why is it stalled?" Nick asked.

"I didn't know it was."

Nick huffed. "Huh. Must be just another bureaucratic snafu. I got an automated message saying the transfer was on hold."

"Well," Bradley said, "I just got off the phone with Derek, and he didn't say anything. I wouldn't worry about it."

"Yeah. Alright," Nick said.

"Hey," Bradley continued, "while I've got you on the phone, have you heard what's going on with Zayt?"

"No. I haven't even heard his name since you left town. It's been kind of nice," Nick said.

At one time, Nick had thought Zayt had a thing for Mara and was none too happy about it, even though it occurred before Nick found the nerve to tell Mara how he felt about her. Apparently Zayt still rubbed Nick the wrong way.

"He's been arrested, Nick. They're charging him with first degree murder," Bradley explained.

"What? He's not one of my favorite people, but even I know he wouldn't kill someone in cold blood. What happened?"

Bradley explained the circumstances and mentioned that he might help in the investigation on his own time.

"Yeah, I imagine you would. Let me know if there's anything I can do. In the meantime, I'm going to try to get this transfer snafu fixed."

They said their goodbyes and hung up.

Thinking about Zayt, Bradley texted him to ask how he made out with the scared woman.

I convinced her to stay in one of the tents overnight, Zayt texted back.

Bradley responded, **Good to hear. I'm heading to Worcester tonight but text me if anything comes up.**

Don't worry about me, Maestro.

Bradley grinned. It seemed Zayt was hung up on nicknames. He remembered how Zayt looked at Tasha when she ran to him at the police station, how he twirled her and kissed her and called her Bunny. Bradley had never seen that side of Zayt before. If Bradley had needed additional motivation to clear Zayt's name, that picture in his head provided it.

TAKE A BACK SEAT

With Rusty fed and taken care of for the night, Bradley left for Worcester according to schedule. Although he found heavy traffic on the Massachusetts Turnpike, it moved steadily and Bradley made good time, arriving at Leah's Ristorante ten minutes early.

He rolled his chair up the concrete ramp of the red brick building, through the door, and to the hostess station where two young women looked to be discussing business.

He mentioned the reservation for Davidson, then handed the hostess his credit card. He asked that she make sure the bill for his table get charged to his card.

"I understand," she responded with a smile.

The second woman showed him to a round table next to a window on the outer brick wall. A space had been cleared for his wheelchair.

He was the first of his party to arrive. The table had been set for five people, which told Bradley that Holly's dad, Mike, and possibly his girlfriend Olivia would join them. He doubted Grace, Holly and John's daughter, would come, as she was in college and probably had more interesting people to spend time with than her honorary uncle.

He saw Mike first. Other than the grey hair on his temples creeping upward, he hadn't changed a bit. Olivia looked dazzling as she always did, her Mediterranean features framed by her long black hair. But it was Holly who brightened the room. She breezed in holding John's hand, and from where he sat, Bradley could feel the happy energy. The smile she sported when she saw Bradley would have flushed away his deepest brood.

She rushed ahead of the others and smothered Bradley with her hugs. "You're here. I didn't want to get my hopes up. I wasn't sure you would come," Holly said with a hint of remorse.

"I guess I deserved that. I've never been very reliable about getting together," Bradley said, as if in apology.

"You're looking good, Bradley. You look so relaxed," Holly said.

"And you look stunning, and it makes me happy just to look at you." Bradley smiled.

"Excuse me," Mike said with a grin. "Can we join you two?"

"Mike, it's great to see you and you, also, Olivia. You look as beautiful as ever," Bradley said.

"Thank you, Bradley. You are looking mighty handsome yourself. There's something different about you, but I can't put my finger on it," Olivia said.

Mike and Bradley shook hands, and Mike said, "He looks exactly the same. You haven't aged one bit, Bradley."

"No, something has changed," Holly agreed.

"Nice to see you, Bradley," John said as they shook hands. "Holly has been anxious all day. There's no one else in this world who can throw her off her game like you."

Bradley reached for Holly's hand as she sat in the chair to his right. Olivia sat to his left, then Mike, then John to complete the circle.

"I've missed all of you," Bradley said. "I don't want to dwell on this subject, but I want to say up front how sorry I am that I left the way I did. As much as I felt the need to, I could have done things better."

Holly said, "You're safe and you're home now, that's all that matters. You are home, aren't you?"

Still holding Holly's hand, Bradley replied, "Yes, I'm home."

The waiter appeared with menus, and Bradley ordered two bottles of wine for the table, one red, one white.

Conversation was lively from the moment they sat. Not until they had each ordered dinner did Mike ask the question on everyone's mind. "Where have you been, Bradley?"

Bradley spoke of his travels, the food, the differences in lifestyle, and the peace he found on the road.

"It sounds like an amazing experience," Holly said.

Bradley smiled and said, "I've got the most cultured dog in Massachusetts now. Rusty has meditated in the Himalayas, bathed in the shadow of Buddha, and eaten multiple Canadian beignets."

"As if he wasn't already spoiled enough," Mike said.

"Okay, so my one vice is spoiling my dog," Bradley admitted.

Holly cracked up, "One vice? Is that all you think you have?"

"That's all I'll admit to," Bradley replied. "Help, Mike. Get me out of this conversation. What have you been up to?"

Mike shared a glance with Olivia, then concentrated his look on Holly. "Well, there is something I've been thinking about."

Holly noticed his stare. "Oh?" She asked.

"I'm thinking about retiring," Mike said.

"Mike, that's great!" Bradley responded.

"Since when?" Holly asked.

Mike grasped Olivia's hand and said, "Since Olivia and I decided to get married."

Holly's hands flew to her mouth to stifle the screech that involuntarily escaped her.

"Oh, my God, Dad! You're getting married?" Holly hardly knew what to do. She jumped out of her chair and raced to her father, who wore a wide smile. John went to Olivia and hugged and congratulated her. Holly devoured her father in hugs, then did the same to Olivia.

Bradley reached for Olivia's hand and held it in both of his. "Congratulations, Olivia. You've got yourself one of the finest men I know. And he is lucky to have you."

"Thank you, Bradley. I never thought I could be this happy again," she replied, knowing her statement would resonate with Bradley.

Bradley reached for Mike's hand and shook it. "It's about time, old man," he said with a grin. "I'm so happy for you."

"We weren't sure if we were ready to announce our intentions yet," Mike said so everyone could hear, "but, with you being here, Bradley, we decided this was the perfect time."

"That's it. We need champagne." Bradley smiled as he flagged down the waiter.

Holly dashed off a series of questions without waiting for an answer to any of them.

"When is the wedding going to be? Where is it going to be? Did you tell Grandma and Grandpa yet? When did you decide? What . . ."

"Hold on, sweetheart," Mike said. "I can't keep up," he laughed.

Holly replied sweetly, "Dad, I'm just so happy for you. You have been alone far too long."

Both Mike and Holly thought back to Holly's mother, who died when Holly was just a little girl. And both knew she would be happy Mike had finally found someone.

Mike winked at his only child and said, "Thank you."

Champagne arrived, and the waiter poured. Bradley lifted his glass and said, "To love and the rippling effects of joy it brings. Olivia and Mike, may you always live in the light."

"Cheers!" they said in unison.

Bradley sat back and smiled as wedding ideas lobbed between Holly and Olivia while Mike and John took pleasure in their excitement.

Bradley decided not to mention Zayt's predicament. He did not wish to change the tone of the evening. There's plenty of time for that, he thought.

The ride home provided Bradley a chance to reflect on his priorities. Olivia and Holly had been right to say there was something different about Bradley. It just wasn't something they could physically see. It was the way he saw the world and his place in it as well as how to focus on joy and happiness instead of anger and fear. It was to take immense pleasure in dinner with old friends and celebration of love.

The drive went quickly, and Bradley smiled the whole way home.

The sun had been up for only two hours when Bradley heard the knock on his door. Rusty had not yet returned from his morning run with Zayt, so Bradley had no warning of an approaching visitor.

Bradley opened the door to a thin, black-haired woman of medium height. She wore jeans, an Eminem concert t-shirt, and a well-worn brown leather jacket. But Bradley was instantly drawn to her large, dark eyes. Eyes that were made to keep secrets.

"Whitman, right?" she barked.

"Yes, I'm Bradley Whitman," he replied.

"I'm Cassie Papadakis," she grumbled as she walked through the doorway, squeezing between his chair and the door jamb. "Damien Sullivan sent me."

Surprised by her brazenness, Bradley turned his chair to follow her to the kitchen table where, without his invitation, she took a seat.

"Uh, yeah. Sullivan said you would be in touch," Bradley said, noticing something vaguely familiar about her.

"I'm only here because Damien asked. I work alone. I don't need or want your help," Cassie explained.

"Okay."

"D says you're with the FBI."

"D?"

"Damien, D. Keep up with me, Whitman." She shook her head.

Bradley didn't answer. Instead, he scrutinized her, wondering where he had seen her before.

"What are you looking at?"

"I've seen you before," Bradley said.

"Ha, some field agent you are," she replied.

"Analyst."

"Huh?" she asked.

"I'm an FBI analyst. C'mon, Papadakis, keep up with me," he replied. Then he realized where he had seen her. "You're the thief from the dining hall yesterday," he said as he pointed his finger at her.

"Score one for the analyst," she spat.

"What was that all about?"

"Do I really need to explain it?" she huffed. "This Warrick guy . . ."

"His name is Zayt. Nobody calls him Warrick," Bradley interrupted.

She widened her already huge, dark eyes. "Pardon me," came her acerbic reply. "This Zayt guy surrounds himself with homeless people, one of whom is now dead. What better way to find out if he's a murderer or a stooge?"

"He's neither," Bradley asserted. "He's been framed. And if you think otherwise, you shouldn't be investigating his case." Bradley knew as soon as the words were out of his mouth how asinine he sounded.

"So, Mr. FBI, I should only look for evidence that exonerates the suspect and discard all other evidence? Is that what they teach you at Quantico?"

Bradley shook his head. "You know I didn't mean it like that. Look, if you're not going to let me help, why are you here?"

"I didn't say I wasn't going to let you help. I said I didn't need or want your help. But D insisted."

"Well, he stuck me with you also. And tied my hands. I promised I wouldn't do anything without your knowledge. And that doesn't sit well with me," Bradley said. "But for Zayt's sake, I'll deal with it."

"As long as we understand each other," Cassie replied.

"So, what did you find out by playing the crazy thief?" Bradley asked.

"Nothing yet, but it was just an introduction. I'll hang around and talk with some of my fellow homeless people and see if anyone saw or heard anything. You can't tell your friend what's-his-name who I am. I don't want him to treat me any different than the rest."

"And me? What do I do while you make new friends?" Bradley asked.

Cassie glared at him. "See what you can get from the coroner's office. That doctor is dragging her feet again."

"Who? Reyes?"

"Yeah, that's the one."

Bradley snapped, "She's thorough. She never drags her feet."

"A company man through and through, I see," Cassie rumbled. "You deal with the coroner. And the dead guy has a history. Check out his arrests and see if he has any partners. Talk with the arresting officers, see what they can tell you."

Bradley was not happy about taking instructions from Cassie, but if he wanted to help Zayt, he would have to put up with her.

"Your wish is my command," he stated sarcastically.

"I'm outta here," Cassie shot back as she walked out.

"Jesus, Sullivan, I hope you know what you're doing," Bradley muttered under his breath.

Bradley checked his watch. On a Saturday, it would be hit or miss whether Maria would be working in the Massachusetts General Hospital morgue. If she was, she would be there early in the morning.

Wasting little time after Rusty returned home, Bradley got the dog settled, then headed to the morgue.

She stood over a body with a scalpel in her hand. Bradley knocked on the glass door to announce his presence.

She wore a mask, but her eyes revealed a smile. She waved him to enter.

"Dear God, Bradley. Where have you been?" Dr. Maria Reyes asked.

"At the other end of the earth, Maria. How are you?" Bradley smiled.

Bradley kept his chair at a distance. To avoid contaminating Maria's subject, neither touched the other.

"Very much the same as when you left. Nothing ever changes," Maria said.

Bradley found the statement ironic, as almost everything about his life had changed.

Maria continued, "Donovan told me you were back."

"Ah, well. That answers my next question. How are things going with you two?" Bradley inquired.

"Do you see those flowers over there?" She pointed to a medium-sized colorful arrangement. "Tomorrow I'll get chocolates, and the next day I'll get fruit."

"What did he do this time?" Bradley snickered, remembering it was he who suggested the apology trilogy to Doyle back when Doyle first asked Maria out on a date and then got the days mixed up and stood her up.

"He forgot my birthday," Maria laughed.

"Happy belated birthday, Maria."

"Thank you, Bradley. But I'm guessing this isn't strictly a social call."

"You're right. Although I am happy to see you. You have a Ronald Crayton who died of stab wounds. I was wondering what you could tell me about him. But before you say anything, I am not acting in an FBI capacity. This is a personal matter."

"Ah, well, all I can tell you is that the newspaper accounts are accurate, for once," Maria replied.

"So, you haven't found any other injuries other than the stab wounds to the chest?"

Maria didn't respond.

"Time of death?"

The time of death had already been speculated on the police report, so she answered, "Early morning, probably between five and six."

"What about the toxicology report?" he asked.

"Given his history, about what you would expect," she answered.

"Got it," Bradley said. "I'll get the rest out of Donovan. Let's get together for a drink soon. You can even bring Donovan."

"Do I have to?" Maria laughed.

"Thanks, Maria. I'll let you get back to work."

Bradley closed the door behind him and sat in the hallway for a moment. The last time he had been in that room was to mourn over Laney's lifeless body. He closed his eyes and replaced the picture in his head of Laney on the steel table with one of Laney in a white dress appearing from the ocean.

Heading back to his truck, Bradley concluded that whoever killed Ronald Crayton did so quickly and purposefully. If there had been defensive wounds, Bradley was sure Maria would have found a way to tell him that. And, as suspected, the victim had been using drugs.

Bradley determined that the assailant was known to the victim and most likely male, as it takes great strength to break through the breastbone and pierce the heart. According to the newspapers, that had happened three times. Strong and athletic, Zayt fit the assailant's profile perfectly.

Bradley next visited the Back Bay, Boston, police precinct station on Harrison Avenue. Officer Dixon Hayes of the precinct had arrested Ronald Crayton on three separate occasions. Bradley suspected that if anyone knew who Crayton's friends were, Hayes would be the guy. Hayes was due to finish his early morning patrol within the half hour, so Bradley waited in the lobby for him to return to the precinct.

A six-foot tall, muscle-bound officer with a deep brown complexion strolled into the building, and the desk sergeant nodded to Bradley.

Bradley rolled his chair to intercept the officer. "Excuse me, Officer Hayes. My name is Bradley Whitman. Could I speak to you for a moment, please?"

The officer stared down distastefully at Bradley and replied, "What do you want?"

"I want to ask you a few questions about a man named Ronald Crayton," Bradley said.

"He's dead." Officer Hayes began to walk away. "Nothing left to say."

"Officer!" Bradley shouted.

Hayes stopped dead in his tracks. He apparently didn't like the authoritative tone Bradley used. He turned and scowled at Bradley.

"Nobody barks at me, especially when they can't stand on their own two feet."

Bradley had dealt with his type before. He knew that the more anger he showed, the more it would please Hayes. So, Bradley smiled.

"Ha, that is funny, Dixon," Bradley said, knowing the use of his first name would infuriate the man.

Dixon Hayes grabbed a handful of Bradley's shirt and was about to respond when Bradley lifted his FBI badge and held it in front of Dixon's face.

Once Bradley's identity registered with the officer, Hayes slowly and reluctantly released his hold on Bradley's oxford.

"Having a bad day, officer?" Bradley quipped.

"What do you want?"

"I want to know about Ronald Crayton. I want to know if he had any known acquaintances or enemies. You arrested him three times in the last two years. I figured you could help me out," Bradley said.

"You figured wrong. Crayton was a junkie and a fool. A guy like that doesn't have friends and probably has lots of enemies. He woulda stole from his own mother if her pimp didn't take it all first," Hayes spat. "Nothin' left to say."

Officer Hayes walked through a door marked Do Not Enter and disappeared.

Bradley eyed the sergeant at the duty desk. The sergeant shrugged.

Bradley had had no intention of flashing his badge but knew it was the best way to alleviate a potential problem. Officer Hayes had come through the door angry and left even more so. Bradley wondered if he was just having a bad day or if that was his true personality.

"Excuse me, Sergeant," Bradley said to the man behind the desk. "How well do you know Officer Hayes?"

"Well enough. He's been here for eight years. I've been here for twenty," he replied.

"Is he always that . . . intense?" Bradley asked.

The sergeant chuckled, "You kidding? He's having a good day."

"Thank you, Sergeant," Bradley said before he turned his chair and left.

Bradley tracked down a few more of Crayton's arresting officers but got no more information from them than he had from Hayes. Those who remembered Crayton couldn't identify any accomplices or acquaintances, and other officers just didn't remember him at all.

The day had dwindled, and Bradley would have nothing to report to Papadakis when next he saw her. Bradley decided he needed to talk to Zayt.

He picked Rusty up from the house then drove to the sandpit and parked his truck by the wooden walkway. He steered his chair to the main dining hall, Rusty following beside him. Several residents sat at tables playing cards or reading, but Zayt was not there. Next, he tried the office. As the sun had already set, the office door was locked, and Shea had left for the day.

As Bradley headed to Zayt's cabin, he spotted Papadakis dressed as her homeless alter ego. She spoke with a thin, pale, and sickly-looking man. She eyed Bradley and Rusty as he rolled by. Bradley didn't acknowledge her.

Bradley knocked on Zayt's door. Scowling and holding a broom in his hand, Zayt opened the door.

Rusty's butt wiggled uncontrollably, which wiped the scowl from Zayt's face.

"Hey, come on in," Zayt said.

"Spring cleaning?" Bradley asked.

"The cops made a mess of the place. I keep finding shards of glass on the floor from the lamp they broke." Zayt shook his head in frustration. "You'd better keep Rusty outside."

Bradley motioned for Rusty to stay out, and the dog trotted off to make his rounds.

"I haven't been able to figure it out," Zayt continued. "I've been thinking about it all day, and I can't come up with one reason anyone would want to frame me like this."

"We're going to take care of this, Zayt. You know that, right?" Bradley encouraged.

Zayt flopped onto a scarred wooden chair next to his small round kitchen table. "I don't know, Bradley. Whoever orchestrated this knew what they were doing."

"Maybe it was random," Bradley said. "Maybe someone just saw an opportunity and took it." Bradley saw a look on Zayt's face that he had never seen before. Fear.

"That would be even worse," Zayt said. "How do you find someone you don't know?"

"Hey," Bradley slapped his hand on Zayt's knee. "There's always evidence. There's a thread somewhere. Once we find it, we just need to pull on it until we get our answer. Somebody saw, heard, or knows something—maybe even you. So, let's start from the beginning. Tell me what's been going on since last year, since I left. I want to know everyone you've talked to, done business with, or had run-ins with, no matter how insignificant it may have been."

"You can't be serious."

"I'm dead serious. I know you, Zayt. If anything of consequence happens, you remember it. I want to hear it all."

Bradley pulled a notepad and pen from his chair pocket.

"Alright, we can try. But I've gone through most of this in my head already and came up with nothing," Zayt said.

For two and a half hours, Zayt talked about residents and homeless individuals who caused minor problems, city workers who angered him, a dog that chases him nearly every morning because it's not on a leash while running with its owner, and a woman who yelled at him at the grocery store for buying the last four loaves of bread.

"What about ex-girlfriends or jealous husbands? Anything like that?" Bradley asked.

Zayt shook his head, "No, I hadn't dated anyone for a long time before I met Tasha. And I'd never date a married woman." Zayt eyed Bradley as if he had insulted his integrity.

"Tell me more about the woman and dog who jog every morning," Bradley said.

"There's not much to tell. I see her when I run the long loop."

"The long loop?" Bradley asked.

"Yeah, on even-numbered days I run laps around the sandpit. That's my short loop, but it's harder because I run in the

124

sand. On odd-numbered days, I run the long loop through the streets surrounding the sandpit."

"How come I didn't know that?" Bradley asked.

"I just started doing that about seven months ago," Zayt said. Then, squinting, he added, "You don't think that has anything to do with me being framed, do you? How could it?"

"I don't know. Right now, it's just another piece of information," Bradley replied. "What kind of dog is it?"

"A boxer, maybe a mix. She calls him Dutch. I don't know who she is, but she needs to get a handle on that mutt," Zayt said.

"Have you ever threatened her with calling the dog officer or cops or anything like that?"

"No, man. I wouldn't do that. He's never bitten me or anything."

"What time do you take your runs?" Bradley asked.

"Same time as always. Five in the morning, give or take."

Bradley sat quiet for a moment, then asked, "Did you run the long loop two days ago? On the thirteenth?"

"Yeah."

"Did you see the woman with the dog?"

"Yeah, why?"

"On what street?"

"Um, I was rounding Howland onto Jameson. She was doing the opposite, coming towards me."

"Tell me exactly what your route was that morning," Bradley said.

"You think she may have seen something?"

"Maybe. Tell me your route," Bradley said, excitedly.

"The same as always, I ran up the access road onto Park Street and went right. Then I took a right on Howland, a right on Jameson, a right on Industrial Drive, and then a right on Park and back down the access road—all the way around the sandpit."

"And you didn't see anything suspicious? Other people? Cars?"

"Nothing. Just the woman and her dog."

"The coroner said Crayton died between five and six o'clock. He was found on the side of the road. You would have seen him if he was dead already. But that was at the beginning of your run, so it wouldn't have been much after five, right?"

"Yeah, right."

"And the other woman ran in the opposite direction. It's possible she saw something or someone. What does she look like?" Bradley asked.

"About five feet, six inches tall. She has blonde hair and wears it tied up. I'd guess she's in her early thirties. The dog is white with brown ears and a brown patch on his butt."

"I'll look into it," Bradley said.

"I could do the long loop in the morning," Zayt said.

"If you step one foot outside this sandpit, you'll be back in jail before you round Howland Street," Bradley warned. "Rusty and I will take care of it."

"Damn, yeah. I forgot," Zayt said.

"You stay put. We got this."

"We who? Who's we?" Zayt asked.

"Sullivan's investigator, Papadakis."

"I want to talk to her."

Bradley knew that wouldn't be possible but chose to stall Zayt. "Yeah, I'll let her know. I'm going home. You just relax. This is all going to work out."

PAPADAKIS

Bradley found Rusty sitting near his truck with fully costumed Papadakis by his side. In a hushed voice, she said," We need to talk. I'll meet you up at your house."

Bradley had only been home for minutes when Rusty barked. It was the only notice he received before Cassie Papadakis barged through his door.

"Don't you believe in knocking?" Bradley asked.

"Don't you believe in locking your door?" she replied. "You got anything to eat? I'm living on cereal and bread these days."

Taken back by her request, Bradley hesitated only moments before he heated leftover honey-garlic chicken in the microwave then added broccoli salad to the plate. While Bradley fed Rusty, Cassie sat at the kitchen table and devoured chicken and broccoli.

"Damn, this is good. Did you make this?" Cassie asked.

"Yeah. Listen, I'm going out first thing in the morning to talk to a jogger who may have seen something Thursday morning. She and Zayt crossed paths on Howland Street not long before Crayton was killed."

"Hang on. Who is this person?" Cassie asked.

"I don't have a name. Just that she and her dog jog every morning—or at least every other morning on Howland. I want to know if she saw anything or anyone unusual."

"Alright. What about today? Did you get the coroner's report?"

"I can tell you the victim died between five and six o'clock Thursday morning as a result of three stab wounds to the chest.

The victim also tested positive for drugs in his system. There were no defensive wounds, so it's likely that the victim knew his attacker, who is male and in good physical condition."

"How can you be sure his attacker is male?"

"Three stab wounds through the breast plate and into the heart is not an easy thing to do."

"I figured as much anyway," Cassie stated. "What about interviewing the arresting officers?"

"I didn't get anything. The one officer who arrested him three times is an angry man who didn't want to talk to me, but he did say that Crayton didn't have any friends and probably had lots of enemies. The other officers either didn't know anything or couldn't remember Crayton. What about you? What did you find out?"

Cassie Papadakis brushed the unruly hair out of her face as she took the last bites of chicken. Even though he barely knew her, Bradley could see she contemplated whether to share what she had learned.

"One of the residents heard Crayton bragging about coming into some money. Said he had recently scored fifty bucks and would be getting a lot more soon," Cassie relayed.

Bradley got excited. "Did he say how or from where?"

Papadakis looked up from the empty plate, a hint of a smile gracing her full lips. "He said all he had to do was to hit a guy."

"So Zayt was definitely targeted," Bradley said. "But why?"

Cassie's slight smile disappeared quickly when she asked, "What the hell were you doing talking with Zayt tonight?"

"I wanted to find out what's been going on this last year since I've been gone—to see if he was having trouble with anyone or anything that might have prompted this whole thing."

"You should have talked to me first. That was the deal," Papadakis scolded, then asked, "What do you mean about being gone for a year? I thought you two were friends?"

"We are. I just had to go away for a while."

"How the hell are you supposed to help me if you haven't even been around to know what's going on? What the hell was Damien thinking? Jesus, you're wasting my time." Cassie jumped up from the chair. Rusty rushed to Bradley's side and came to attention.

"Okay, pup," Cassie said. "Easy. I was just leaving."

"Wait a minute," Bradley shouted. "I'm in this thing, and I'm staying in whether you like it or not. Tomorrow morning I'm going to find that jogger and see what she can tell us. That frees you up to find out who gave Crayton the fifty bucks. I'm sure Damien gave you my phone number. Call me when you want to meet. Otherwise, I won't know what you want me to do next, will I?" Bradley grinned, knowing he had her cornered. He as much as said that if she wanted to run the investigation, she would have to keep in touch with him.

"Fine!" Cassie barked, "but don't do anything else until you hear from me. That means no talking to Zayt. We don't need him trying to work this case."

"I understand," Bradley answered.

Cassie stomped out the door.

"I'm going to have to teach that woman to meditate," Bradley said to no one.

The forecast was for rain. His truck's digital clock read 5:02 when he, with Rusty, parked on the corner of Howland and Jameson streets. Figuring he would be more approachable and perceived less of a threat to the woman jogging if she saw him in his wheelchair, Bradley opted to get out of the truck. He donned his rain jacket and left Rusty inside with the window down.

Ten minutes passed before he saw the woman and her dog make their way down Jameson Street. The dog spotted Bradley and charged toward him. Rusty began to bark at the fast-approaching dog so loudly that Bradley could not hear the woman calling for her dog to stop.

Bradley's only option was to cross his arms in front of his face for protection.

Accelerating to a full run, the woman yelled, "Dutch, no!" several times.

Dutch skidded to a stop in front of Bradley and stood. The dog's hind end wiggled uncontrollably, back and forth causing his short tail to repeatedly circle. Bradley saw playfulness in Dutch's eyes.

When Dutch stopped running, Rusty ceased barking. Bradley held out his hand to the dog, allowing Dutch to make the first move. Dutch sniffed Bradley's chair, sneakers, and legs.

By the time the woman reached the two, he and Dutch were fast friends. Bradley stroked Dutch's head and back.

Breathing heavily, the jogger said, "I'm sorry. He just loves people. He gets excited."

"No, he's fine," Bradley answered, "I love dogs," he said, pointing to Rusty in the truck.

"He's beautiful. What's his or her name?" she asked.

"His name is Rusty, and I'm Bradley," Bradley said, holding out his hand to shake hers.

"This is Dutch, and I'm Jennifer," she said as they shook hands. "I hope he didn't scare you. He loves to run with me but hates the leash. That's why I run so early in the morning. We usually only run into one or two people this early."

"Actually, that's what I wanted to talk to you about," Bradley said.

"You wanted to talk to me?" she asked, showing confusion.

"Yes. I'm investigating the death of a man who was found in the early morning on Howland Street three days ago. I was hoping I could ask you some questions," Bradley smiled.

"Yes, I read about that. But I heard they arrested someone," she said. "Are you with the police?"

"The police did arrest someone, but, no, I'm not with the police. I'm working with a private investigator," Bradley replied. "Would you mind telling me, did you run that morning, Miss . . . ?"

"Cornwell, Jennifer Cornwell."

"Miss Cornwell, did you run that morning?"

"Yes, I run every morning, unless the weather is really bad."

"Did you see anyone during your run that morning?"

"Just the regular guy that runs every other day. A big black guy. He looks like he's in the military. He's very polite. We passed each other on Jameson. Hmmm, come to think of it, I didn't see him yesterday. Oh, no! He's not the person who was killed, is he?"

"No, Miss Cornwell, he's fine. Did you see anyone else that morning?"

"Yes. I saw two police officers standing outside a cruiser way down the other end of Howland. I didn't think much of it until I saw the newspaper the next day."

"You didn't jog past them?"

"No, I live right over there." Jennifer pointed to a house diagonally across from where they talked. "I was finishing my run when I saw them. I only noticed because I try to watch ahead for people so I can catch Dutch before he takes off." She shrugged her shoulders." I didn't see you until it was too late. But I did see them in time."

"What time was that?"

"Right around this time, 5:10 or 5:15, I suppose. I'm a creature of habit."

"Can you think of anything or anyone else you may have seen that morning?"

Jennifer tilted her head and looked away, then said, "No. That was it."

"Miss Cornwell, can I have your phone number in case I have any additional questions?"

"Of course."

Bradley reached for two of his business cards, wrote her number on the back of one, and his cellphone number on the other. He handed the card with his phone number to Jennifer.

"You're with the FBI?" she asked.

"That's my day job, but this is not an FBI case. That's my personal number on the back of the card. Please call me if you think of anything else. And thank you for your time." Bradley smiled.

"I will, and you're welcome," she replied.

"See you later, Dutch," Bradley said as he returned to his truck.

Back home, knowing he had committed himself to Sunday dinner at his parents' house, Bradley made himself a light breakfast. His cellphone chimed with a text message just as he put the first spoonful of instant oatmeal into his mouth.

Coming into town today. Would like to see you. The text came from Derek.

Bradley texted back. **Is Cate coming with you?**

Yes. Landing at Logan at 10am.

Dinner with Mom and Dad?

Sounds great!

I'll pick you up at the airport, Bradley replied.

Bradley checked the time. His parents would be getting up soon to get ready for church.

He called them after breakfast.

"Good morning, Dad," Bradley said.

"Good morning, Bradley. Please don't tell me you are calling to cancel dinner. Your mother will be so disappointed," his father said.

"No. Actually, I'm calling to tell you that Cate and Derek are coming home this morning and I took the liberty of inviting them to join us for dinner. I hope that's alright," said Bradley.

"You know it is. Your mother will be thrilled," Doug replied.

"We'll be there around noon or so. Let me know if you need me to pick anything up."

"See you soon, son."

About to wash his breakfast dish, Bradley was interrupted by his ringing cellphone. The telephone number showed as blocked.

"Hello?" Bradley answered.

"What did you find out?" the brash voice asked.

"Papadakis?" Bradley asked.

"Who the hell else would it be?" Cassie asked.

"Oh, almost anyone else," Bradley replied, a bit more snidely than intended.

"Well, excuse me for not knowing how popular you are," Cassie replied just as snidely. "Do you think you can tear yourself away from all your friends to tell me what you found out this morning?"

Bradley decided against matching wits with Papadakis and opted to take a more professional approach.

Bradley began. "Her name is Jennifer Cornwell. On Thursday the thirteenth, she and Zayt passed each other on Jameson Street just after 5 a.m. He was headed toward Industrial Drive, and she ran toward Howland. She then rounded the corner of Jameson and Howland where she said she saw a patrol car parked roughly sixty yards down the street with two officers standing outside the vehicle. Then she went into her house."

"And what time did she say she saw the patrol car?" Cassie asked.

"Maybe ten or fifteen minutes after five."

"That's bullshit," Cassie said.

Bradley flinched. "Excuse me?"

"That's bullshit, I said. The cop didn't get there until almost six-thirty."

"How do you know that?" Bradley asked.

"How the hell do you think? I got a copy of the police report. Your witness is wrong about the time or is lying," Cassie stated.

Bradley found it difficult to keep his composure. "Why didn't you show me the police report? It could have helped in the interview," he said with clenched teeth.

"Doesn't matter. She's wrong," she huffed.

"Dammit, Papadakis! Do you really want to find out what happened here or just jerk me around?" Bradley shouted.

Cassie laughed. "Jerking you around is just a bonus, Agent Whitman. I'm going to find out what happened."

Bradley took a few deep breaths to calm himself, then said, "She was positive about the time. She stays on the same schedule every day. Besides, it confirms the timeline Zayt gave me."

"I want to talk to her," Cassie said.

"I want a copy of the police report," Bradley replied.

"Alright. But for your eyes only."

"And I want your phone number," Bradley said.

"Nobody gets my phone number," she replied.

Nobody in their right mind would ask for it, Bradley thought. Then said, "I need to be able to get in touch with you."

"Dammit. If you start bothering me, I'll change it," Cassie said.

Bradley spurt, "You don't need to worry about that."

Cassie gave Bradley her telephone number, and Bradley promised to call her with a time when they could talk with Jennifer. As much as he wanted to be done with their conversation, Bradley needed to find out if Cassie had made any progress. "Did you find out where Crayton got the fifty dollars?" he asked.

"Not yet. But it's clear he planned to meet with the person again. He told some residents that he would be making another score the following day."

"So, whoever he met may be the murderer," Bradley said.

"And you deduced that all by yourself, did you?"

Bradley sighed, "Just send me the police report. And I'll make inquiries to see if there were any patrol cars in the area around 5 a.m."

"Suit yourself. But she could just be a ditz who can't tell time."

"Goodbye, Papadakis!" Bradley said and hung up.

Bradley found his conversations with Cassie Papadakis exhausting. But he did have to admit that they probably would not have found out about the fifty-dollar payment had she not gone undercover.

He dialed Jennifer Cornwell's phone number, listened to a recorded message, then left a message asking her to call him at her earliest convenience.

The clock seemed to advance quickly that morning. Having done it many times before, Bradley precisely timed his arrival at Logan Airport shuttle pickup terminal. Cate and Derek had been standing on the sidewalk for only minutes when Bradley arrived. They carried just two small bags which Derek placed on the backseat next to Rusty.

Cate joined Rusty in the backseat and gushed over him.

"We really appreciate you picking us up, Bradley," Derek said.

"I thought we could go directly to my parents', and then I'll bring you home after dinner. Does that sound alright?" Bradley asked as he pulled into the heavy airport traffic.

"It sounds wonderful," Cate answered. "I can't wait to see Lynn and Doug. It's been too long. And I must tell you, Bradley, that I am extremely jealous that you were able to be present when Mike made his big engagement announcement. I would have loved to have been there."

"It was pretty special. Holly is so happy. She and Olivia started making wedding plans even before the meal came," Bradley chuckled.

"How are things going with Zayt?" Derek asked.

"We're making progress, and Zayt is taking things in stride or at least seems to be. You never really know with him," Bradley said. "Sullivan's investigator is a piece of work, though. She's fighting me every step. She won't give up one bit of control and is hoarding information like a packrat."

Derek and Cate exchanged amused glances that did not escape Bradley's notice.

"What was that look for?" Bradley asked.

Derek grinned. "You just described yourself to a tee."

"No. No way. Not like her. She's brash, secretive, untrusting, and annoyingly good at her job," he replied.

Derek stared at Bradley with a grin.

Bradley continued, "Come on! I was never like that." Then he paused. "Okay, maybe I was a little untrusting and possibly secretive, but I was never controlling."

"You're kidding, right?" Derek laughed. "Shall I start at the beginning, when we met? You were tailing me, Bradley. At age twelve, you played detective and didn't tell anyone. Then there was the Joshua case, the Branson murder weapon, the . . ."

"Alright!" Bradley interrupted. "I get your point. But trust me. Papadakis is different. She's exhausting to deal with."

A snicker emerged from Derek's direction.

As soon as Bradley said it, he regretted it. In hindsight, Bradley knew he had caused Derek many sleepless nights.

With a slight grin, Bradley said, "That's it. I'm taking you two back to the airport right now. I don't need this abuse."

"What do you think, Cate? The shoe is on the other foot, and Bradley doesn't want to wear it. I think we finally have the upper hand," Derek laughed.

"Bradley, don't pay any attention to my husband. He is overworked and sleep deprived," Cate pouted. "I'm dying for your mother's cooking."

"Alright, Cate. But only for you," Bradley chuckled.

Doug met them at the door and gave Cate, Derek, and Bradley each a hug. For Rusty, he brought a dog treat. Lynn was in the kitchen when she heard them arrive.

Wearing a daisy-covered apron, she rushed into the living room to greet them.

"Oh, we've missed you both so much. I'm so happy you could come today," Lynn said.

"We are happy to be here. I hope it wasn't too last minute. This was kind of a spur of the moment trip. Derek surprised me with it," Cate explained.

"Not at all. You know I always have enough food for an army. Doug, get them a drink. Dinner will be ready shortly," Lynn said and returned to the kitchen.

"Can I help, Lynn?" Cate asked.

"No, honey, you sit and relax. Plane travel can be exhausting no matter how short the flight," Lynn said.

"That's so true," Cate replied.

Lynn returned to the kitchen while the others gathered in the living room and Doug opened a bottle of wine.

"How is Washington, Derek?" Doug asked.

"Busy. I have a new appreciation for what Paul Davis was going through all the years I worked under him," Derek said.

"He's working himself to death, Doug. Just look at him." Cate's concerned voice did not go unnoticed.

"You do look a little pale, Derek," Doug replied. "And tired."

Derek put his hand on Cate's knee and said, "Cate was saying the same thing when I worked in Chelsea, Doug. I'm fine. Well, maybe a little tired but otherwise, fine."

"What the two of you need is a trip to Bhutan or India," Bradley piped in. "Watch a sunrise from Tiger Hill, and you'll never be the same. Words can't describe the feeling of complete inner peace I achieved that morning."

"That sounds wonderful," Cate smiled. Then turning towards Derek asked, "When will we be able to take a trip like that?"

Derek could not picture himself ever being that far away from Washington while holding his current position. He smiled and replied, "I guess we'll have to see."

Cate rolled her eyes, stood, and walked into the kitchen.

Bradley caught Derek's eyes and said, "She seems lonely."

"I know," Derek said with frustration. "I need to make more time for her. I knew this job would be tough, but I never thought it could be this time consuming."

Bradley nodded in sympathy with Derek's plight. "Here's the thing, Derek. There's always going to be a case that requires your attention. They never stop. So, now and then you need to stop. If you don't, soon you won't be able to take care of your cases or your wife."

Doug's heart warmed at Bradley's advice. "That trip had a real impact on you, didn't it, son."

Bradley smiled and replied, "It did, Dad. I realized what a small world I had made for myself. And in our line of work . . . " Bradley alternated his pointed finger between himself and Derek, " . . . a small world can be very dark. Once I broadened my world, I created a lot more light."

"That all sounds great, Bradley, but you know it's much easier said than done," Derek said.

"It is. And I don't know if I'll be able to find that balance myself, but I'm going to give it a try. And I'm going to continue to remind you to try, too, Derek," Bradley said.

Lynn and Cate heard Bradley's remark and eyed each other as they walked into the living room.

"Balance what?" Lynn asked.

Bradley chuckled. "My life, Mom. I'm going to find balance in my life. Sahani is helping me."

Eyebrows raised around the room. Stunned by Bradley's admission, the others were speechless.

Lynn finally asked, "You're seeing Doctor Kumar?"

"Yes. We had a nice long talk the other day when I went into the office. She's really quite intuitive."

"Wait a minute," Cate said, glancing from Bradley to Derek. "I thought you disliked Sahani Kumar?"

Derek shrugged in confusion.

"I wasn't in the best state of mind last year. I misunderstood her motives. And I guess I was somewhat . . . controlling."

Lynn said, "Well, I'm very happy you're talking to Sahani. She was extremely helpful for me. I just hope you don't jerk her around like you did the psychologists we took you to when you were a boy."

Bradley laughed. "No, Mom, I won't. But you have to admit that, at the tender age of eight years old, I fooled every one of those doctors."

"What?" Cate screeched. "What's this about Bradley fooling psychologists?"

"Let's move to the dinner table, and we'll tell you some stories," Lynn said.

As they enjoyed a prime rib dinner, Lynn and Doug relayed the stories of how Bradley would choose a different disorder for each doctor and mimic the symptoms. His visits resulted in diagnoses of oppositional defiant disorder, obsessive compulsive disorder, and the most disturbing, early signs of a serial killer.

"You didn't!" Cate chuckled as she glanced at Bradley.

Bradley laughed. "I did. You should have seen the look on the doctor's face when I asked him if I should feel bad about wanting to skin a rat."

"Bradley! Please. We're eating!" Lynn exclaimed.

"Sorry, Mom. But his expression was priceless. That was the last doctor they took me to."

Derek shook his head. "Why doesn't any of this surprise me? Even at eight years old you were outsmarting the professionals."

A satisfying grin spread across Bradley's face.

"That's when I started losing my hair," Doug said as he passed his hand over his bald head, causing laughter.

"Well," Cate said, "I for one am happy to see some of that rakish young boy in you again, Bradley. I've missed him."

Bradley replied, "So have I." Bradley gave Cate a sweet smile. "By the way, Mom, Dad. I have some news for you. I wanted to see your faces when I told you. I had dinner with Holly, John, Mike, and Olivia the other night. Mike and Olivia are getting married."

"It's about time!" Lynn said with a big smile. "When is the wedding?"

"I don't know. You'll have to talk to Holly and Olivia about that. I'm not sure Mike will have much say in the matter," Bradley laughed.

They spoke of how nice it would be to attend another wedding and how happy they were for Mike and Olivia. After dinner, Lynn, Doug, and Cate began to clear the table. Derek took the opportunity to ask Bradley if they could talk.

"Of course," Bradley said. "What's up?"

"Can we go outside?" Derek asked.

"Alright," Bradley said, then called for Rusty. They moved to the back deck.

Derek sat in a deck chair, and Bradley turned his wheelchair to face him. Bradley kept Rusty on a long leash so he could explore but not go too far.

"What's the secret?" Bradley grinned.

"Your transfer has been held up," Derek said.

"Still? I thought Nick was taking care of that?" Bradley asked, then noticed the serious nature of Derek's gaze. "Derek, what's wrong? Are you saying the FBI doesn't want me back?"

Bradley had to admit he had never given that a thought. But he had abruptly disappeared for a year without much explanation. He suddenly wondered if he had burned his bridge.

"No, that's not it. If anything, it's the opposite," Derek replied.

"I don't get it. What are you trying to tell me?"

"Sam Houghton wants you to work for the National Security Branch. He wants you to transfer to his team, Bradley."

Bradley didn't speak. He repeated in his head what Derek had just said out loud.

Derek continued, "It would mean moving to DC. You would have a new title, higher security clearance, and most likely a pay raise. He thinks your talents are being wasted."

"I . . . I'm not sure what to say," Bradley stammered.

"You don't have to say anything right now. I'm here to relay the message. I told Sam I would talk to you, but this decision is yours to make. Take some time to think about it. I told Nick that your transfer got mired in paperwork and you couldn't start for a few more days."

"But I promised Nick," Bradley said.

"I'm taking the hit for this, not you," Derek explained.

"Move to DC? I don't know. What about my parents? What about Zayt?"

"I know. There's a lot to think about." Derek hesitated before he continued. "There's more. Sam asked me to bring you in the loop about the Times Square and Mall of America bombings."

"Bombings? I thought the Mall of America was a fire in the construction area?" Bradley said.

"That's what the media was told," Derek said. "Both were bombings. And both have been attributed to Ali al-Haqani. We think he used Washington as a diversion."

Bradley bobbed his head. "That's why we were able to capture them so easily. It was a setup."

Derek nodded. "We haven't heard the last of him."

"And Sam wants me on the case?" Bradley asked.

Derek nodded.

Doug opened the deck door and asked if either of them wanted coffee.

"Yeah, Dad. Coffee sounds great. We'll be right in," Bradley answered. Doug retreated to the house, and Bradley asked, "Who else knows about this?"

"Nobody. You, me, and Sam."

"How long are you here?" Bradley asked Derek.

"We're leaving in the morning."

Bradley sunk his head to his chest. "Jesus, Derek. I need you to talk this through with me. I can't make this kind of decision without you."

Derek looked Bradley in the eye and said, "I can't help you with this one, Bradley. I'm not a neutral party. I'm not sure I can be impartial. All I'll say is you got a glimpse of what the job would be like. It's up to you to decide if it will give you the balance and the satisfaction you're looking for. Maybe it wouldn't be a bad idea if you talked to Sahani about this." Derek stood. "Sam wants you to call him tomorrow so he can discuss the position with you."

Derek walked into the house. Bradley sat quiet for a moment wondering how his life had gotten so complicated so quickly.

THE ONE OR THE MANY?

Bradley dropped Cate and Derek at their Medford home. He wanted desperately to talk about the job offer with Derek but knew he shouldn't bring it up in front of Cate. Once the front seat became available, Rusty occupied it.

"What do you think, Rusty? Would you want to live in Washington, DC? I know you would miss Zayt and your friends at REACH. But you would get to see Cate and Derek more often."

Bradley's focus then changed from his job dilemma to Ali al-Haqani. Al-Haqani proved himself to be a much more perilous adversary than Bradley had hoped. Al-Haqani had anticipated the bureau's abilities and took advantage of them. He was smart and ruthless, and he was just getting started. Could I really sit on the sidelines knowing what I know now? Bradley wondered.

And what about Zayt? No, I can't go anywhere while Zayt is in trouble, Bradley decided. Okay, that's it. I can't take the job.

Relieved, Bradley spent the remainder of the drive thinking of Zayt's case. Once home, he checked his phone messages.

"Hi, this is Jennifer Cornwell returning your call. I'll be home the rest of the day if you need to speak with me," the recording said.

Bradley checked the time and was surprised to see it was not yet six. Before returning Jennifer's call, he checked his email for the police report Cassie had promised to send. When he saw it in his inbox, he smiled.

"I think I've figured out how to deal with Papadakis, Rusty," Bradley said.

Rusty cocked his head.

The police report stated that, on the morning of the murder, Revere police officer Eugene Higgins responded at 6:25 a.m. to a call from the city's tip hotline that a homeless person was sleeping on the side of the road across from 34 Howland Street. When the officer arrived at the scene, he found the body of Ronald Crayton. The report described the body as having trauma to the chest. The officer wrote that he then radioed the police station, where an officer arranged for the coroner and detective to arrive on scene.

Bradley shuffled through the report again and again.

"The officer was alone?" he said out loud.

So, Bradley thought, not only is the time of the police car arrival off, but Jennifer said she saw two officers standing outside the cruiser. No wonder Papadakis thinks she's lying.

But Bradley did not concur with Cassie's conclusion about Jennifer. He thought Jennifer seemed completely truthful about what she had seen. It was time to call Jennifer Cornwell back.

"Hello?" she answered.

"Hello, Miss Cornwell. This is Bradley Whitman calling back. Thank you for getting back to me. I wondered if it would be possible to talk to you again tomorrow morning. I could meet you at the same place, same time. It shouldn't take too long. I just have a couple more questions."

"Yes, of course."

"Thank you. I'll see you in the morning then," Bradley said.

Bradley texted Cassie Papadakis, **Meet me at the corner of Howland and Jameson tomorrow morning at 5.**

In return, Bradley received a thumbs up emoji from Papadakis.

Bradley booted his computer and searched the Revere police department log for Thursday, August 13, the day Ronald Crayton was found dead. He looked for any instances where a police cruiser may have been called to the area of Howland Street at five o'clock in the morning. He found none.

Unable to find an explanation for what Jennifer said she saw, Bradley considered the small chance Cassie may have been right. But he decided to wait until morning before committing to the idea.

Rather than chase the unknown, Bradley diverted his attention to the bombings at Times Square and Mall of America. Using the willing media as objects of misdirection, information in both instances had been contained well by the FBI. The Times Square bombing was being portrayed as performed by a disgruntled ex employee of the city. The incident at Mall of America had been attributed to hazardous combustible materials accidentally igniting and exploding.

He tapped into the FBI incident reports but quickly realized that he did not have access to all available information. Hadn't Derek said something about higher security clearance with the new job? That would be nice, he thought.

The files he had access to did not include any surveillance video from the mall or Times Square. Bradley knew there would have been video. The omission made him think there was something worthwhile on it. If it didn't show anything obvious, it wouldn't be highly classified.

He called Derek.

"Hey, Bradley," Derek answered.

"Derek, have you seen the video from the two related incidents we discussed earlier?" Bradley was careful not to reveal anything over an open telephone line.

"What makes you think there was video?" Derek asked.

"Really? Come on, Derek."

"Yes, I've seen it," Derek replied.

"Just tell me this much. Was there only one suspect in each of the videos?"

Derek paused before he answered, "Yes."

"And they probably weren't homegrown," Bradley stated.

"Right."

"Okay. That's good to know," Bradley said.

"So, you're delving into it, huh?" Derek asked.

"Just to satisfy my own assumption. It doesn't mean I'm going to make a move. Jesus, Derek. I wish we could talk about this."

Derek said, "I don't want to influence you in any way. Call Houghton tomorrow and hear him out. Then take some time to think about it."

"Alright, thanks."

Bradley had gotten the answer he was looking for. Ali al-Haqani did not believe he would succeed in Washington. That's why he used homegrown terrorists to carry out the diversion plan. He didn't wish to sacrifice any of his own men.

If he tries that again, I'll be ready, Bradley thought. He looked forward to having access to the classified information that he didn't yet have clearance for.

Snapping himself from his thought process was the fact that he was thinking about the case as if he were going to be working it. It happened naturally and without forethought. He wondered what that meant. Had he already subconsciously made up his mind to take the job?

Inside an hour's time, Bradley had laid out a case both to take the job and not to take the job.

Bradley reached for his phone to text Sahani. He saw he had a text from Nick. It read, **Derek says transfer still on hold. Don't know why!**

Bradley replied to Nick, **Guess I got at least one more day of freedom?**

Bradley wanted to downplay the delay as much as possible. He didn't want to worry Nick, but he felt bad about not being honest. He was going to need Sahani's help with the decision. He typed a text.

Can we meet somewhere to talk tomorrow afternoon? I can't come to the office. Her reply came quickly.

How about 4pm? I can come to your place???

Perfect, thank you. See you then, Bradley returned.

Sure that his text must have puzzled Sahani, he also knew he needn't worry about her saying anything to anyone.

With a fresh brewed cup of coffee, Bradley and Rusty moved to the backyard. Rusty gazed at Bradley for approval before heading down the steep bank into the REACH community. At Bradley's back, the sun shone the day's last rays on the tiny homes and would soon duck below the horizon for its nightly nap.

As he tried to clear his mind, Bradley found it difficult to stop thinking about the decision before him. He thought back to what his father had said about being able to change his life's direction if he wasn't happy with it. But he wasn't willing to make a decision based on the existence of an exit strategy. It wouldn't be fair to whomever he worked for or with. Whatever he decided, he needed to commit fully. And he couldn't commit to anything without knowing details, which he wouldn't have until the following day.

There was a time, Bradley thought, that I wouldn't hesitate before taking the position Sam Houghton was offering, even without knowing the full details. He had always aspired to be a cog in the wheel that could potentially save the world, possibly even the wheel itself.

But if Bradley had learned anything in the past year, it was that no one action or decision is any more or less important than any other because each connects to the other. So, no matter what route he chose, he could still do his part to make the world a safer and better place at least within his small piece of it.

The question for Bradley then became, What do I want to do, as opposed to What should I do? And that was a much more formidable question for him to ponder.

The sun still hid below the horizon when Bradley and Rusty drove to meet Jennifer. By the side of the road at the corner of Howland and Jameson stood a scraggly, black-haired woman in shabby clothes.

"Good morning, Papadakis," Bradley said as he pulled alongside her. "I see you're wearing your Sunday finest."

"Easy there, prep boy. I don't think you're qualified to get into a fashion debate with anyone," Cassie replied.

Together, Bradley and Rusty rode the truck's ramp to the pavement.

"Well? Where is she?" Cassie asked.

"Relax. We're early." Bradley checked his watch. "She should be coming around the corner on the other end of Jameson in a few minutes." Bradley neglected to warn Cassie about the dog that would inevitably come running to greet them.

Almost on cue, Bradley saw Jennifer round the corner some eighty yards away.

"There's got to be an explanation, Papadakis. She was telling me the truth yesterday," Bradley said.

"And you know this how?" she asked skeptically.

"Because I can read people reasonably well," he answered. "I'd stake my reputation on it."

"Which reputation? The one where you nearly got people killed? Or the one where you got a six-month suspension?" Papadakis stared him down.

Had he had time, Bradley may have tried to explain the circumstances of those instances. But, he thought, it's just as well. He would have sounded like he was justifying bad choices. Besides, Dutch had spotted them.

From nearly forty yards away, the dog launched into a full run. Having experienced the situation the day before, Rusty did not bark but sat still in front of Bradley.

The closer the dog came, the wider Cassie's eyes opened. When Dutch was within twenty yards and showed no signs of slowing, Papadakis howled, "Jesus Christ," and reached for the handgun inside her layers of clothing. She drew a .45 caliber Smith & Wesson M&P compact and concentrated the barrel on the approaching dog.

"What the hell!" Bradley yelled, reaching for her raised arm. "He's friendly, for chrissake. Put that thing away."

Eyes still bulging, Cassie lowered the firearm, then moved behind Bradley's chair.

"Hey, Dutch," Bradley said as the dog skidded to stop at his and Rusty's feet. Rusty and Dutch exchanged sniffs. Then Dutch placed his two front paws on Bradley's lap and waited to be petted. Bradley pulled two dog bones from his pocket and gave one to each dog.

Cassie slowly replaced the M&P into its holster.

After finishing the bone, Dutch crowded Cassie looking for attention. Bradley could tell Cassie was angry and embarrassed.

"You knew he was going to do that, didn't you?" she asked.

"I figured he would."

"And you didn't think to warn me?"

"I thought about it," Bradley said.

"I might have killed that stupid dog," Cassie barked.

"No," Bradley said. "You wouldn't. Instinct had you pull the gun. You weren't going to shoot him."

Before Cassie could reply, Jennifer slowed her pace and approached the two. Her eyes fixed on Cassie.

"Good morning, Miss Cornwell," Bradley said. "Thank you for meeting with me again. This disheveled looking person is Cassie Papadakis. She is an investigator working the case of the deceased man."

"Ahh! Good morning," Jennifer said, seemingly relieved by Bradley's introduction.

"Miss Cornwell, can you tell Miss Papadakis what you told me yesterday? Specifically, what you saw at the end of your run, please?" Bradley asked.

Jennifer relayed how she saw a police cruiser with two police officers standing outside of the car about sixty yards from where the three conversed.

In what Bradley perceived to be her most amiable conversation tone, Cassie said, "I'm sorry, Miss Cornwell, but the report said that the patrol car didn't get on the scene until almost 6:30. And there were no other calls in the area that morning. Are you sure about the time?"

Jennifer nodded. "I'm positive. I was just finishing my run. The first car was there a little after five. The second one, the blue one, didn't show up until later. That must have been the one you're talking about."

Bradley and Cassie exchanged glances.

Bradley asked, "The second one? Are you saying you saw two different police cruisers in that same area that morning?"

"Yes. When I left for work, the dark blue police car was there," Jennifer added. "That would have been around 6:30."

"Why do you say dark blue? Was the other car a different color?" Bradley asked.

"Uh huh, yes. The car earlier was white with a blue stripe on the side. That's the one where the officers were standing outside. That must have been when they first discovered the . . . the . . . you know." Jennifer shuddered at the thought.

Cassie asked, "What can you tell us about the two men standing by the car?"

"Not much. They were pretty far away. And I didn't pay that much attention. I was trying to keep Dutch from running at them," Jennifer said.

"Right," Bradley said. "Jennifer, could you do me a favor?"

"Sure."

"If I hold on to Dutch so he won't go anywhere, could you close your eyes and think back to that moment when you saw the two men?" Bradley asked.

"I can, but I don't think it will do any good," Jennifer said.

"Let's just give it a try, alright?" Bradley smiled.

"Alright."

Bradley grabbed hold of Dutch while Jennifer stood before him with eyes closed.

"Okay. It's Thursday morning and you were jogging down Jameson toward home. You saw that man, the military guy who runs the opposite direction of the same route you do. He was running toward you. Dutch ran to greet him. You acknowledged each other as you passed. You continued down Jameson, and as you turned the corner onto Howland, you noticed people up ahead. Don't pay attention to Dutch now, I've got him. Stay focused on the two men. What do you see?"

Jennifer's eyes shot open. "One of the guys is really tall and big. Not overweight, but big. Kind of like the military guy but only taller. And the other guy wasn't wearing a police hat. He was shorter. Not short, but shorter than the big guy. The big guy had a police cap on. I could tell by the shape.

"I can't believe that worked," Jennifer chuckled. "Does that help at all?"

Bradley smiled. "It is a big help. You did great. Would it be alright if we contact you again if we have any questions?"

"Of course. That was kind of interesting. I might have to try that method at work to see if I can remember where I put the Rottman file," Jennifer laughed.

"Thank you for your time, Miss Cornwell," Cassie said politely.

"Jump in the truck," Bradley said to Cassie.

With Rusty in the back seat and his door almost closed, Bradley and Cassie shared an intense glare.

"She saw the killer and the victim," Cassie said.

Bradley nodded. "White cruiser with a blue stripe. That's a Boston Police Department cruiser. There's no reason a Boston cop should be in Revere at five o'clock in the morning, is there?"

"We're looking at a cop for the murder of a homeless man." Cassie shook her head.

"Not only that," Bradley said, "he's got to be the one who gave Crayton the fifty dollars to punch Zayt. When Crayton showed up to collect what was owed him, the cop killed him.

And he timed it just after Zayt jogged by so witnesses might point him out. That's a hell of a setup."

"But why?" Cassie asked.

"I need to talk to Zayt," Bradley said.

Cassie gave it some thought, then replied, "I'm coming with you."

"What about your undercover status?"

"I think we are beyond that now," Cassie said.

"He's not going to be happy you deceived him."

"He'll be less happy when I tell him you knew."

"You know you make it really hard for me to keep my dark side at bay." Bradley shifted the truck into gear.

"Please, don't hold back on my account. I'd like to see what happens when prep boy blows his stack. Do you pop a few buttons?"

Bradley quietly smoldered for the short drive to the sandpit while Papadakis rode shotgun and discharged a satisfied grin.

Not seeing Zayt on his morning run around the sandpit, Bradley assumed he had finished and gone back to his cabin. Bradley, Papadakis, and Rusty waited outside Zayt's door as Bradley knocked.

With wet hair and wearing a bathrobe, Tasha answered the door.

"What are you doing here?" she asked Bradley.

"I need to talk to Zayt," he answered.

Tasha turned her attention to Cassie. "Okay. But what is she doing here?"

"She needs to talk to Zayt, too," Bradley said. "Can we come in?"

Tasha reluctantly let them inside. Zayt had been dressing in the bedroom when he heard the knock. He walked into the only other room in his cabin, which became quite crowded.

"Hey, Bradley," Zayt said, then looked at Cassie with a befuddled expression.

"Zayt, we need to talk to you." Bradley eyed Tasha.

"Okay," he replied.

"Um, alone, Zayt," Bradley said.

Tasha couldn't hold back. "Oh, no, you don't. You don't come in here and kick me out. I've got as much right to know what's going on as anybody. More than you do," Tasha said pointing to Bradley. "I didn't abandon Zayt for a year. I've been here the whole time."

"Tash, easy," Zayt said. "Come on, Bradley. She's as important to me as you are. I want her to know what's going on."

Bradley looked to Cassie, who nodded.

Zayt caught the exchange, glared at the homeless woman he had been trying to help, and asked, "What the hell is going on?"

"Zayt, this is Cassie Papadakis. She is Damien Sullivan's private investigator."

Zayt's jaw dropped as did Tasha's.

Tasha reacted first. "Why you lying sack of shit!"

Before Zayt could stop her, Tasha lunged toward Cassie and grasped the outer sweater layer of her disguise. Tasha would not let go. As Zayt pulled Tasha away from Cassie, the sweater stretched beyond its capabilities and tore from Cassie's back. Cassie fell, causing her nose to smash into the floor and spurt blood. Cassie jumped up and leapt toward Tasha, still held by Zayt. Bradley tried to maneuver his chair so he could grab Cassie, but the trio moved too quickly around the kitchen table.

"Rusty, stop her," Bradley said to the dog.

Rusty ran to Cassie and took hold of the remaining clothing she wore. He latched on to her loose-fitting shirt from behind and yanked. Cassie fell backwards onto the floor as Bradley placed himself between her and Tasha and Zayt.

"Zayt? Can you handle Tasha?" Bradley asked.

Zayt pulled Tasha into the bedroom and closed the door. Cassie, furious that Bradley used Rusty to stop her, stood up and punched Bradley in the face. Rusty bared his teeth and released a throaty growl. Ready to pounce on command, he placed himself between Cassie and Bradley.

"Down, boy," Bradley commanded.

Rusty sat but did not break eye contact with Cassie.

Bradley wiped the blood running from his lip. Then he reached into his pocket, pulled out a handkerchief, and handed it to Cassie.

"What's wrong with you?" Bradley asked Cassie. "How can you do what you do if you let people get to you that easily?"

Cassie wiped blood from her nose. "She took me by surprise. I didn't expect it."

"For chrissake, Papadakis. It's not even 6 a.m., and you've pulled your gun on a dog and gotten into a cat fight. What's next? Are you going to wrestle a pony?"

"You used your dog to attack me," she barked.

"No, I used my dog to stop you. If I could've done it myself, I would have. Sometimes Rusty has to be my legs." Bradley could feel his lip swelling. "That's a nice little right hook you've got there."

"Yeah, well." Cassie had nothing more to say.

Zayt came out of the bedroom, Tasha followed.

Zayt asked, "Are we under control out here?"

"We'll see," Bradley said.

"Well, then, will someone tell me what the hell is going on?" Zayt asked.

"Like I said, Papadakis is Sullivan's private investigator. She went undercover to see what she could find out from the homeless community about Ronald Crayton," Bradley explained.

"Why didn't anyone tell me about this?" Zayt asked with obvious irritation.

Bradley looked at Cassie to answer.

"I needed to see how you interacted with the residents," Cassie replied.

"And?" Zayt asked.

"And, nothing. My job is to find out why someone framed you for the murder of Ronald Crayton. That's what I'm doing. I don't care if you like my methods. I don't work for you."

"The hell you don't," Tasha spat.

Zayt quickly subdued Tasha's oncoming outburst with a glance.

"Look, can we just skip the hurt feelings and get to the point?" Bradley asked.

"I wish you would," Zayt said.

"Papadakis found out that someone paid Crayton to take a swing at you," Bradley began. "She also found out that Crayton was expecting to receive additional funds once he completed the task."

"Who? Why?" Zayt asked.

"That's what we're trying to figure out, but we need your help," Bradley said to Zayt.

"First, we need to know everything you saw the morning of your arrest when you went for a jog. From beginning to end," Bradley said.

"I've been through this with you," Zayt said to Bradley.

"Then go through it with me," Cassie said.

Zayt told of how he woke that morning and jogged the long loop, ran into Jennifer and Dutch, and returned to the sandpit.

"Did you see anything unusual on or just before you turned onto Howland Street?" Bradley asked.

"No," Zayt said immediately.

"Think about it, Zayt. Recall that morning. Was there anything out of place? A car or truck that didn't belong in the area. Anyone hanging around a street corner?"

Zayt closed his eyes and pictured his route that morning. When he opened them, he said, "Nothing. I didn't see anything unusual."

Bradley and Cassie's shoulders slumped.

Tasha's body language said she wanted to throw the two of them out the door.

"What have you found out about this guy Crayton? I had never seen him before that day," Zayt said.

"The regular residents didn't know him either," Cassie said. "Maybe that's why he was stupid enough to brag about being paid to hit you? Well, he didn't say you, specifically. That's conjecture."

"He's got a lengthy record, mostly small stuff," Bradley said. "I spoke to a few of the arresting officers. Most of them didn't remember him. And the one guy that did was unhelpful." That sparked an image in Bradley's head of the six-foot tall angry, muscular cop in the Back Bay precinct.

"Huh," Bradley uttered.

Nobody spoke, each of them waiting for Bradley to explain his utterance.

"Well?" Cassie asked.

"What?" Bradley questioned.

"What was the 'Huh' all about?"

"Jennifer said the guy was tall and muscular," Bradley said.

"Who's Jennifer?" Tasha asked.

Bradley ignored the question and continued his thought. "And he drove a white cruiser with a blue stripe."

"That's a Boston Police Department cruiser. That's what we drive. What's that got to do with a murder in Revere?" Tasha asked.

Bradley again ignored Tasha and continued, "Officer Hayes had an attitude. And he wasn't interested in answering any questions about Crayton."

Tasha lifted her hands to her mouth and gasped, taking a step back from the other three. All eyes turned to her.

"Tash? Are you alright?" Zayt asked. But he knew she wasn't. Her body had begun to quiver, and fear widened her eyes. "Tash, what's the matter?"

"This is all my fault!" Tasha spat. "Oh, my God, Zayt. I'm so sorry. This is all my fault."

IT'S THE LAW

Zayt took Tasha by her shoulders and pulled her toward him. "What are you talking about? Baby, you're shaking. What is it?"

She gazed into Zayt's eyes and said, "It's Dixon."

Bradley's "huh" had just panned out. "Dixon Hayes," Bradley said. "Let me guess, Tasha. He's the cop you told Zayt about."

Tasha nodded, unable to speak. Her trembling brought with it uncontrollable sobs. Zayt wrapped his arms around Tasha and tried to calm her.

"What the fuck are you three talking about?" Cassie asked.

Bradley said, "Let's go outside and give them a few minutes. Rusty, come."

Bradley, Cassie, and Rusty went outside, closing the door behind them.

"What the hell is going on? Who's this Dixon guy?" Cassie asked.

"I don't know the whole story," Bradley said, "but Zayt told me Tasha had been in a very abusive relationship with a cop before she met him. Zayt said it took her a long time to get away from the guy, but she would never tell Zayt who it was. Now we know."

"And nobody thought to bring this up?" Cassie asked.

"Nobody was focused on Tasha," Bradley replied. "We were focused on Zayt. It's not like it's a new relationship. They've been together for eight months without a problem."

"Tell me about this Dixon Hayes," Cassie said.

"He came off as an angry and arrogant man. If I had to profile him based on that one conversation, I'd say he has a God complex. He thinks he's better than everyone around him. That would fit with his abusive nature."

"He's a cop, though. Could he kill someone, unprovoked?" Cassie asked.

Bradley gave it some thought, then answered, "Yes, I believe he could. If he's been this way his whole life, he was bound to escalate especially due to the perceived power he holds, you know, being a cop."

"Shit! This isn't going to be easy."

Zayt walked out the door and closed it behind him.

"How is she?" Bradley asked.

"She's pretty torn up. She's blaming herself for this whole thing. I tried to tell her it's not her fault, but it's not helping," Zayt paused. "Bradley, I'm afraid of what she might do. Tasha's a very protective person. She's going to want to confront this guy."

"She can't do that," Cassie said adamantly. "She can't let him know what we know. Not if we're going to nail him."

"Zayt, we're going to need to talk to her," Bradley said. "We need to know everything we can about the guy. You must convince her to trust us."

Zayt dropped his head and took a deep breath. "You'll have to give me some time. She doesn't trust easily."

"Okay," Bradley said, "but not too much time."

"Are you crazy?" Cassie nearly screamed. "We don't have the luxury of babying her. Zayt could end up in prison for a very long time."

"Papadakis," Bradley said, "we can press her now and get a little or let Zayt talk to her and potentially get the full scoop on the guy."

Cassie shook her head in defeat. "It'd better be a double scoop. You've got two hours," she said before she walked away.

Bradley turned to Zayt. "I'm sorry about Papadakis. I didn't know until two days ago. I wanted to tell you but . . ."

"I get it. Just keep her off Tasha, or we're going to have a problem," Zayt said.

"I'll do my best, but she's a bit stubborn."

"Sounds like someone else I know," Zayt said as he glanced at the closed door. "I'll see you in a couple hours." Zayt returned to his cabin.

When Bradley and Rusty returned to Bradley's truck, they found Cassie leaning against the driver's door.

"Our only hope is the coroner's report," she said. "If they find DNA on the body, we know who to check it against. If there's no DNA, we've got nothing."

"There is another possibility. It's possible Hayes's police cruiser was equipped with a GPS tracking device. If we can get that report, it may show that Hayes was on Howland Street around the time of Crayton's death."

"That's great. How do you propose we get our hands on the report?" Cassie asked sarcastically.

Bradley smiled. "That's the easy part."

Cassie eyeballed Bradley as if he were a lunatic. "Easy, yeah. All we have to do is walk in and ask the Boston Police Department for it, I suppose?"

"No, not the BPD. How about the FBI?" Bradley grinned. "If we can come up with enough circumstantial evidence that Dixon Hayes, a Boston police officer, was involved in the death of Ronald Crayton, the FBI will have to investigate. It's their jurisdiction along with police internal affairs, of course."

For the first time since Bradley met Cassie, he saw her natural smile. It nearly threw him out of his chair. Even though she dressed as a hobo about to board a moving train, Bradley could see the beauty she so desperately tried to hide. He couldn't help but smile in return.

"Okay," she said. "So, we have the homeless man Crayton bragged to about the money. We have Jennifer Cornwell who saw the cruiser and two people on Howland Street. And we have a connection between Officer Hayes and Zayt. How much more do we need?"

"More," Bradley said. "Is Sullivan going to call you when he gets the coroner's report?"

"Yes. We're hoping to get it today, but who knows. The coroner's office is so backed up."

"Let's go back to my place and work up a strategy. We'll need to know just the right questions to ask Tasha. And maybe we can find something online about Dixon Hayes. A guy who's that angry has had to have public complaints against him."

"I'm hungry. Let's stop for something first," Cassie said.

"I've got plenty of food. I'll make us some breakfast while we talk."

"You're going to make me breakfast?"

Bradley chuckled. "Yeah, Papadakis, I'm going to make you breakfast."

Back at Bradley's, Cassie wolfed her western omelet and home fries faster than Rusty gobbled his dog treats. She finished by downing a full glass of orange juice. "Damn, Whitman, you sure can cook."

Only half finished with his meal, Bradley replied, "Thanks. I enjoy it."

"Hey, have you got a t-shirt or something I can change into?" she asked. "These rags are really itchy."

"Yeah, sure." Bradley pointed to the dresser by his bed. "Top left drawer. Take your pick. The bathroom is through that door to the right."

Cassie brought her plate to the kitchen sink, then went to choose a shirt. "Hey, you've got a Led Zeppelin shirt in here."

"Why do you sound so surprised?"

"I don't know. I guess I figured you for a classical music sort of guy."

"Jazz. But I like all music," Bradley said.

Cassie disappeared into the bathroom, and Bradley finished his breakfast. Bradley watched as Rusty got up and moved to the bathroom door to wait for Cassie. It caused Bradley to smile.

Their discussion up to that point had been focused on what it would take to get the FBI involved in the case. Bradley wanted to steer the conversation to Tasha's knowledge of Dixon. As it turned out, he didn't have to.

With her hair combed and wearing Bradley's Led Zeppelin t-shirt, Cassie looked like a different person than the one who sat across from him and ate breakfast, even if she did still wear torn green army ranger pants that were two sizes too big.

"Tasha had to have seen or heard something about Dixon that we can use against him, wouldn't you think?" Cassie asked.

"Yes, I would think so. We're going to have to approach her carefully, though. She feels guilty about this whole thing, so I suggest we go very easy on her."

Cassie shook her head and sighed. "She's a cop, not a daisy. What is it with men? You all think woman are so fragile and need your protection."

"That's not at all what I meant," Bradley stated. "I just think we need to gain her trust first."

"Look, Whitman. I hate to burst your Superman bubble, but she's never going to trust you. At least not for a long time. So, stop thinking she will, and let's make our plan from there."

Bradley thought about Cassie's assessment of Tasha and realized she was probably right.

"How do you think we should handle it?" Bradley asked.

Cassie widened her eyes and pointed her finger at herself, mocking him. "Me? Are you asking me what we should do?"

"Jesus, Papadakis, you are exhausting. Yes, I'm asking you what we should do."

Bradley saw just a hint of her smile.

"We need to stress that no matter how much we believe Dixon Hayes killed Ronald Crayton, it doesn't do any good if we can't prove it. We need to impress upon her the danger of Zayt spending the rest of his life in jail. We may even need to convince her Dixon may come after her next. We need to scare the shit out of her."

Bradley shook his head. "No. I don't like it."

"Then you can stay here," Cassie said. "I can't have you contradicting me."

Bradley didn't have much of a choice. He had agreed to the terms of Cassie taking lead on the investigation. He was stuck.

"Alright. But Zayt isn't going to like it," Bradley said.

"Zayt isn't going to be there. He can't be present when we're questioning a witness, for chrissake. Even he must understand that."

They went on to discuss specific questions to ask, but mostly they agreed they would see where the conversation took them.

Tasha was in the driver's seat. She was the one who knew what information was pertinent. Cassie just needed to root it out of her.

After two hours had passed, Bradley left Rusty at home while he and Cassie went back to Zayt's.

"You're going to have to leave, Zayt," Cassie said.

"I'm staying right here," Zayt growled.

Tasha, who looked as if she had just seen her pet rabbit stewed, said to Zayt, "I don't want you to stay. I'm going to have to say things that I don't want you to hear, Zayt. You, either." Tasha pointed to Bradley.

Bradley was about to object when Cassie caught his eye. "Why don't you and Zayt go for a long walk."

Bradley couldn't stop himself from glaring at her.

"Christ, I didn't mean. . .walk," Cassie said, rubbing her forehead. "You know what I meant. Go do something for a while." Cassie's tone then softened. "I'll text you when we're done."

Bradley looked up at Zayt and asked, "Do they need help in the kitchen serving lunch?"

"They can always use more help," Zayt said.

"Alright, let's go," Bradley said as he pushed his throttle and rolled out the door.

Zayt gave Tasha a hug and lightly kissed her forehead. "Are you sure you want me to go?"

Tasha nodded, unable to say the words.

Zayt shut the door behind him.

JACK IN THE BOTTLE

Lunch had long since been served and the dining room reset for the following day when Bradley's phone chimed with a text.

"They're done," Bradley said to Zayt.

Zayt jumped from the bench and sprinted out the door of the common room.

He held Tasha tightly when Bradley entered the cabin. As she watched them, Cassie revealed an empathetic look that Bradley found uncharacteristic.

Cassie spotted Bradley observing her, which caused the expression to quickly disappear. "Let's go, Whitman."

Once in the truck, Bradley asked, "How many people have you got in there?"

Her eyebrows pinched, Cassie asked, "What?"

"You are a conundrum. I can read most people easily, but you? Just today I've seen three, maybe four distinct personalities in you. Which one is the real you?" Bradley asked.

Cassie turned to look out the passenger window. "Nobody sees the real me." She regretted it as soon as she said it.

Bradley had no response because he knew exactly what Cassie meant.

They didn't speak until they got back to Bradley's house. Bradley let Rusty out knowing he would head to Zayt's. He hoped Rusty could help Tasha and Zayt through this difficult time.

"I need a drink," Cassie said.

"You realize it's not even two o'clock in the afternoon, right?" Bradley said.

"What am I, a fucking child? I want a drink. What have you got?" Cassie snapped.

Her eruption took Bradley by surprise. "Um, I've got beer. Or how about some wine?"

"Christ, don't you have any big boy drinks in this place?"

Bradley paused, then said, "In the cabinet behind the couch. Pick whatever you want," Bradley said.

Cassie chose a bottle of Jack Daniels. Bradley provided her with a glass.

"Do you want something to mix with that?" Bradley asked.

Cassie sat at the kitchen table and poured three fingers of whiskey.

"How about some ice?" Bradley asked.

She didn't respond.

The first swig relieved the glass of half its contents.

Bradley pulled his chair to the kitchen table but didn't speak. He could tell Cassie needed some time to think. Why, he didn't know.

Finally, after another swig, Cassie said, "This guy is a piece of work. But the problem is that he's smart. He covers his bases. I'm sure he's got some story worked out why his car was on Howland Street that morning. The GPS thing may backfire if we try to use it."

"What did Tasha tell you?" Bradley asked, concerned about Cassie's reaction.

"He's a serial rapist. He raped her more times than she could count. He beat her and raped her and used her for his dirty side business—drugs. And he shared her with his business partners. By sharing, I mean, allowed them to rape her, too."

"Jesus Christ," Bradley murmured.

"She was his prisoner. For four fucking years," Cassie said before she emptied her glass and refilled it.

"But she's a police officer. Why didn't she say something to someone?" Bradley asked.

Cassie's head shot around quicker than a lightning strike. "She couldn't tell anyone. She was straight out of the academy. Who would believe her? He had pictures of her with him and other men. He threatened to embarrass her, get her fired, and then kill her if she said anything. That's how this shit works, prep boy."

"But the bruises. Someone must have noticed," Bradley said.

"You haven't had to deal with many abusers, have you?"

"No. None, in fact."

"They always hit you where it won't show. The gut, the small of your back, your crotch. If it's part of your body that's typically covered, they will exploit it," Cassie said and took another gulp.

Bradley sat back in his chair. He suddenly understood Cassie's reaction to Tasha's story. His eyes softened as he brushed his hand over his face.

Cassie saw the change in his demeanor.

"What?" she asked. "What is it?"

"You said, 'you.'"

"What?"

"They always hit you where it won't show . . .your body. Not 'them' . . . 'you.'"

Cassie became flustered. "It's just a figure of speech."

"One that takes two whiskies to talk about?"

"Goddamn it." Cassie gulped the last of her drink and threw the glass against a kitchen cabinet. Bradley instinctively shielded his face with his arm. The glass shattered and sprayed the kitchen with shards. Cassie jumped up and stormed out the door, slamming it behind her.

After surveying his surroundings, Bradley muttered, "Good going, prep boy. You're about as sensitive as a meat grinder."

He retrieved his kitchen broom and started sweeping. He wasn't overly worried about his wheelchair tires, as they were built to withstand sharp objects. But he needed to make sure he got every piece of glass off the floor before he let Rusty back inside.

A few minutes later, he heard his door open, and Cassie walked in. She had been crying, evidenced by her puffy eyes. She didn't say anything but took the broom from Bradley's hands and started sweeping. Bradley cleaned the countertops and kitchen sink. Neither of them said a word.

When finished, Cassie walked to the kitchen door. Bradley followed her. "I'm sorry," she said as she reached for the door handle. "I'll bring your shirt back tomorrow."

Bradley reached for her arm and held it. "Hey, I'm sorry, too."

Cassie wouldn't look at him, and that saddened Bradley greatly.

Two very strong, independent, and capable women, both victims of abuse. Bradley realized how little he knew of the world around him. He had worked cases that included sexual abuse but had never spoken nor interacted directly with the victims. He had been shielded, and because of that, he found himself completely inept at communicating with Cassie.

After reviewing the morning's events, Bradley glanced at the clock. The day moved quickly, and Bradley still had not reached out to Sam Houghton. It was time he made the call.

"Houghton," Sam answered.

"Director Houghton, this is Bradley Whitman."

"Bradley, great to hear from you. I assume you've talked to Derek?"

"Yes, but he couldn't tell me much."

"I want you on my team, Bradley," Houghton replied. "I think you could do a great deal of good here in Washington working cases that affect the entire country. You've seen a little of what we do here. I need people like you to help keep this country safe."

"Director Houghton . . . ," Bradley started to say.

Houghton interrupted, "Call me Sam."

"Sam, I just got back into the game after a year away. I don't know if I'm ready for the big league."

"Oh, you're ready," Sam chuckled. "Bradley, you have a sharp mind, a keen sense of intuition, and you think outside the box. Those are all qualities we need here. And I think your recent trip abroad could prove to our advantage."

"How did you know I . . . " Bradley began to ask.

"You're an FBI agent. You must have known the bureau would monitor your movements outside the country," Sam said.

"Actually, I never thought about it. I suppose it makes sense. So, when Derek said he was keeping tabs on me . . . "

"Yeah, he was doing his job. Well, he was helping me do mine. So, the job comes with a substantial pay raise and two jumps in clearance level. You'll have access to some of the most highly classified material we have in this country. Imagine what you could do with that."

"But," Bradley said, "I'd have to move to DC."

"Well, yes. This isn't a position that could be handled remotely. Things move too fast. But you've already got friends here, right? And it's a great opportunity for advancement."

"Look, Sam, I don't know how much you know about my career, but I've made a couple of bad decisions in the past," Bradley said.

"I've read your file, Bradley. And I've talked to Paul Davis about you. He highly recommended you for this position."

"Director Davis? The same Davis that wanted me out of the bureau?" Bradley asked.

Sam chuckled. "Yeah, Paul could be a hard ass, but he knows good agents. He told me you are one of the best as long as you can keep to the script. This job would keep you out of the line of fire, so to speak. And trust me, if he wanted you out, you would have been out."

"Well, that's a recommendation I never thought I'd get. Sam, I've got a service dog. He goes everywhere with me. Would that be a problem?" Bradley asked.

"Not at all," Sam said.

"When would you want me to start?"

"Yesterday. But I understand you have things you need to take care of. How about next week?"

"Can I have a couple days to think about it?" Bradley asked.

"Of course. But, Bradley, I've got new information on Ali al-Haqani. Don't wait too long."

"You don't play fair, do you, Sam," Bradley chuckled.

"Not when I really want something, no."

Bradley told Sam he would be in touch as soon as he made a decision. He had never felt so conflicted about a job in his life.

Sahani was due to show in less than an hour. Bradley had a lot to think about before she arrived, and it served only to confuse him more.

"Is everything alright?" Sahani asked once she came through the door.

"Yes, everything's fine. It's just that I have some decisions to make that pertain to my job, and I didn't want to talk about them in the office," he replied.

"Oh?"

"Yes. Would you like a cup of coffee or something?"

"No, thank you. So, tell me what's going on."

Bradley led Sahani to the couch.

"I've got a major decision to make, and I need to talk it through with someone."

"Isn't that something you usually do with Derek?" Sahani asked.

"Exactly," Bradley said, as if someone understood him for the first time. "But Derek won't talk to me about this. He says he doesn't want to influence my decision."

"Maybe you better tell me what the issue is," Sahani said.

"I've been offered a job with the FBI National Security Branch."

"With Sam Houghton?" Sahani asked.

Impressed, Bradley said, "Do you know everyone in Washington?"

"I was there for a long time."

"Did you like it there?" Bradley asked.

"Yes, I loved it."

"If you don't mind me asking, why did you leave?"

"Because Derek said he needed me here."

"But you stayed here."

"I did," she simply agreed.

"So," Bradley said, "this is the dream job that I've always wanted, a chance to make a major difference in the world. A few years ago, I wouldn't have thought twice about taking it. Now, I don't know what to do."

"What's changed to make you hesitate?"

"Me. My priorities. My relationships. And, I guess, a sense of belonging. But to be honest, if I were going to make a move, this would be the perfect time."

"Why?"

"Because I've created a natural break. I've been gone for a year already."

"True," Sahani said. "But what about rebuilding those relationships. Isn't that something you said you wanted to do?"

"It seems the most damaged relationship is mine and Cate's. She's still holding some resentment. So, going to DC would help with that."

"What about your parents?" Sahani asked.

"Yes, that would be tough. But it's only an eight-hour drive home. Rusty and I could come back on some weekends if I'm not working. And if I get a big enough place in Washington, they could come and visit."

"What about Rusty?" Sahani asked.

"Sam said he wouldn't be a problem. And he does really well adapting to new places. And he loves Cate and Derek."

"Okay, then. Who else in your mind is holding you here?"

"My friend, Zayt. He's in trouble right now, and I need to help him."

"What if he wasn't in trouble?" Sahani asked. "Would you still feel the need to stay for him?"

"I don't know. He certainly doesn't need me for anything. And he's got a girlfriend that seems to be the real deal. I guess I wouldn't feel too bad about leaving. Again, I could always come home and visit."

"So those are your relationships. What about your priorities? Which job would support those better?"

"I would like some balance in my life. Both Laney and I struggled with that. In the past, I allowed some of my cases to become personal. So much so that I would do almost anything to solve them, and I wouldn't rest until I did. The cases I'd be working on with national security would be broader, less personal, but with far greater costs if I fail."

"You talk as if you are the only one who would be culpable for failure. You can't take on that kind of responsibility, no matter which job you choose," Sahani offered.

Bradley pursed his lips and nodded his head. "I know. It's a hard habit to break. I'm working on it. Which brings me to another problem."

"What's that?"

"You. I was beginning to like the idea of having someone I could talk to on a regular basis. And if I go to Washington, that won't be possible if you are here," Bradley said.

"There are multiple ways of dealing with that, Bradley. We could meet online, on the telephone, or make arrangements for one of us to visit the other now and then. There are also many qualified FBI psychologists in DC."

"No. I don't want to start over." Bradley shook his head.

"Can I ask you to do something for me?" Sahani asked.

"Of course."

"Close your eyes and think of the conversation we just had. Think of the conversation as if it happened between two strangers. Then I want you to profile the person who has the job offer. Tell me what you think."

"Okay."

Bradley closed his eyes and was silent for several minutes. Sahani could see his eyes darting back and forth behind his lids signaling the conversation shifting from one person to the next.

A smile indicated that Bradley was about to open his eyes and reveal what he had learned.

"You know, I used that same technique for a different reason on someone this morning," Bradley said.

"Did it work?" Sahani asked.

"Both then and now."

"What did you come up with?"

"The person who was offered the job obviously wants to take it," Bradley said.

"What makes you say that?"

"Because I answered every question with a justification for taking the job. Except for one. One big one," Bradley said.

"Which is?"

"Zayt is in trouble, and I need to help him."

"At the cost of your dream job?" Sahani asked.

"Yes, if it comes to that," said Bradley.

"Well, I guess you have your answer," Sahani smiled.

"I guess I do, thank you." Bradley paused, then asked, "Sahani, now that my question is answered, can I pick your brain about another subject?"

"Of course."

"I'm going to open some wine. Would you like some?" Bradley asked.

"If it's red, I'm in," Sahani grinned.

"Pinot Noir, coming up. The questions I have concern male sexual abusers and their female victims. I haven't had much experience with either, and I was hoping you could give me some insight into what to look for."

"Okay. Well, some sexual abusers exercise power and control that they lacked in their childhood. A large portion of abusers were abused themselves."

"A vicious cycle," Bradley added.

"Yes. Some are fairly easy to profile. They have a bad temper, and are insanely jealous, verbally abusive, and unpredictable. Some believe women are inferior and don't deserve to be treated as equals. But there are those who hide their dark side well. To the outside world, they adore their wife or girlfriend, all while raping or beating them behind closed doors. In both cases, the victims are held hostage. Not always physically, but emotionally."

"But how can they have that much control over these women?"

"The abuser finds a way to make it difficult for them to leave. They threaten to blackmail, discredit, embarrass, ruin financially, or even kill their victims."

Bradley handed Sahani a glass of wine.

"What about the victims? What is the lasting effect on a woman who has gotten away from her abuser?" Bradley asked.

"In most instances the victims feel guilt, shame, embarrassment, and fear. A lot of women isolate themselves rather than seek help, which is another kind of hell. Without counseling and support, these women may live with depression and anxiety and even develop suicidal tendencies. Then there are the physical problems: high blood pressure, eating disorders, insomnia, and somatization."

"Somatization, what's that?"

"When someone feels physical pain caused by psychological or emotional factors, we call it somatization."

"What if the women are strong, smart, and independent? How is it they fall into the abuser's trap?"

"Most male abusers look for a vulnerability in women. It doesn't matter if they are smart, strong, or whatever. All people, men and women, have vulnerabilities, and the abuser preys on that. Whether male or female, abusers are master manipulators. They will find that vulnerable thread and give it a tug just a little at a time so as not to cause notice. Later, they slowly begin to unravel the thread until they have it tied around their victim's throat."

Bradley bobbed his head back and forth trying to reconcile the idea of getting lulled by an abuser. Sahani sensed a common metaphoric explanation might help.

"Think of it like this," she continued. "If you threw a frog into a pot of boiling water, the frog would instinctively jump out, right?"

"Yes, if possible."

"Okay. Now, put that same frog into a pot of water at room temperature. The frog will adjust to its surroundings and get comfortable."

"Okay, so?"

"If you slowly and periodically turn up the heat under the pot, the frog will continue to adjust to its environment, thinking it normal, until it's too late and the frog boils to death."

"I see what you mean." Bradley nodded. "Tell me, is it possible the abuser will find another woman if their victim does somehow escape?" Bradley asked.

"Not only is it possible, but it's probable. Sometimes the abuser dumps one woman for another, probably younger one, leaving the first woman stripped of what little stability and self-worth her abuser provided and unable to care for herself. Without support, a lot of these women don't make it." Sahani took a sip of wine and studied Bradley.

"Bradley," Sahani continued, "I can see your wheels turning so I'm guessing this conversation isn't hypothetical."

"That's right, it isn't."

"You do remember what we talked about the other day, that you can't save the world on your own?"

Bradley grinned slightly and said, "I remember. I'm not going to do anything stupid. I'm more concerned about the victims at this point. Someone else can deal with the abuser."

"Well, whoever these women are, they're lucky to have you on their side," Sahani said.

"Thank you. I appreciate your help," Bradley said. "I have one more question."

"Alright."

"Can these women ever grow to trust a man again?"

"That's a difficult question to answer, Bradley. Many abuse survivors suffer from post-traumatic stress disorder. Much like soldiers coming home from war, the events of their lives are imbedded in their brain. Although it is possible to rewire negative messages to your brain, it is never easy and not always successful."

Making fists with his hands, Bradley said, "It makes me so angry that a human being could do these things to another human being."

"You're assuming that the abuser sees his victims as human beings. You're wrong to think that. And that's what makes them so dangerous."

Bradley's mind flashed back to Cassie throwing the whiskey glass against the kitchen cabinet. He wished there were some way he could erase her pain. Then he thought of Tasha and the trust she had placed in Zayt, and it gave him hope.

"Thank you, Sahani. You've been very helpful with everything."

"I'm always happy to help," Sahani smiled.

"Would you like to stay for dinner?" Bradley asked.

"Although I understand that you are an amazing cook, I can't stay. I have a date tonight. Shortly, actually."

Bradley smiled, "I hope he treats you to a nice dinner."

Sahani stood, grinned, and said, "She always does."

"Ah, I apologize for my presupposition." Bradley's wide smile indicated his delight at being allowed a glimpse into Sahani's personal life.

"No need," Sahani said as she walked to the door.

"Thank you, for everything. Enjoy your evening."

After Sahani left, Bradley sat and pondered how he made assumptions about people. He had thought Cassie a crude, egotistical, and unfriendly person. Then he finds that she may just be in survival mode. And Tasha? Well, he had newfound respect for her as well.

Just another part of me that needs work. Will I ever be the man I want to be? Bradley thought.

As far as the job went, Bradley had decided not to accept it as long as Zayt was under indictment for murder. If by some miracle they were able to exonerate him in the next two weeks, he might rethink his position. He would need to call Sam Houghton the following day and explain the situation.

Wondering where the heck Rusty was, Bradley went out the back door, closed it, and whistled. He watched as a moment later Rusty came running from behind one of the tiny homes in the sandpit and bounded up the steep grade to Bradley's backyard.

"Hey, buddy. You've been gone a long time. Did you visit everyone down there?" Bradley asked Rusty.

Rusty tilted his head.

"Are you hungry?"

Rusty ran to the slider door and waited for Bradley to open it.

While Rusty ate his dinner, Bradley prepared his own. In boiling water, he cooked penne pasta until al dente, then set it aside. Using a saucepan, he heated olive oil, butter, and minced fresh garlic.

He then added sliced shallots, zucchini, summer squash, blanched broccoli florets, shredded carrots, and sauteed it with Chardonnay. With the heat lowered to medium, he seasoned the mixture with salt, pepper, and Italian seasoning, and just as the vegetables began to soften, Bradley poured heavy cream into the saucepan. As the cream heated, he added a generous handful of grated Parmesan cheese and stirred it together until the cheese blended with the other ingredients.

He finished off the sauce by mixing in two hefty spoonsful of tomato paste. The blush-colored sauce began to thicken. He stirred in the cooked penne, turned the heat to low, and covered the saucepan.

Rusty's head shot up, and he began to bark. A moment later, the doorbell rang.

The last person Bradley expected to ring his doorbell, mostly because she had previously just walked in unannounced, was Cassie. But there she stood, grasping a folder and Bradley's t-shirt.

Her silky black hair wove into a French braid, and she dressed in clean, form-fitting jeans with a rust brown cowl-neck knit top. Her normally dark-rimmed eyes were highlighted with light eyeshadow, and Bradley could see her eyes were similar in color to her sweater. Her cheeks resembled the color of Bradley's newly made pasta sauce, blush. Cassie Papadakis looked completely different than Bradley had ever seen her.

"We got the coroner's report. I thought you would want to see it right away," Cassie said.

Still stunned, Bradley replied, "Ah, yeah. Come on in."

Cassie's head snapped toward the kitchen as the aroma of garlic enveloped her senses.

"What is that?" She lifted her head slightly and took a deep breath through her nose.

"Dinner. Are you hungry?" Bradley asked.

"I'm always hungry," she said. "But you've already cooked for me once today."

"Papadakis, I can never cook for one person. I'll be eating this for a week unless you help me out. I'm getting you a plate. Sit down."

Bradley tossed the t-shirt onto his couch.

"Alright, but only because you're making me," she nearly smiled.

"What does the report say?" Bradley asked as he served the pasta.

"There's no DNA, but they found fibers stuck in some kind of oil on Crayton's shirt around the stab wounds. They are still analyzing both. Other than that, there's nothing in the report that can help us," Cassie frowned.

"But the fibers could help," Bradley said.

"Oh, my God, this is unbelievably good," Cassie said with a mouthful of pasta.

Bradley chuckled and shook his head. "You don't get to eat much home cooking, do you. Sorry I don't have any bread or rolls. I haven't made any since I've been home."

"You make your own bread?" a wide-eyed Cassie asked.

"Yes, usually," Bradley said as he watched Cassie stick an overloaded fork of food into her mouth. "How the heck do you stay so thin when you eat the way you do?"

With her mouth full, Cassie's eyes darkened, and for a moment, she stopped chewing. When she continued, she did so slowly.

Bradley sensed he had said something wrong, so he continued in a casual tone, "I love cooking for people. I get joy out of watching them eat. Sometimes I can be annoying that way."

Cassie swallowed and replied, "Annoying? You?"

"Alright, I threw you a softball. Let it go, or when I make my homemade bread, I won't give you any."

Seeming to relax, Cassie shoveled the pasta into her mouth as fast as she could. Bradley wondered if Cassie had at one time been denied food. After his talk with Sahani, he wouldn't discount anything.

She moaned as she cleaned her plate.

"Can I get you more?" Bradley asked.

Bradley could see a conversation happening inside Cassie's head. "Well, maybe just a little," she replied.

Bradley nearly filled her plate again. Cassie's eyes lit.

"So, what are you going to do next?" Bradley asked.

"What do you mean?" Cassie asked, startled.

"About Hayes? What's the plan?" Bradley asked.

"Oh. I don't know yet. I may tail him for a couple days."

"He's probably abusing another woman. I understand most abusers will do that and move on to someone else, I mean. If we can find her, maybe she could help us," Bradley said.

"No. It's doubtful she'd be able to help us. But maybe we can help her."

"Yeah, we need to do that," Bradley said.

Cassie finished her second plate as Bradley polished off his first.

"What do you call that dish?" Cassie asked.

"Um, I don't know. It's kind of a cross between pasta primavera and an Alfredo, I guess. With a little tomato paste thrown in."

"Where did you learn to cook like this?"

"I cooked a little bit with my mother when I was a kid. But mostly I taught myself. It relaxes me. Do you want some coffee?"

"Sure. Why not? Do you mind if I use your bathroom?"

"Of course not," Bradley smiled, then gathered the dishes and brought them to the sink.

She had been in the bathroom for only a minute when Bradley noticed Rusty get up and walk to the bathroom door. He sat and waited.

Bradley had never known Rusty to do that before with company, and here he had done it twice in one day. Bradley rolled his chair over to Rusty to see what it was that interested him so much.

It was faint, but it was unmistakable. Bradley heard Cassie getting sick in his bathroom. Then he recalled Sahani talking about some victims developing eating disorders.

Shit! What did I say to her? Something about how she stayed so thin. Goddamn you, Bradley.

When he heard the toilet flush, he rode his chair back to the kitchen. Rusty stayed.

When Cassie emerged from the bathroom and Rusty returned to his bed, Bradley asked, "Do you use milk or sugar?"

"No, thanks. Just black."

Other than the mint she sucked on, she showed no sign of what she had just done. He wouldn't have known if he hadn't heard it for himself.

Bradley handed Cassie a cup of coffee, then said, "I was going to do a search for possible complaints lodged against Hayes. Do you mind if I do that now?"

"Great idea. Let's find a picture of this guy, too. I want to see what he looks like," Cassie said. "So, how are you going to get the information? Are you going to use the FBI database?"

"No. I can't do that. It's not an official FBI case. I'm going to use the database that the local newspaper has amassed."

Cassie wrinkled her nose. "What database?"

"When circumstances caused law enforcement officers to be closely scrutinized, Boston Globe reporters requested Boston Police Department public records concerning disciplinary actions, internal investigations, and other records so they could compile their own database. There are ten years of records dating from 2010 available online. All I have to do is search his name."

"Why didn't I know about this?" Cassie asked.

"Well, I don't think it's something that has been heavily advertised," Bradley said. "Besides, I imagine you get most of your information from Damien."

Bradley typed Dixon Hayes into the search box. Hayes had twenty-nine complaints against him, including excessive force, conduct unbecoming, pointing a firearm, and others.

Of the twenty-nine accounts, fourteen were sustained, which meant the department found sufficient evidence in support of the complaint. Hayes had been suspended ten times and received four reprimands.

"How is this guy still on the police force?" Cassie asked.

"Just think how many of his victims didn't report his actions. I imagine he does his utmost to discourage that from happening."

Bradley printed out two copies of the report and gave one to Cassie.

"He cooks and he's resourceful. Who knew?" Cassie said.

"Have I finally impressed you?"

And there it was, the smile that lit up her face. It lasted only a few seconds, but it shone brilliantly. "Find me a picture of the guy, and we'll see."

It took a little digging, but Bradley came up with a newspaper article written three years prior detailing a raid performed on a suspected drug dealer. Officer Dixon Hayes looked as if he posed for the photographer.

"Here you go." Bradley printed two copies and handed one to Cassie. Then, with a smirk, asked, "Well?"

Cassie eyed Bradley, and without a twitch of a smile said, "I'll call you tomorrow, Whitman. Thanks for dinner." And before Bradley could respond, she headed out the door.

Bradley typed eating disorders into his search engine. He quickly found what he was looking for—bulimia nervosa. People with the disorder typically eat large amounts of food in a short period of time and then force themselves to purge.

A profound sadness filled Bradley and a sense of guilt for his initial conclusions about Cassie. She was a survivor just trying to find her way in the world—different from him but also very much the same. He wished he could figure out a way to put her in a room with Sahani.

NO GOING BACK

He performed a vigorous morning workout, but his shower soothed him. Bradley couldn't pinpoint why he felt so aggressive. Maybe he projected his anger regarding Dixon Hayes and whoever abused Cassie. Or maybe it was the fact that he might miss out on his dream job. Either way, it provided a good workout.

Rusty had already returned from his morning run with Zayt and eaten his breakfast, signaling time for a nap. He fluffed his bed, circled it five times, and lay down.

Bradley picked up his telephone. He had repeated the same conversation several times in his head that morning, and it came out the same each time. He dialed Sam Houghton's telephone number. Sam's assistant put Bradley through right away.

"Bradley, good morning," Sam said.

"Good morning, Sam," Bradley replied. His voice sounded weak.

"Maybe not. I don't like the tone of your voice, Bradley."

"I want to accept the job, Sam, but I can't. I have a commitment here at home that I need to take care of. And I don't know how long it will take."

"What kind of commitment?" Sam asked.

Bradley thought it only fair he tell Sam the reason. "My friend has been accused of a murder he didn't commit. I need to help him clear his name. I can't leave this to the local PD, Sam. The person that framed him has done a really good job."

"You know who did it?" Sam asked.

"I'm ninety-five percent sure, yes."

"Then finish it up. The job will be here when you're done," Sam said.

"Sam, this could take a year. Maybe more," Bradley said.

"I'm betting on you, Bradley. The job is here, and it's yours. Let me know if there's anything I can do to help," Sam said.

"Thank you, Sam."

Bradley put the phone down and sat startled. The conversation did not go at all as he expected. And the result? Bradley just accepted a job with the FBI National Security Branch. At some point in the future, Bradley would be moving to Washington, DC.

Derek. How am I going to tell Derek? Bradley wondered.

He knew if he thought about it too long, he wouldn't have the nerve to do it, so he selected Derek's office number in Washington and pressed it.

"Director Richards's office. How can I help you?" Madelyn Cross asked.

"Hello, Madelyn. This is Bradley Whitman. Is Derek available?"

"Hello, Bradley. Yes, he is. I'm sure he has a few minutes for you. One moment, please."

The next voice Bradley heard was Derek's.

"Hey, Bradley. Is everything alright?" Derek asked.

"Yes, everything's fine. Why is it that's the first thing people ask me when I call?"

"Because you never call," Derek said. "To what do I owe this unusual honor?"

"I just got off the phone with Sam."

Derek paused. "Oh?"

"I told him I couldn't take the job because of the situation with Zayt. But . . ."

"But what?" Derek asked.

"He said he'd hold the job for me, Derek. And I didn't say no."

Another pause. "Well," Derek said, "Sam's no idiot. Congratulations, Bradley. It's a heck of a step up. I'm happy for you."

"I'm sorry, Derek. Everything has happened so fast I don't know what to make of it. I just know that I love working for you and I . . . I'm really going to miss it."

"Yeah, me too. But there's nothing to be sorry about, Bradley. Let's look at the bright side. You'll be here in Washington. I'll tell Cate to keep the spare room ready." Derek feigned a laugh.

"What about Nick? Do you want to tell him or should I?" Bradley asked.

"I'll give him a call and explain everything," Derek said.

"This whole move might take a long time. If we can't come up with concrete evidence against this guy, then I'm not going anywhere."

"You've got a suspect?" Derek asked.

"Yeah. I'm pretty sure we know who's framing Zayt. Once I'm a hundred percent sure, I'll let you know."

"Hey, what do your parents think about the new job?"

"I haven't told them about it yet."

"Nothing? You didn't talk to them about it first?"

"No. The only person I talked to was Sahani," Bradley said.

"I don't envy you that conversation. Listen, I've got to get back to work. I'm happy for you, Bradley. Really."

"Thanks, Derek."

Bradley hung up and let out a sigh. As difficult as that conversation felt, the one with his parents would be much worse. But he didn't have to do that just yet.

Bradley needed a distraction, so he moved to his desk and booted his computer. The printout of Dixon Hayes lay on his keyboard. The man stared from the photo as if mocking Bradley.

"He even looks like an asshole," Bradley uttered. Then thought, He really does. That's not a forgettable guy.

"Hey, Rusty. Let's go for a ride," Bradley said.

Rusty jumped from his bed and was at the door before Bradley could make a move. Bradley made three copies of Dixon's picture before he and Rusty drove down to the REACH community and searched for Zayt.

Finding him in the office, Bradley showed Zayt the picture of Dixon Hayes and said, "Is it possible this guy could walk through this entire community before getting to your cabin and plant evidence without anyone noticing him?"

"Is this him? Is he as big as he looks?" Zayt's face cinched.

"At least six feet and bulky. And his face isn't exactly . . . pleasant," Bradley answered while nodding.

"I'll show the picture around."

"Here, I made multiple copies. Give one to Shea and anyone else you trust. If Hayes didn't plant the evidence, we have another rat out there. While you do that, I'm going to look into Hayes and see who his friends are, if he has any," Bradley said. "Is Tasha going to be around today?"

Zayt shook his head. "She's working a double shift."

"I'll investigate his partners. When you talk to Tasha, tell her I'd like to talk to her, alright?"

"Yeah."

"We're going to nail this son of a bitch, Zayt. We just need to be patient," Bradley said.

Back at the house, Rusty returned to his bed while Bradley tried to reach Cassie on the phone. It rang four times before her voicemail picked up.

"Hey, it's Bradley. I wanted to let you know I gave Dixon's picture to Zayt and Shea. They're checking to see if anyone saw him in the community around the day the evidence was planted. Call me."

In searching the web, Bradley found an Excel database of Boston police officers. The list was long, and it was four months old, but it would do. What it didn't list was who partnered with whom. To get that information, Bradley would have to talk to someone in the department or with Tasha.

Bradley didn't have Tasha's contact info, and he wasn't sure Zayt would give it to him. Tasha hadn't exactly warmed to Bradley. Instead, he called Boston police headquarters and asked if he could speak to her or leave her a message.

"She's not in today. She's not due back to work until Thursday. Do you still want to leave a message?" the voice on the phone asked.

"No, thank you," Bradley answered, then hung up the phone. Zayt said she was working a double shift today. Why would he lie to me? Or, did she lie to him? Bradley thought of possible reasons Tasha would be untruthful.

Maybe she was seeing a psychologist and didn't want anyone to know? But that didn't make sense. It wouldn't take all day, and why would she want to hide it from Zayt if it were true?

Maybe, knowing that her ex-boyfriend framed him, she just couldn't face Zayt. She was probably feeling guilty. That's got to be it, Bradley thought. She just couldn't face him.

Cassie must have her number, he thought. I'll ask her for it when she calls me back. Or, I'll ask Cassie to ask Tasha about Dixon's past partners with the BPD.

While he pondered his next move, Bradley's cellphone rang. It was Nick.

"Shit," Bradley muttered, then answered.

"Hey, Nick."

"What the fuck, Bradley?"

"Nick, I'm sorry I didn't . . ."

"What? Didn't what? Tell me a fucking thing? Give me a heads up?"

"I didn't know until this morning whether I would take the job. What did you want me to say? I might, maybe, someday be moving to Washington? Come on, Nick."

"Fucking DC?" Nick questioned.

"I know. It doesn't sound like me, does it?" Bradley scoffed.

"Jesus, Bradley. I know it's a great opportunity. And if I wasn't so pissed off, I'd be happy for you."

"What have you got to be pissed about? You're living the dream, buddy. You've got a beautiful wife, a baby on the way, and a great job. What more can you ask for?"

"My fucking partner. What the hell am I going to do without my partner?" Nick asked.

Bradley's throat constricted, and he found it hard to swallow. He had never considered himself anyone's partner and had no idea anyone thought of him that way. But Nick spoke as if it were common knowledge.

Bradley cleared his throat and said, "I've been gone for a year, Nick. You've done fine without a . . . without me."

"But that's because I knew you would be back someday. What the hell am I supposed to do now? There's no one who knows me better than you."

"Well, I think Mara would take issue with that. But Nick, you don't need me. You haven't needed me for years, not since the Vince Vega days," Bradley chuckled. "Remember that? You took over like the pro that you are. You filled Derek's shoes without missing a beat, and that was a heavy burden. It's been all you, Nick. I'm just a problem solver who plays with information and data. And I'll always be available if you have a problem."

"I haven't told Mara yet, Bradley. This is going to be a big blow to her. You know that, right?"

"Yeah, well, we have time. I'm not leaving for a while yet. Not until this thing with Zayt is cleared up."

"Yeah, how's that going?" Nick asked.

"We think it's a cop who's framed him. And he did an excellent job."

"A cop? Why haven't you made a formal complaint? We could look into it if you do?"

"I know. We just want to make sure. We're close to having enough circumstantial evidence."

"Who's we?" Nick asked.

"The lawyer's private investigator and me. We're almost there," Bradley said.

"Keep me posted. We'll be ready to jump in when you do."

"You're ready to help Zayt? I thought you couldn't stand the guy," Bradley grinned as he spoke.

"True, but he's your friend, and you're my friend. Let's leave it at that."

"Thanks, Nick. Give Mara a hug for me."

"Yeah."

Bradley had not been prepared to deal with the impact of his new job so quickly. In fact, everything seemed to be moving quicker than expected. He knew, though, he would need to deal with his parents before they accidentally found out from someone else.

Once again, he picked up his phone.

"Hey, Dad," Bradley said.

"Bradley? Is everything alright?" Doug asked.

Bradley chuckled. "Yes, Dad, everything is fine. I wondered if you and Mom were busy tonight. Maybe we could meet for dinner somewhere?"

"What's the matter?"

"Nothing, Dad. I just want to talk to you and Mom about something, that's all. It's nothing bad," Bradley said.

"Why can't you tell me now?" Doug asked, still suspicious.

"Dad, do you want to meet for dinner or not?"

"Yes, sure, of course. I just don't want any more surprises, that's all."

Bradley sunk his head. Well, you may not like this one then, he thought.

"How about we meet at Emelio's at six?" Bradley asked.

"Alright, son. We'll be there. You promise everything is alright?"

"Yes, Dad. I promise. I'll see you tonight." Bradley hung up the phone.

A chuckle escaped him before he could pull it back. He began to understand how his past actions had affected the people around him. He looked forward to the day when his father could answer his phone calls without saying, What's wrong? or Is everything okay? The same with his friends. He knew he would need to work hard to dispel expectations he had created all those years.

THE PLAN

At noon, the public park parking lot packed a plethora of vintage eighties vehicles belonging to strung-out mothers who brought their kids to the playground. An old black Jeep Wrangler blended in perfectly with the pickup trucks pieced together from junkyard parts and with the ancient Toyota, Ford, and Pontiac sedans. Cassie had bought the used Jeep when she left college in her sophomore year and worked as a bouncer in a strip club.

"That's it, right there," Tasha said from the passenger seat. She pointed to the brand-new silver Chevrolet Camaro.

"Yeah," Cassie replied, "that wasn't too hard to figure out," glancing sideways at Tasha.

"Hey, I found him, didn't I?" Tasha asked.

"Yeah, I'm sorry. I'm just not used to doing this with anybody else. I usually go it alone, you know?"

"I get it," Tasha replied, "I'm the same. If the department didn't make me have a partner, I wouldn't. He's a dick. One of those goody-two-shoes guys, you know? Married, two kids, pretty wife, and everybody's happy."

Cassie scowled. "Nobody's that happy. There's got to be something else going on, right?"

"That's what I think, too. He's got to have a girl on the side or maybe a gambling addiction or something," Tasha said. "But he plays it straight, you know?"

"They all do until they get comfortable. Then, wham!"

"Maybe not all. Zayt isn't like that. He's the real thing. He's been through some shit, you know, in Afghanistan. But he went the other way. He protects people instead of shitting on them. That's why we need to fix this. I need to fix this," Tasha said angrily.

"Does Dixon always do his transactions in this park?" Cassie asked.

"No. He has a couple places. But this one is his favorite. A lot of junkies and homeless people hang out here. There he is," Tasha said as she sank down in her seat. "Coming from the tree line."

Cassie lifted her camera and snapped as many pictures as she could get before Dixon Hayes and an unknown male companion got into his Camaro and drove away. She put the Jeep in drive, then followed from a distance.

"Where would he go now after making the deal?" Cassie asked.

"Out drinking. He does the same thing every Tuesday, Wednesday, and Friday. He'll go to a bar and get drunk—play at being the big man—then go home and either beat the crap out of whatever woman is there waiting for him or he'll rape her. Maybe both. Then he'll sleep, go to work, and do it all over again."

"So the best time to get him is when he's drunk and leaves the bar, but before he gets home?" Cassie asked.

"Yeah. If you want to get him to talk, that's the best time. He lets his guard down a little when he's drinking. I can get him to talk. He'll want me to know it's him that's screwing with Zayt," Tasha said.

"Okay, but we need to plan this right. He's got to be alone, and we'll need to be able to debilitate him once we get what we need," Cassie explained.

"I've got a taser and my personal 9mm. I'm going to have to get close to him anyway. And, if those don't work, your .45 caliber is my backup."

"That all sounds great, but where and how will all this play out? We don't even know where his drug deal will take place."

"That doesn't matter. There's only one street leading to his house, and it's secluded. I can slam my shitbox of a car into that nice new shiny Camaro," Tasha grinned.

"Wait, slam into? What the fuck are you talking about?"

"How did you plan on stopping him? Stick your thumb out?" asked Tasha.

"I thought we'd take him by surprise—fake an accident or something," Cassie said.

"How? No, I'm going to ram him. I'll get out of the car all pissed off about what he's doing to Zayt. He'll think it's funny and want to brag about it. I'll record it, tase him, and that will be it."

"What about traffic?" Cassie asked.

"There are only two houses on the street, and the neighbors are old and rarely leave their home. I'll wait parked on his street. You can tail him and call me when he leaves whatever bar he ends up at. Then you follow him home but hang back when he turns onto his road. I'll ram him. When you hear it, and you will, you block him in with your car, then sneak up behind him. You'll be my safety net."

"I want to see this road. I want to know exactly where you plan to stop him. We're not leaving anything to chance, alright?"

"Okay, we'll go there tonight after he goes to work. His shift starts at eleven o'clock," said Tasha.

Dixon backed his Camaro out of the parking space and headed for the exit.

"Aren't you going to follow him?" Tasha asked.

"No. Why take the chance if we already have a plan. Did you recognize the guy with him?" Cassie asked.

"No, but I didn't get a good look at him."

Cassie brought up the clearest picture from her camera and showed Tasha.

Tasha cringed. "Yeah, I've seen him before, but I don't know his name." She looked away from the camera.

"Is he a cop, too?" Cassie asked.

"No. He's a car thief. Dix uses him for deals sometimes, so he doesn't have to show his face. He's got a couple guys for that. I wonder if he was using Crayton?"

Cassie's phone buzzed.

"Shit. That's Whitman again. If I don't answer him soon, he's going to get antsy. I'm going to take this, but you need to be quiet," Cassie said.

Tasha nodded.

"What the hell is so important that you can't leave me alone for a minute," Cassie answered the phone.

"Easy, Papadakis. You're the one who doesn't want me doing anything without you knowing. I'm just trying to comply, that's all," Bradley explained.

"What is it? What's your big move?"

"I gave Zayt and Shea a copy of Dixon's picture to show around the REACH community. That guy stands out. If he's the one who planted the evidence, chances are someone would have seen him. Otherwise, we have another unsub."

"Unsub?"

"Unknown subject. Don't you watch TV, Papadakis?"

"That's it? That's why you've been bothering me all morning?"

Cassie could hear Bradley sigh. She found he did that when he tired of the banter and decided to let her have the last word.

"No. We may have a problem with Tasha," he said.

Cassie glanced at Tasha and widened her eyes.

"What kind of problem?"

"I wanted to ask her about Dixon's partners or possible accomplices, so I asked Zayt to call her. He told me she was working a double shift today. So I called her at work to leave a message, and they said she's not working and won't be back until Thursday."

Cassie paused, looked at Tasha, then said, "So, you think we have a problem because a woman lied to her boyfriend about having to work? Are you that naïve, prep boy? Shit like that happens all the time. Show me a relationship without lies, and I'll show you a poorly written 1950s sitcom. What else have you got?"

"Seriously? That doesn't bother you?" Bradley asked.

Cassie thought about Bradley's reaction and figured the best way to keep him at bay was to appease him.

"Alright, if you're that worried, I'll give her a call. Just know that you're probably going to be disappointed to find out she just needed a break from Mr. Greenjeans."

Bradley began to reply to her remark, but Cassie noticed he pulled his comment back and simply said, "Call me back," before hanging up.

"He knows you lied about working today," Cassie said to Tasha.

"Did he tell Zayt?" Tasha asked worriedly.

"It doesn't sound like it. Not yet anyway. We need a story, a good one. Have you got a sick mother or something?"

"No family. Zayt knows that. What about a doctor's appointment? I could say I went to see a therapist and I was embarrassed about it," Tasha said.

Cassie's eyes brightened. "No, but I've got it. A foolproof excuse. One that even Bradley Whitman could not second guess."

"Well?" Tasha asked.

"We're going to tell Bradley that you are at the doctors' because you might be pregnant. And that he can't tell Zayt because you don't want to worry him right now. Not with everything going on."

Tasha's eyes furrowed, bringing her forehead with them. "Do you think he would keep his mouth shut? Not tell Zayt? He can't tell Zayt."

"What difference does it make?" Cassie asked.

"No, we can't use that. Come up with something else. Just say I'm sick and I didn't want to worry Zayt," Tasha said.

"Alright. I'll call him later. I have to make it seem like it took a while before I talked to you. But I still think the pregnant story would work better. I'll drop you at your car. Send me the address to meet you tonight. We'll make our final plan there," Cassie said.

Odd, Bradley thought. Cassie is not a trusting person. According to Bradley's profile of Cassie, finding Tasha in a lie should have set off all kinds of alarms in her brain. Maybe I was wrong about her, he thought.

An hour later. Cassie texted Bradley a picture of Dixon Hayes and another man. She wrote, Can you find out who this car thief is?

His first thought was to send the picture to Nick to have him run it through the FBI database, but he then realized that would be inappropriate.

"Doyle!" Bradley stated aloud, causing Rusty to lift his head from his resting position.

Bradley dialed the Revere police precinct and asked for Sergeant Doyle.

"Yah!" Doyle barked.

"Now there is that soothing voice the public likes to hear when they call their local police department," Bradley quipped.

"Who the hell is this?" Doyle asked.

"Come on, Donovan. Life can't be all that bad," Bradley said.

"Whitman. What do you want?"

"I need to see you. Can I come over?" Bradley asked.

"I'm swamped. Is it important?"

"It could help you make detective. How's that for important?"

Doyle paused. "I can give you fifteen minutes."

"I'll be right there," Bradley answered.

Doyle looked more harried than usual, Bradley thought, when he got to the precinct.

"Are you getting anywhere on the Crayton case?" Bradley asked.

"I hope that's not why you came here, Whitman. You're wasting my time and yours. You know I can't talk to you about that."

"I'm here to talk to you about it, Donovan. And it's a game changer. You may want to sit down for this. I know that you know Zayt is being framed. You just don't know by whom. Well, I do."

Donovan Doyle sat.

"Go on," Doyle said.

Bradley told Doyle about Tasha and Dixon Hayes, about his encounter with Hayes, and Hayes's connection to Ronald Crayton. He also told him about a witness who saw the Boston police cruiser on Howland Avenue just before Crayton was killed.

"This guy is bad news, Doyle. He's running drugs, been suspended a bunch of times, and has had countless complaints brought against him. And he likes to hurt women. A lot," Bradley stressed.

"And you have proof of all this?" Doyle asked.

"Circumstantial. I can't prove anything yet, but I'm working on it. I need your help with something," Bradley said as he showed Doyle the picture. "This is Officer Dixon Hayes," Bradley pointed to Hayes in the photo. "I need to know who the other guy is. I'm told he's a car thief."

Doyle took Bradley's cellphone and used his thumb and forefinger on the screen to increase the size of the photo. "That's Ricky Lansford. Car thief, drugs, stolen property, and a ladies' man. He also takes bets on the horses. We've picked him up twice for solicitation. I'm told he likes to get rough, too."

"That makes sense. Hayes likes to share. Maybe he shares with Lansford. Listen, Doyle, is there a way you can get the city's camera footage from that morning? A Boston police cruiser wouldn't go unnoticed, and it's impossible to get to Howland Avenue without using Park Street which has a camera at every streetlight. If we can put Hayes in the area along with the eyewitness, we might have enough to go to internal affairs."

"I'll put in the request. It might take a day or two."

Bradley hesitated to bring up his next question, but he had to. "What can you tell me about the Revere police officer who searched Zayt's cabin, the one who found the evidence?"

Doyle's face grew stern. "Are you accusing one of my guys of planting evidence?" Doyle stood and pounded his hands on his desk.

"I'm just asking the question, Doyle. If you remember, it wasn't long ago we had our own dirty FBI agent right under our nose. I want to be thorough, that's all," Bradley exclaimed.

"Officer Folk has been with us for three years. Chris is a dedicated and exemplary officer. He's a family man, a couple kids, nice wife. He works two jobs. Does that sound like a dirty cop to you?"

"What's his other job?" Bradley asked.

"He works full-time with the Boston Police Department." Doyle held up his hand before Bradley could say anything. "I know what you're thinking. Alright, I'll look into him. But I'm not going to like doing it."

"And Donovan," Bradley said, "slow down some. You're a basket case, for crying out loud."

Doyle's eyes popped. "That reminds me, I have to order a fruit basket." He reached for his desktop phone.

"Stage three of the apology bomb?" Bradley grinned. "Honestly, I don't know what Maria Reyes sees in you."

Doyle scowled and said, "Maybe she really likes fruit!"

Bradley laughed all the way to his truck where Rusty waited for him. When he got home, a black Jeep sat in his driveway.

"That Jeep suits you," Bradley said to Cassie as she got out.

Bradley opened the door and waved his arm to suggest Cassie enter before him.

"Such a gentleman," Cassie said. "Let me ask you something. Are you for real or is this some kind of game you play?"

"What are you talking about?" Bradley's face crinkled.

"This nice guy act, Mr. Perfect—whatever you want to call it." Cassie spat.

"First of all, I am a nice guy. And second, I'm far from perfect and never portended to be."

"You mean pretended."

"That too, yes."

"Well, stop it. It's unnerving."

"What's unnerving?"

"You! It's not natural."

"What's not natural?"

"Being pleasant all the time."

"Pleasant? We've done nothing but bicker most of the time."

"What bickering?"

"This bickering."

"Then stop it."

"Stop what?"

"Whatever it is you're doing, just stop it!"

Bradley sat with his mouth hanging open as if his jaw were on strike and refused to close.

"What did you find out?" Cassie asked.

He covered his face with both hands, then slowly slid them down, rubbing midafternoon stubble on his cheeks, then down his neck. He finally placed his hands in his lap.

"To which subject are you referring?" Bradley asked.

"Christ, Whitman, pick a subject."

After a heavy sigh, Bradley replied, "I haven't heard anything from Zayt yet. That means he hasn't found anyone who saw Dixon that morning."

"Okay. What about the guy in the picture?"

"His name is Ricky Lansford. He's not only a car thief but a bookie, a drug dealer, a fence, and he likes to beat up women," Bradley stated with a stoic expression.

"How the hell did you come up with all that this quick?" Cassie asked.

"It's what I do," Bradley said, not wanting to let on that Sergeant Doyle was helping with their investigation. "What did you find out?"

"About what?"

"About Tasha! For chrissake, she lied," Bradley said frustratingly.

"Oh, Tasha. Yeah, she's pregnant. Well, she might be. She had a doctors' appointment today. She didn't want to tell Zayt because she didn't want to give him something else to worry about."

Bradley's jaw malfunctioned again.

"Are you alright?" Cassie asked. "You look pale. It's not your kid, is it?"

"What? No! Are you out of your mind? I would never . . . Zayt's my friend. Why would you think . . . " Bradley stopped and shook his head.

"I'm going to find your flaw, Whitman. That would have been a good one," Cassie said.

"Zayt should know about this," Bradley said.

"No, you can't. I promised Tasha I wouldn't. She may not even be pregnant. Why worry the guy if she isn't, right?"

"But she must be scared to death, going through this alone," Bradley said.

Not anticipating Bradley's concern and wanting to make sure Bradley wouldn't talk, Cassie made up another lie.

"She's not alone, she's staying with a friend."

That seemed to appease him, Cassie thought.

"Wow! Zayt might be a father," Bradley smiled.

"Easy there, fairy godfather. It could be indigestion. I've got to go." And without another word, she was out the door.

Completely drained from their conversation, Bradley sat back in his chair and meditated.

EXPECTING THE IMPOSSIBLE

Bradley was a half hour early, arriving at Emelio's at five-thirty. The hostess showed him to a table and removed a chair to accommodate his. When the waiter approached, he wasted no time ordering a beer. He no sooner got his beer when he saw his parents enter the restaurant. He waved to get their attention.

"You're early," Bradley said as they drew near.

"You're earlier," Doug said.

Lynn leaned down to kiss Bradley on the cheek.

"This is a pleasant surprise, Bradley. Your father assured me everything was alright, but please, tell me it is," Lynn said.

Bradley's smile had just a hint of sadness behind it. "Everything is great, Mom. I hate that you worry when I call you. I'm sorry I've done that to you."

Lynn let out a light gasp, put her hand to her chest, and said, "No, honey. I'm sorry if I come across that way. I didn't realize. It's nothing you've done. It's something a mother never stops doing, worrying."

"So, what did you want to talk about, son?" Doug asked.

"Why don't you order a couple of drinks first," Bradley said as he saw the waiter walking over.

Doug eyed Bradley. "That bad, huh?"

"No, that good!" Bradley replied.

"Well, then," Doug smiled. "A Chardonnay for my wife, and I'll have a bourbon, neat."

Bradley loved that his father ordered for his mother. Of course, if she hadn't wanted the Chardonnay she would have spoken up and chastised him for not asking her what she wanted. But that scenario rarely played out.

"How does it feel to be back at work, Bradley?" Doug asked.

"I haven't gone back yet. There was a bit of a hang-up."

Lynn questioned, "What kind of hang-up?"

"A job offer, Mom."

Confused, Lynn said, "But you have a job."

Bradley chuckled and said, "I've been offered a different job with the FBI. A really good job with the National Security Branch. That's what I wanted to talk to you about."

"The NSB?" Doug asked. "Wouldn't that be working with terrorists and national security threats?"

"Against terrorists, yes. They also protect the country from weapons of mass destruction, foreign intelligence operations, and espionage. It's the job I dreamed of as a kid. It's my Super Bowl, Dad. And they want me."

"Will Derek be working there, too?" Lynn asked.

"No, Mom. Derek would be staying in his current job."

"That's too bad, because it would be nice to have him and Cate back home," Lynn said.

Doug gazed at Bradley, then at Lynn.

"Lynn," Doug said, "I don't think this job is based in Chelsea."

Lynn turned to Bradley. "Oh?"

"That's right. The job is in Washington, DC."

The waiter returned with the drinks and asked if they were ready to order dinner.

"Give us a few minutes, will you?" Bradley asked.

"But you just got home, Bradley," Lynn said.

"I know, Mom. I don't have to leave right away. I told them I have to take care of some things first," Bradley said.

"So," Doug said, "you've accepted the job."

207

"Yes, Dad. I did. It all happened so fast, but I think it's the right decision."

"How can you know that?" Lynn asked. "How do you know you won't hate it?"

Without going into detail, Bradley explained what brought him back from India, how he worked with the team, how much he enjoyed it, and the great satisfaction he got from it.

The third time the waiter came back, they felt compelled to order dinner. None of them had looked at the menu. Each ordered something familiar. Dinner would merely be a distraction from the discussion.

"It's only eight hours away. I can come back on weekends, and you can come visit." Bradley tried to make it sound exciting. "I'm going to get a big enough place so you can come and stay with me whenever you want. Maybe I can find a house with one of those in-law apartments, huh?"

"Excuse me," Lynn said as she got up from the table and headed to the restroom.

Bradley lowered his head.

"Hey, she'll be alright," Doug said. "When she has time to think about it, she'll be happy for you. Right now, all she is hearing is that you're leaving again."

"And you?" Bradley asked.

Doug chuckled, "Pretty much the same. But, Bradley, I am so proud of you." Doug put his hand on Bradley's arm.

"Thanks, Dad."

The meals arrived before Lynn returned. Bradley and Doug waited until Lynn sat before they began to eat.

"You know, Lynn," Doug said, "if you hadn't brought the boy up to believe he could be anything he wanted to be, we wouldn't be in this mess."

Bradley nearly spit his food onto the table.

"Douglas, that's not funny. Bradley, wipe your mouth, then tell me about the in-law apartment."

Cassie met Tasha at a convenience store not far from Dixon Hayes's home. Tasha got into the Jeep and directed Cassie to Dixon's street. Cassie moved the vehicle slowly as she tried to take in the landscape.

"This is creepy," Cassie said, "even for me."

"Yeah, well, it isn't a night on the town for me either," Tasha said. "Here. Do you see this first bend in the road? Not long after the corner is a small pull-off." The Jeep inched forward. "There, see?"

Cassie noted an area that looked like cars made a U-turn to correct the mistake of pulling in to that road to begin with.

"I'll wait there in my own car," Tasha said. "When I see him come around the corner, I'll floor the gas pedal and ram into him. I won't be going fast enough to hurt him, but his car will be messed up. You can wait around the bend."

Cassie shook her head. "I don't know about this. So many things could go wrong."

"Like what?" Tasha asked.

"Like he could pull his gun and shoot you on sight," Cassie said.

"It'll be the middle of the day. He won't shoot me. Besides, you don't know Dix. He'll want to hurt me, yeah, but not quickly. He'll want to make me suffer. But he's not going to get the chance. Once he talks, I'll put him down."

"I don't know," Cassie reiterated.

"He'll head home around three o'clock so he can sleep off the booze before work. You can watch from the corner. If anything goes wrong, you step in. Please, Cassie, I owe this much to Zayt."

"Alright. Let's get out of here," Cassie said.

They rode in silence. When they got to Tasha's car, Cassie asked, "Are you positive you want to do this?"

"More than anything."

"Okay, I'll talk to you in the morning."

The phone woke him from a sound sleep. The clock read 12:02.

"Yeah," he answered.

"Bradley, it's Sam Houghton. Turn on your TV."

"Okay, give me a minute," Bradley said as he slid himself to the side of his bed and maneuvered into his wheelchair.

Still holding the phone, he turned on his television. A news station showed film of something engulfed in flames. Bradley couldn't tell where or what it was. But the text on the bottom of the screen read San Diego, California.

"Sam? What's on fire?" Bradley asked.

"The USS *Midway* aircraft carrier. It's now a museum and moored at Navy Pier," Sam said.

"Any warning?"

"No. But he's crowing about it now."

"Casualties?"

"Still counting. Thank God the museum was closed. Look, I know you're busy with another case, but if I send you some information, will you take a look at it?" Sam asked.

"Yes, send it," Bradley replied.

"I'll put Agent Noor on the first shuttle in the morning. Text me your address."

"No, I'll pick her up from Logan. Tell her it's the white Chevy Silverado."

"We need to find a connection between his targets. Somehow, we have to get in front of him," Sam said.

"Got it. I'll do what I can," Bradley said.

His alarm woke him next.

The first shuttle from Washington wouldn't arrive until 7:30, so he had plenty of time to get his workout in while Rusty joined Zayt in the sandpit for his morning run.

Bradley had planned to see Zayt early that morning to give him the picture of Ricky Lansford, but Sam's call changed that. Instead, when Rusty returned and after eating breakfast, the two got into the truck and drove to Logan Airport.

Naila carried only a backpack and briefcase. She headed straight for the truck.

"Good morning, Naila. How was your flight?" Bradley asked, then added, "Oh, and you remember Rusty?"

Rusty lifted his paw for Naila to shake.

"Nice to see you again, Rusty. My flight was short. That's the best thing I can say about any commercial flight."

"You've been spoiled by Cessy."

"I have," Naila agreed.

"What's the plan? How long are you here?" Bradley asked.

"At least overnight, but the rest depends on you. I made a reservation at the Revere Motor Lodge. Sam said you lived in Revere, so I picked something close," Naila said.

Bradley laughed. "No, you're not staying at the motor lodge. You're staying with me. If you set foot in the motor lodge, it would take years to wash away the stench. Their rooms are usually rented by the hour. The clerk must have got a good laugh when you made the reservation."

Naila smiled. "He did sound a little surprised. But I don't want to put you out. I can stay somewhere else."

"We'll get more done if you stay with me. I promise, I won't bite. The worst I'll do is make you eat my cooking. What can you tell me about last night?"

"We won't know for sure if it was Ali al-Haqani until we can examine the devices."

"Devices? Plural?"

"It's a big ship. Luckily the bombs didn't go off until evening when the museum was closed and most people were off the docks. The death count is up to twenty-three."

"How soon until the Terrorist Explosive Device Analytical Center will examine the devices?"

"We're hoping TEDAC will have them tomorrow or the day after. The ship is a big hunk of smoldering metal right now."

"But I assume we are confident this is al-Haqani's work?" Bradley asked.

Naila nodded as she said, "We must be. I'm here. I haven't seen what's in this file. I got it just before boarding the plane. Some of it may be background, but I'm assuming there's something new. Sam seemed rattled, and he doesn't rattle easily."

"I'm in the middle of something here. Not an FBI case but a personal one. A friend is in trouble, so I'm working with the lawyer's private investigator to clear him. I was clear with Sam that my friend's case is my priority right now. I just wanted you to know, because I might get called away."

"He told me. He also gave me leeway to help you in any way I can," Naila said.

"Leeway?" Bradley questioned.

"That translates to mostly outside of the bureau."

"Good to know. I've got to stop and see my friend Zayt on the way home, so you'll get to meet him. Then we'll go to my place and get to work."

Breakfast was winding down when they arrived at the REACH community. Bradley had explained to Naila a little about the place and Zayt's predicament.

"I'd be happy to help you put that guy away," Naila stated. "I had a cousin who was abused. She's out now, but that bastard is still walking the streets. She can't turn a corner without fear that he'll be there."

"There he is." Bradley pointed to Zayt, who had just walked out of the community dining room and headed toward his cabin. "Hey, Zayt," Bradley called.

Zayt stopped and turned. By the way Zayt carried himself, Bradley could tell something was wrong. When they caught up to him, Bradley asked, "What is it? What's wrong?"

Zayt eyed Naila, then answered, "I haven't been able to get Tasha on the phone. I've left her five messages and nothing. I'm about to break out of here and go find her."

"You can't do that, Zayt. You'll end up back in jail. Doyle wouldn't have a choice."

"Something's not right," Zayt said, then added, "Who's this?"

"Sorry. Zayt, this is Naila. She's a colleague from DC. She's here to help if we need her." Bradley thought that the easiest way to explain her presence. He didn't want to get into conversation about his pending new job. "Look, Tasha's probably just busy working. I'm sure she's alright."

"I didn't hear a word from her all day yesterday or this morning, Bradley. That's not like her. I think he got to her. And if he did, can you imagine what he's doing to her right now?" Zayt began to pace. His body became rigid as rebar. "I have to go find her." He headed toward his cabin.

Bradley moved his chair swiftly to keep up with Zayt. Naila followed. "She's fine, Zayt. Papadakis talked to her yesterday afternoon," Bradley said.

Zayt stopped. "What did she say? Where is she?"

Bradley didn't want to betray a confidence, but he also didn't want Zayt thrown back in jail for no reason. If Bradley couldn't calm him down, he would tell him about the doctor's appointment.

Turning to Naila, Bradley asked, "Would you excuse us for a minute? Rusty, stay with her."

Naila and Rusty waited outside Zayt's cabin while Bradley and Zayt went in. Zayt gathered his wallet and his jacket.

"Zayt, you can't leave. Tasha is perfectly fine."

"Bradley, she calls me every day like clockwork. She hasn't responded to any of my messages. That tells me she can't. And that tells me Hayes has gotten to her and is beating the crap out of her. There's nothing you can say to stop me. I'm going to find her."

Bradley found himself blurting, "She didn't work a double shift yesterday. She went to a doctor's appointment!"

Once again Zayt stood like a statue, "What? How do you know that?"

"Because I called the precinct, and they said she wasn't at work and wouldn't be back until Thursday. So, I asked Papadakis to call her."

"And she said she had a doctor's appointment?" Zayt asked, suspicion in his voice.

"Yes," Bradley said.

"What happened to her? Is she alright? Did he hurt her . . . I'll kill the motherfucker!" Zayt's eyes began to widen, and Bradley could feel the rage building.

Bradley had no choice. He would have to tell Zayt the truth.

"Zayt, calm down. She's not hurt. She's pregnant!"

Zayt paused to take in what Bradley had just said.

"What the fuck are you talking about?" Zayt spat.

"Papadakis told me Tasha thinks she might be pregnant. So, she went to the doctor. That's all. She's fine. She's staying with a friend. She didn't want to throw this at you right now."

Zayt stood quietly. His expression changed from hate to fear to anxiety. Bradley was uncertain how Zayt was taking the news. He didn't seem pleased.

When Zayt finally spoke, his monotonous voice alarmed Bradley.

"Dixon Hayes beat Tasha to within an inch of her life. She was in the hospital for three weeks. Because of that beating, the doctors told Tasha she would never be able to have any children. And Tasha doesn't have any friends to stay with."

It was Bradley's turn to freeze. He stared into Zayt's angry eyes as his own grew larger and larger until he whispered, "Papadakis."

Bradley reached for his phone and called Cassie. He got her voicemail and left a simple message, "Call me."

"You said Tasha didn't go to work yesterday?" Zayt asked.

"Right. So, I called Papadakis," Bradley paused, "and she lied to me. Why make up such an elaborate lie?"

"It doesn't make sense," Zayt said. "Why use a story she knew I wouldn't believe?"

"Tasha didn't. Cassie did. And she told me Tasha swore her to secrecy and that I couldn't tell you either. Cassie made it up. She doesn't know Tasha can't have kids. But why would she lie about that? And why would she cover for Tasha? It's not like they're best of friends."

Bradley tried to recall their telephone conversation. "I told her that Tasha lied about working a double shift and Cassie didn't sound concerned. I found that odd, but she made it sound like it was normal."

"When we first started dating, Tasha would ghost me when I started asking questions about Hayes. Whenever I brought him up, she would disappear for a couple . . . days. Fuck, Bradley! We have to find them. We have to find them now! They're going after Hayes!" Zayt hollered.

It took only a moment for Bradley to play it out in his head. Zayt was right. Everything pointed to Cassie and Tasha teaming together to go after Dixon Hayes. But when? And how?

"You can't, Zayt. Doyle will have you picked up inside a half hour. Just give me a minute. Let me think."

A dreadful feeling seethed in Bradley's gut, and it took him a moment to understand why. It felt like déjà vu. He and Zayt had once gone on their own to try to catch a murderer. Bradley had lied to Derek and his co-workers to keep them in the dark about their intentions. Cassie and Tasha were doing the same thing. But Bradley and Zayt had learned by experience that even the best plans rarely play out as expected. He knew he had to find them before it was too late.

He opened the door and asked Naila to join them in Zayt's cabin.

Bradley asked Naila, "This leeway Houghton gave you—does it include tracking a personal phone?"

"Probably not, but I have some outside sources that may be able to help. It might take some time, though," she replied.

"How much time?" Bradley asked.

"Maybe a few hours. He's not exactly a sanctioned user. And it will cost," Naila said.

With Zayt pacing, Bradley worked through his thoughts out loud.

"They won't go after him at his house. Cassie would want neutral ground."

"Tasha wouldn't go back into that house," Zayt added.

"Naila, get it started. I'm going to give you two cellphone numbers. I'll pay whatever he asks. I'll pay extra if he can have either one of their positions to me in the next two hours. Zayt, give Naila Tasha's phone number."

Bradley pulled paper and pen from his chair pocket and gave it to Zayt, who gave Naila Tasha's number. Then he wrote Cassie's number on another slip of paper and handed it to Naila. Naila went outside to call her source.

"I can't just stand here, Bradley. I've got to do something," Zayt said.

"And you will when the time is right. But right now we need to think like Tasha and Cassie. What's their plan? Did Tasha ever tell you about Dixon's habits or anything that might help?"

"Tasha won't do anything illegal—she won't try to kill him, I mean," Zayt said.

"Well, that's good to hear. I can't say for sure Papadakis wouldn't at least think about it." Bradley felt a knot in his stomach.

"Jesus, Bradley. This feels too much like the Joshua thing. And we both know how that turned out," Zayt said.

Zayt referred to the same previous incident Bradley had been thinking about—when he decided to use himself as bait for a murderer and asked for Zayt's help. Nothing went as planned, and both could have died. Bradley had lied to Derek to implement his plan much like Cassie had now done with Bradley. He didn't like being on the other side.

"I know. But we're going to find them and stop them," Bradley insisted. "Now, tell me everything Tasha ever told you about Dixon Hayes."

I CAN EXPLAIN

"How are you holding up, Tasha?" Cassie asked over her cellphone.

"I'm ready. This can't happen fast enough for me. Where is he now?" Tasha asked.

"He's still at the drug drop. He's got a different guy with him this time. I haven't been able to get a picture of him. He's average height and build, brown hair, and dresses like a . . . like Whitman. Any ideas?"

"Yeah, half the men in Boston!" Tasha replied.

"Yeah, well. I'll call you when we're on the move. Wait a minute. Here he comes. The other guy isn't with him. He's alone. Let me call you back," Cassie said as she started her Jeep.

She followed Dixon's Camaro out of the parking lot to Parker Hill Avenue. He headed west, away from the city, avoiding the busy streets and driving through neighborhoods. He knows the area well, Cassie thought. Even better than I do.

After twenty minutes, Dixon pulled into the parking lot of an Irish pub in West Roxbury. The brick structure sported a black awning reading Patsy's Pub. Two levels of pale yellow clapboarded apartments sat atop the pub.

Cassie parked across the street and watched as Dixon walked inside. She lifted her phone.

"We're at a place called Patsy's in West Roxbury," she told Tasha.

"He likes their whiskey selection," Tasha said with a sense of dread.

"Is that good or bad?" Cassie asked.

"Good, because he will definitely be drunk but also bad, because he's nasty when drinking whiskey."

"Well, we won't give him a chance to get nasty, will we."

"Down and dirty. I'm leaving now. I want to be in place in case he cuts his drinking short," Tasha said.

"I'll call you when he's leaving."

Cassie checked her firearm three times as she sat across the street from the pub. She visualized the plan. She would follow Hayes from a distance but not too far behind. When he turned down onto his street, Cassie would follow but stop short of the curve in the road. She should be able to hear the crash of Tasha's car into Dixon's. She'd get out of her car and walk along the edge of the road using trees as cover. Dixon wouldn't be looking for a second person as he'd be preoccupied with Tasha. If Tasha pegged him right, he would spill his guts. Then, if Tasha had any problem with her taser, Cassie would make her presence known.

Simple, yet effective, Cassie thought.

As her job required numerous hours of surveillance, Cassie was used to sitting for long periods. Nevertheless, she found herself becoming anxious. The capture was important to her for many reasons. First, she would prove a man innocent of murder. Second, she would free Tasha of the emotional chains that still bound her. Third, she would finally get some justice—not justice for herself like she always hoped she would get, but justice for Tasha.

Dixon nearly stumbled when he stepped out of the darkened pub and into the bright sunshine. Cassie hoped it was a sign of inebriation and weakness. "We're on the move," Cassie said into her cellphone.

The clock in her car showed the time as 3:46.

"I'm in position," Tasha replied.

"You take care of this asshole, Tasha. I've got your back."
Cassie hung up the phone.

Dixon took a different route heading back to his hometown of Roxbury. Still only on back streets, the ride seemed short to Cassie. She worried Tasha might not have had enough time to ready herself.

He slowed his car as he approached his street, then turned. Cassie followed at a safe distance and parked her Jeep in the middle of the dirt road just before the curve. As she stepped out of her Jeep, she heard the crash. A smile formed on her lips. Walking along the edge of the road and ducking inside the tree line as she rounded the corner, she made her way toward the bend.

Although she couldn't hear what they said, Cassie could see Tasha standing next to her crunched car while Dixon, presumably screaming obscenities, stood at the front of his mangled front end.

As Cassie walked closer, she could decipher the conversation.

"You always were a little fucking crazy, you bitch! This one is going to cost you some skin!" Dixon yelled.

"You fucking framed him, didn't you?" Tasha fished.

Dixon let out a howl. "Is that what this is about? Your boyfriend? GI Joe? Mr. I'm-better-than-you-are? He deserved it! He's a fucking sissy hanging around with all those losers."

"So, you admit it! You framed Zayt. You killed Ronald Crayton," Tasha said.

Dixon's expression changed. Tasha cursed herself for going too far too fast. That wasn't her plan.

"Come on, Tasha, baby. What is it? Are you wired? You got a recorder or something? Come on, baby. Let's go to the house and talk this out. I've missed you," Dixon said as he moved closer to Tasha.

"You just stay where you are, Dix. I know you framed Zayt. You just hate the idea that you can't control me anymore. And do you want to know something, Dix? Zayt is better than you at everything," Tasha showed a wry smile. "And I mean everything!"

Dixon's anger deepened the color of his dark skin. He arched his back and held his head high, attaining every inch from his body's frame.

He yelled, "Take her!"

Tasha looked around her but saw no one. As Dixon lunged at her, she reached for the taser secured behind her back. With her hand firmly on the grip, she held it in front of her and pulled the trigger.

Seeming to anticipate a weapon, Dixon turned sideways as he continued to lunge. He grabbed Tasha's arm. The spent electrical charges lay harmless in the dirt. In one fluid move, Dixon took Tasha's waist and ripped the shirt from her body.

"No wires. Where is it?" Dixon growled.

Tasha struggled to get free but knew she would not win the battle. She frantically looked for Cassie.

Then she saw her. Blood dripped down Cassie's face from a gash in her head. A man of average build with brown hair and wearing an oxford shirt held a gun as he led her towards them.

When Dixon saw the look of defeat on Tasha's face, he grinned.

"Did you really think you could outsmart me? That was easier than framing your boyfriend. If you want to hang with losers, you become a loser."

He backhanded Tasha across the face. She stumbled but did not fall. Dixon stuck his hand into Tasha's bra and removed a small recording device. With a harsh laugh, he dropped the recorder on the ground and stomped on it. Then he punched Tasha in the stomach.

Cassie struggled to free herself and yelled, "No!" as Tasha doubled over.

"Hey, asshole! You want to hit someone? How about me?" Bradley yelled as he appeared in his wheelchair from the wooded tree line.

Startled, Dixon and his accomplice's attention were diverted long enough for Naila to appear and place the barrel of her gun against the accomplice's head. "Drop it," she said.

The accomplice complied.

Dixon let go of Tasha and reached for his gun. Before he could level the firearm at Bradley's head, Bradley yelled, "Get him."

From behind the car, Rusty attacked. First, he sunk his teeth into Dixon's gun-wielding arm, prompting Dixon to drop the pistol. Next, while struggling to loosen the grip of the dog, Dixon tripped and fell backwards, allowing Rusty to release the hold he had on the arm and latch on to Dixon's groin.

A horrendous scream nearly drowned police sirens from the three Boston cruisers that came around the corner. The police vehicles followed an old, beat-up Toyota. As the cars got close, the Toyota stopped, and Zayt jumped out of the driver's seat. He knelt on the ground and put his hands behind his head. But he never took his eyes off Tasha.

A police officer handcuffed Zayt and put him in the backseat of his police car. The other officers concentrated their weapons on the array of people in front of them.

"Rusty, enough!" Bradley yelled.

Rusty let go his grip on Dixon and returned to sit by Bradley's side.

"I want to see hands, everybody's hands in the air," said the shortest and oldest of the six officers.

Bradley was first to raise them. Already having holstered her weapon, Naila held up hers followed by Tasha, Cassie, and the accomplice. Dixon's hands were attached to his groin.

"Can somebody get her a coat, please?" Bradley yelled toward the officers as he motioned his raised hand toward Tasha.

"Get her a blanket," the officer told his partner.

Another police vehicle approached, but it didn't belong to the Boston Police Department.

Bradley watched as Sergeant Donovan Doyle emerged from the Revere police cruiser and approached the Boston officer in charge.

"Finn, how the hell are you? I haven't seen you in ages. How's the family?" Doyle asked.

"Good to see you, Donovan. Family's good. We got your guy in the cruiser over there, but we seemed to have stumbled into a bit of a mess," Finn said.

"It usually is when these characters are involved," said Doyle. He turned to Bradley and asked, "Whitman, what's going on?"

"Can we put our hands down now? I don't want to get shot before I have a chance to explain," Bradley said.

"Oh, by all means. I wouldn't miss this for the world. I see a half-naked woman, a man bleeding from his private parts, a head gash over there," Doyle swung his arm in Cassie's direction then turned toward Naila, "and an unknown female with a holstered weapon who, judging by the way she's dressed and her demeanor, has FBI written all over her. Let's have it."

"First, some of these people need medical attention," Bradley said.

"Shit, Whitman, do you think all cops are slow? They called it in three minutes ago. Ambulances are on the way."

Bradley throttled his wheelchair over to Finn and Doyle. Rusty followed. Cassie took a jacket from one of the officers and went to Tasha to help her cover herself. Naila kept an eye on Dixon and the accomplice.

"Okay, it's really quite simple," Bradley said, and Doyle huffed.

"The guy with the torn-up groin is the one who framed Zayt." Bradley continued. "He's a Boston police officer."

"Jesus, is that Hayes?" Finn asked.

"Yes, Dixon Hayes. He was Tasha's ex-boyfriend. Tasha is now Zayt's girlfriend."

"Are you saying a Boston cop framed a guy for murder because he stole his girlfriend?" Doyle scowled.

"No. Just let me finish."

Bradley went on to explain the abusive nature of Tasha and Dixon's relationship and his side business of drug dealing, among other illegal activities.

"So, who's this guy?" Finn asked.

Doyle shook his head in disgust. "He's one of yours and mine. His name is Officer Chris Folk. If I'm reading this right, he is the person responsible for planting the evidence against Zayt.

Bradley nodded. "That's right. Anyway, Tasha and Papadakis over there decided to get Dixon to confess so they could record him and use the recording to exonerate Zayt. Luckily, we figured out what they were planning and followed them, because things didn't go so well."

"Imagine that," Doyle said sarcastically.

Bradley ignored his comment and continued, "We used Zayt to get you guys here when we needed you."

"You could've called, Whitman," Doyle said.

"It would have taken too long to explain, Doyle. You're not always the easiest sell, you know."

"Did you get his confession?" Doyle asked Tasha.

Cassie interrupted to answer. "Yes, but the bastard found the recorder and smashed it." She pointed to the crushed pieces in the street.

"Well," Tasha said, "he found the one I wanted him to find," then reached into her waistband and retrieved a second recording device.

"Son of a bitch!" Cassie smiled.

"Okay, now we know all the players except one. Who's she?" Doyle asked, pointing to Naila.

Naila eyed Doyle. A thin smile graced her lips.

"Sergeant Donovan Doyle," Bradley responded, "meet Agent Naila Noor from the National Security Branch of the FBI, Washington, DC. And . . . Sergeant Finn, is it?"

"Sergeant Finn Murphy," he corrected.

Two ambulances arrived. EMTs lifted Dixon Hayes onto a gurney and took him away, but not before one of Finn's men handcuffed him to the gurney and escorted him into the ambulance.

The EMTs tried to get Cassie into the second ambulance, but she wouldn't go. Seeing the commotion she created, Bradley excused himself from Donovan and Finn.

"Papadakis, what's the problem?" Bradley asked.

"I don't need an ambulance. I'm fine."

"You've got blood gushing out of your head. I'd hardly say you were fine."

"I'm not going to the hospital in an ambulance. Besides, they should take Tasha. She took a couple tough shots," Cassie said.

Bradley spoke with the EMTs, and they loaded Tasha into the ambulance.

"Let's go," Bradley said to Cassie.

"Where?"

"My truck is just down the road. I'm taking you to the hospital."

"But what about all this?" Cassie waved her arm around the scene.

"Doyle, we'll be in the emergency room at Mass General. Could you find it in your heart to let Zayt see Tasha? Hasn't he gone through enough? Naila, can you help Papadakis to my truck, please? Rusty, let's go."

"I don't need any help?" Cassie replied.

"I think we've established that you do," Bradley said with a stern voice.

Naila tried to grasp Cassie's arm, but Cassie resisted until she wobbled and nearly fell.

"Alright, maybe a little help," Cassie whispered.

Once they were on their way to the hospital, Cassie asked, "How did you know?"

His voice indicating his displeasure, Bradley replied, "Zayt knew Tasha wasn't pregnant."

"You told him? I told you that in confidence," Cassie spat.

"Oh, no you don't. You're not going to throw this back at me. You lied to me. An out-and-out lie that almost got you and Tasha killed."

"He wasn't going to kill us," Cassie said.

"Of course he was, Cassie. You didn't leave him a choice," Bradley yelled.

Cassie paused, then said, "You're really pissed off, aren't you?"

"Damn right I am!"

"You've never called me Cassie before."

"What?" Bradley hollered.

"I said, you've never called me . . ."

"I heard what you said," Bradley huffed.

An uncomfortable silence followed. Then Cassie leaned from the back seat of the truck and glared at Naila, who sat in the passenger seat. "Who the hell are you?"

"I'm the one who saved your ass today," Naila said.

Bradley could feel Cassie's blood boiling and, wishing to prevent Cassie from jumping over the seat, held up his hand to signal Cassie not to move. Then he said, "This is Agent Naila Noor. She's from the Washington office."

After another short pause, Cassie asked, "How did you find us?"

"We pinged your phones," Bradley said.

"That's illegal," Cassie said.

"Go ahead, file a report," Bradley shot back. "We picked you up at the park, followed you to Patsy's and then to the scene of your brilliantly conceived plan," Bradley explained.

"It was a good plan. But somehow, Dixon was ready for us," Cassie said.

"That's because Officer Folk followed you from the park, too," Bradley said. "You really need to watch your rear, Papadakis. A caravan of vehicles followed you the whole time, and you didn't notice."

"That's not possible," Cassie said. "I would have seen someone following me on those side streets."

"Apparently not," Bradley replied. Naila cast him a questioning glance.

MOVING ON

The emergency room was ready for them when they arrived and took Cassie into an examination room right away.

While they sat in the waiting area, Naila asked Bradley, "Why did you tell her we followed her? Why not tell her the truth, that we staked out Dixon's house?"

"Because she needs her confidence shaken. A hefty dose of humility might make her think twice before doing something this stupid again," Bradley said, then added. "It worked for me!"

When she furrowed her brows, Bradley knew Naila wanted to ask what he meant. Instead of explaining, he said, "Long story."

The emergency waiting room doors opened, and Sergeant Doyle walked in, followed by Zayt. Bradley noticed that Zayt's ankle monitor had been removed. Zayt went directly to the receptionist, who brought him to see Tasha.

Doyle joined Bradley and Naila in the waiting room.

"So," Doyle said, "do you want to start at the beginning? Or are we going to have to do this the official way?"

Bradley detailed events leading up to Cassie and Tasha's ill-advised attempt at getting a confession from Dixon, including the circumstantial evidence they had acquired. Instead of mentioning the illegal telephone tracking, he emphasized the information that Tasha had told Zayt about Dixon's habit of afternoon drinking followed by a brutal beating.

"We were lucky enough to find them in time," Bradley said.

Doyle shook his head. "You know, Whitman, at first glance your escapades seem like chaos. But when all is said and done, they make sense. Messy, but they make sense. At least I always know what to expect. Sergeant Murphy is going to need you both to make a statement. I told him you would stop by his precinct when you were done here: District B-2 in Roxbury. Don't make a liar out of me."

Doyle stood to leave.

"What about Zayt?" Bradley asked.

"Those damn ankle monitors malfunction all the time," Doyle replied.

"Thanks, Donovan."

Doyle turned and walked out the door.

Tasha had two broken ribs, and Cassie's contusion caused a concussion. They heard no news on Dixon's condition.

To the others in the emergency room waiting area, Bradley said, "We'd better get over to the precinct and give our statements."

"The officer already took Tasha's statement," Zayt said. "I'm going to grab a cab and take her back to my place."

"Alright, I guess it's just the four of us?" Bradley said.

"Four?" Naila questioned.

"You, Papadakis, me, and Rusty," Bradley smiled. "They might want to study Rusty's takedown tactics."

"I just hope Rusty detached some of Dixon's parts," Cassie said.

Bradley winced and shook his head.

An hour and a half after arriving at the B-2 district on Washington Street, Bradley pulled his truck into traffic and headed toward Revere.

"Hey, I need to get my Jeep at impound," Cassie said.

"Not today, Papadakis. You've got a concussion. You're not driving anywhere," Bradley said.

"Fine," she grumbled. "Just drop me off at home."

"No," Bradley said.

"No? What do you mean, no?" Cassie asked.

"I mean you're not going home alone, either. You're staying at my place tonight where we can keep an eye on you," Bradley said.

"The hell I am! Whitman! Take me home. There's no way I'm spending the night alone with you."

"Oh, we won't be alone. Naila's staying with us, too," Bradley said.

"What the hell. Is this some sick fantasy of yours? Have you been dreaming about a threesome?" Cassie spat. As soon as she said it, she regretted it on account of not knowing if Bradley was able to have sex in the conventional way.

"You can try and piss me off all you want. It won't work. Give it up. The doctor said you need to be watched. I'm going to watch you," said Bradley.

"I've been to your place. All you have is a bed and a couch. How do you see this thing playing out?" Cassie asked.

"We'll work it out," he said. "Besides, I may be working most of the night."

"I can still get a hotel," Naila said.

"We'll get more work done if you stay. There's plenty of room for one night. Can we all just relax now?" Bradley pleaded.

Ten minutes passed before Cassie asked, "Are you going to cook?"

"Yes, I'm going to cook," Bradley answered.

"Alright, I'll stay," Cassie said.

But I'm going to see to it that you keep your food down, Bradley thought.

Bradley prepared homemade manicotti and meatballs topped with his own tomato sauce pulled from his freezer.

Alongside a chopped salad tossed with fresh vinaigrette dressing, it made a pleasing and filling meal.

During dinner, he adeptly interrupted Cassie by asking her questions to slow down her eating. Cassie didn't seem to notice what he was doing. Bradley wasn't sure if Naila's presence kept Cassie from a second helping or the concussion did, but he was glad of it. He wouldn't feel as bad doing what he knew he had to do next.

Immediately after she finished her plate of food, Cassie excused herself from the table.

Bradley did the same and followed her across the room. When she neared his bed, which sat just outside the bathroom, he stopped her.

"Cassie."

Not realizing he had been following her, she turned and said, "I can go to the bathroom by myself, you know."

"Please, sit down for a minute," he said softly, so only Cassie could hear. He pointed to the bed.

"But I . . ."

"Please," he said again.

"Okay," Cassie said warily as she sat on the bed.

"I want to ask you a favor. A big one," Bradley said.

"Alright. But can I go to the bathroom first?" Cassie snapped.

Bradley took her hands. "No," Bradley whispered. "As a favor to me, I'm asking you not to go into the bathroom." He stared straight into her large copper eyes.

When she saw his plea, she knew her secret was no longer. Fear filled her eyes, and she pulled her hands away from him. But she could not pull her eyes away.

Still quietly, Bradley said, "Please! Just one time. Just once." Then, raising his voice and without breaking eye contact with

Cassie, he said, "Naila, could you take Rusty out to the back yard, please? His leash is on the counter."

"Sure," Naila replied.

When the door closed behind Naila, Cassie said, "You don't know what you're asking, Whitman. I can't do that."

"I think you can," he replied.

"It's none of your business. Who do you think you are, anyway?"

"I'm your friend, and I'm asking you to do this for me. Right here, right now." Bradley debated whether to add the next. He did. "You owe me, Papadakis."

"You're a bastard, Bradley! That's not fair."

Bradley answered. "You must really be mad. You used my first name." Then he smiled.

"Tomorrow. I'll do you the favor tomorrow. Today I've got a splitting headache, and I feel sick to my stomach. I promise I will do you the favor tomorrow," Cassie said.

"Sorry, no, Cassie. I'm collecting right now."

A tear fell from Cassie's eye, and it took her by surprise. "I can't."

"You can. You just need to realize you are as strong as the person you project to others." Bradley wiped the tear away. "Come on. Help me clean up."

"What happens when I really have to go to the bathroom?" Cassie asked.

"You're not a prisoner, Cassie. You are in control. That's the whole point," Bradley said. "Take back your control."

Leaving Cassie to think about her next move, Bradley wheeled to the kitchen table. To Bradley's delight, she joined him there.

Bradley opened the slider, told Naila she could let Rusty off the leash, and asked if she wanted some coffee. While the three cleared the table, Naila noticed an anxiousness in Cassie and wondered, only for a moment, if she had some sort of addiction. Then, Naila decided it to be none of her business.

Bradley cleared a workspace for Naila next to him at his desk. He booted his computer and turned on all three of his overhead monitors.

"I need to lie down," Cassie said. "This headache just won't quit."

"Concussions will do that. Take some pajamas out of the bottom dresser drawer. You can sleep in my bed. Don't worry. The sheets are clean," Bradley grinned.

Without strength to argue, Cassie donned a pair of Bradley's pajamas and chose the side of the queen bed where she assumed Bradley did not sleep. She slid under the covers. Bradley dimmed the lights everywhere in the house except the office area, and he left the backyard light on. Rusty arrived home an hour after Cassie fell asleep.

"We're getting a late start, but with Zayt's problem cleared up, I can devote all my time to this," Bradley said quietly. "Let's take a look at those files."

For hours, Naila and Bradley combed through confidential reports from Washington, New York, and Minnesota. They watched camera videos captured from each location's terrorist attack. Details of devices and detonators, exact locations of bombs, and casualties were difficult to read, and view, without prompting a sickening feeling.

Bradley felt how Cassie had looked when she went to bed. As he glanced at her, he was reminded that catastrophic circumstances are not limited to terrorist bombs, murderers, or enteroviruses. Sometimes they happen within.

The horrific photographs, once seen, could not be forgotten. Body parts in the streets of New York provoked a fury Bradley had rarely felt. But he knew he had to gather his composure and remove himself from the emotional aspect of the case. If he intended to stop the bloodshed, he had to become the bad guy— the terrorist. He had to think like Ali al-Haqani.

The file held a thumb drive with a new al-Haqani video. Inserting himself into the video as the main character, Bradley watched it multiple times.

After the typical opening accounting of his hatred for western countries, Ali al-Haqani ambiguously relayed his intentions on how to bring the infidels to their knees.

> I will attack where they most feel it: personally, financially, politically, and academically. Soon I will draw the United States into war, destroy the infidels, and establish a single Islamic state using all that was given me by my heart and brain. Praise Allah!

Bradley went back to the original profile that he had developed of al-Haqani. The profile suggested he's arrogant, egocentric, and will risk everything to succeed. His mission is personal, not theological. Yes, Bradley thought, he is using the Muslim religion to further his cause, but it is not his driving force. His driving force is personal glory.

"I will do this. I will do that," Bradley said, quietly.

"What?" Naila asked.

"Sorry, I was just thinking out loud. This guy is the worst kind of terrorist to be up against."

"Why?"

"Because he doesn't answer to anyone. He is self-motivated, self-financed, and self-absorbed. He's another Osama Bin

Laden," Bradley continued to whisper in case Cassie were still awake. "And we didn't stop Bin Laden until thirteen years after the 1998 US embassy bombings in Tanzania and Kenya."

"We can't give this guy that much time," Naila replied.

"We won't. There's one big difference between Osama and Ali."

"What's that?"

"Ali tips his hand because he is so personally invested and arrogant."

"What is it, Bradley. What do you know?"

"I didn't see it until a couple minutes ago. He's told us how he intends to hit us: personally, financially, politically, and academically. But the files tell us where he'll strike. While in school, here in the states, we know Ali al-Haqani also traveled to DC, Texas, Florida, New York, California, Minnesota, and Louisiana. Texas is where the ordinances arrived, DC was a diversion, and attacks were made in New York, Minnesota, and California. That leaves Florida and Louisiana."

"So, one of those states is next?"

"It's possible. He was also in Massachusetts. But there's got to be more to it. How did he pick the bombing sights? I can understand Times Square. New York is the financial capital of the United States, a high-profile target and always with heavy traffic."

Bradley paused. The video played again in his head: personally, financially, politically, and academically.

"If New York was the financial hit, then the Minnesota bomb could be considered a personal target. In one of his earlier videos, al-Haqani complained about how vain and wasteful the American people are. What better place to attack than America's largest shopping mall?

"And, if both of those assumptions hold true, then the bombing of the retired USS *Midway* might be considered a political objective. It certainly carries weight with the military and gives the government a black eye. Which leaves us with academics.

"Florida, Louisiana, and Massachusetts have large, well-known academic institutions. One of them could be the next target."

"A college?"

"Or any school. Children are our greatest and most vulnerable asset." Bradley paused, then continued. "Al-Haqani's school in Asadabad was destroyed. That would make the objective both highly personal and academic."

"But it's the middle of August. Most schools don't open until September."

"Which doesn't give us much time to figure out which school might be targeted. College students usually move into their dorms at the end of August before classes begin."

"Where do we start?" Naila asked.

"Find out exactly where Ali al-Haqani went during his visits to both states. Check credit card statements, hotel bills, and car rentals. We'll start in the cities with the largest schools and go from there. But not tonight. It's 2 a.m. We need to get some sleep. You can have the sofa bed."

"Where are you going to sleep?"

"I'm going to sleep in my bed with Cassie. The medication they gave her should have her sleeping soundly. I'll be awake before she is. It shouldn't be a problem."

Naila chuckled, then said, "You like to live on the edge, don't you, Bradley."

After shutting down the computers, Naila changed and crawled under the blanket on the sleep sofa.

Bradley changed into gym shorts and t-shirt before quietly lifting himself onto the bed from his chair. He plugged the wheelchair charger into the nearby electrical outlet and turned out the lights.

What first he mistook for Rusty snoring Bradley soon realized was Cassie—not a harsh, loud, or grating sound, but a soft, methodical, soothing whisper of a snore.

Bradley smiled. It had been a long time since he shared a bed with a woman. He closed his eyes and dreamed of Laney.

ANOTHER CHANCE

"Jesus Christ," came the scream that woke Bradley from his slumber.

Startled, Bradley turned his head to his left and saw Cassie clutching her body while glaring at him and backing herself onto the edge of the bed. Rusty jumped and raced to Cassie, placing himself in front of her to protect her from unknown danger, his eyes darting right to left. Naila threw her covers off and reached for the pistol that lay in its holster on the coffee table.

Bradley lifted his upper body from the bed and held himself upright.

"It's alright, Cassie. It's just me. I'm sorry. I didn't mean to scare you. Cassie, I'm sorry," Bradley said, feeling dreadful for upsetting her.

Jumping out of bed and placing her back against the wall, Cassie slid down to the floor. Rusty snuggled up beside her. Still clutching her chest, she said, "Okay. I'm okay. It's okay."

But distant and dark, her eyes told a different story. And Bradley suddenly felt like one of the bastards that caused the darkness.

"Jesus, Cassie, I'm so sorry," Bradley repeated. "I didn't think . . . I shouldn't have . . . I'm sorry."

Naila had put her weapon back in its holster and watched with concern.

"It's alright," Cassie said, her anxious breathing slowing to normal. "It's just waking up in a strange place. And then . . ."

"Yeah, I get it. I feel like an asshole."

"Let's just forget about it, okay?" Cassie said without lifting her gaze from the floor.

"No, I was thoughtless and stupid and . . ."

Cassie yelled, "Enough apologizing!" Then, in a softer tone, "Relax. Please, just stop."

"Okay," Bradley replied.

Cassie lifted herself up from the floor and went into the bathroom.

Bradley moved himself from the bed to his chair and unplugged the charger. "Shit!" he muttered as he rolled to the kitchen. The clock read 7 a.m. He couldn't remember the last time he slept that late. "It had to be today, didn't it?" he chastised.

"Is she going to be alright?" Naila asked.

"Yes, I just scared her. I should have thought it through better," Bradley said, forgetting Naila likely had no idea what he was talking about. But Naila had begun to realize that Tasha wasn't the only female in Bradley's circle who had previously been abused.

Bradley made a pot of coffee and, so upset with himself, threw together a vegetable and cheese quiche accompanied by roasted red potato home fries.

While preparing the food, he heard his shower running. He was happy Cassie felt comfortable enough to use it.

"I think I should go home this morning and get to work on the al-Haqani research," Naila said.

"Okay. I can drive you to the airport. Why don't you see what the earliest flight is?"

"11 a.m.," she replied. "I already booked it."

"Okay. I'll drive you to Logan after breakfast. Then I'll give Sam a call. I still have a few things to iron out here, but I can probably be in Washington tomorrow," Bradley said.

Cassie ate in silence and did not vigorously devour her food as Bradley had previously witnessed. Bradley took it as a deliberate attempt to control her impulse and surmised it took immense concentration to restrain herself.

Once showered, dressed, and fed, Bradley, Cassie, and Naila discussed the travel arrangements.

"Why don't you stay here with Rusty, Cassie, while I drop Naila at Logan. Then I'll come back here, and you and I will get your Jeep out of impound. How does that sound?" Bradley asked.

"That works for me," Naila answered.

"Why don't you drop me and Rusty off at Zayt's. I'd like to see how Tasha is doing?" Cassie said.

"Perfect," Bradley smiled.

It had been twenty minutes since Cassie took the last bite of her breakfast, and she hadn't gone back into the bathroom. Bradley took notice and felt hopeful.

When Bradley arrived back at REACH community to pick up Cassie, Zayt told him she and Rusty had gone back to his house. Zayt tried to hide a smile, and Bradley assumed Zayt got the wrong idea of why Cassie spent the night at his house. But then, as Bradley pulled into his driveway, he knew what the smile was all about.

His parents' blue van was parked in front of his house.

"Thursday!" Bradley spat. Had Bradley remembered it was Thursday, he would have realized that his parents would be cooking breakfast for the residents of REACH. And now they sat in his house with Cassie.

"This isn't going to be good," Bradley uttered as he lowered himself out of his truck.

Doug, Lynn, and Cassie stood just inside the doorway. Rusty lay on his bed.

"Bradley, sweetheart, come in and give me a hug," Lynn said.

"Hi Mom, Dad. What are you doing here?" Bradley asked.

"We finished work and found this delightful young woman and Rusty waiting for you to pick her up. We offered to give her a ride," Lynn replied.

Cassie's eyebrows raised, and she smirked.

"Where have you been, son? Was Logan busy?" Doug asked.

"Yeah, Dad. It usually is."

"Cassie was saying she needed to wait for you so you could bring her to pick up her Jeep," Lynn smiled.

Bradley could see Lynn's ecstatic expression, that of a mother who just found out her only son had gotten himself a girlfriend. He had seen it a few times before. Those times, it was warranted. This time, he considered, his mother would be disappointed.

"Cassie and I have been working together, Mom. On Zayt's case."

"Oh, but Zayt told us that was settled already," Lynn said.

"Yes, it is," Bradley started, "but . . ."

"Well, it's so nice you are keeping in touch," said Lynn, a warm smile gracing her hopeful face. "We don't want to keep you two from anything. Come on, Doug. Let's go."

"Mom, it's not . . ." Bradley began. But it was too late. Lynn pushed Doug out the door before they could even say goodbye.

Bradley shook his head and glanced at Cassie. "I'm sorry about that. My mother . . ."

". . . wants you to be happy." She paused. "I'm sorry about your fiancée. I didn't know," Cassie said.

Bradley closed his eyes and took a deep breath, "How could you?"

"And you're moving to DC?" Cassie asked.

"How long did you spend with my parents? Did they tell you about the pet rock I had as a kid, too?" Bradley asked, only half joking.

"They're fun people. Happy people. I don't know too many happy people. It's nice to see they still exist," Cassie said.

"Yeah, well. Shall we go pick up your Jeep?" Bradley asked.

"Why didn't you tell me you were moving to DC?"

"I didn't think you would care," Bradley said, surprised by the question.

Cassie turned and moved further into the room. "When I was in your shower this morning, I got so angry at myself for reacting the way I did when I woke up next to you."

"At yourself? You should have been angry with me," Bradley said. "I was the inconsiderate one."

"Whitman, you are a lot of things, but none of them are inconsiderate. Although you should let me finish without interrupting," Cassie said, then flashed the striking but seldom seen smile. "I got angry at myself because it was the only time in my life when I woke up in bed next to a decent man, a good man, a man who cares enough about me to ask me not to throw up in his bathroom."

Cassie's lips formed a slanted grin.

"And I blew it," she continued. "In the middle of washing my hair, I thought, 'That's it. That was my last chance.' And now you're moving to DC."

Bradley brought his chair closer to her. It was a side of Cassie he had not seen before. Of all the personalities she projected, this one felt genuine.

"I'm leaving tomorrow. I have work there," Bradley said.

"Tomorrow?" Cassie's face scrunched and she whispered, "So soon?"

Bradley watched as Cassie struggled with a thought. Her copper eyes widened and slid from side to side as she contemplated something only she was privy to. She then concentrated her gaze on Bradley and moved toward him. Standing in front of his chair, she pivoted the chair arms to point straight up, as she had seen Bradley do when he needed to get them out of his way.

Before Bradley could react, Cassie straddled him, took his head in her hands, sat on his lap, and kissed him hard.

Bradley's eyes shot open. It wasn't a long kiss nor particularly good kiss, as Bradley did not fully participate.

Cassie pulled her lips away, touched her forehead to Bradley's, and said, "I'm sorry. I just had to do that. I would have hated myself forever if I didn't."

She began to stand, and Bradley pulled her back down on his lap.

"You took me by surprise, Cassie. I . . ."

"Look, I don't know what your physical situation is, and I don't care. I just like being around you. You make me feel . . . good. And I haven't experienced that very much."

Bradley drew her to him and kissed her gently. Confusion stirred inside him, but he recognized her passion and could not dismiss it. He kissed her again and again, harder each time and with more emotion.

Cassie leaned into his kisses and delighted when she could feel him swelling beneath her. She had her answer, and she was grateful for it.

Bradley cut his last kiss short, looked at Cassie's straddled body on his lap, and said, "I haven't been with anyone since Laney died."

"And I've never been with anyone who hasn't given me a black and blue before the first kiss. No strings, no relationship. Let's just think of this as . . . therapy," she said as her smile lit his heart.

Bradley dropped the left chair arm just enough to rest on Cassie's thigh and used the throttle to take them to his bed. Cassie removed herself from his lap and lay on his bed. Bradley watched her body stiffen.

Using his considerable upper body strength, Bradley positioned his chair next to his bed and hoisted himself onto the mattress. He lifted each leg one at a time and straightened them below his waist.

He turned to Cassie, who lay on her back looking at the ceiling.

Bradley positioned himself to lie on his side, facing her. "Are you sure about this?" he asked. "We can just lie here if you want."

She turned to face him.

"I want this more than I've ever wanted anything," she murmured. "I'm just nervous."

"Me, too," Bradley realized. "You are a special woman, Cassie Papadakis."

Cassie chuckled, "A nutcase, you mean."

"No. I mean a beautiful, caring, and sometimes very scary woman," Bradley said, a smile punctuating the end of the compliment.

Cassie laughed, a sweet, happy melodic, laugh. It was the first time Bradley heard her laugh.

He leaned to her and gently kissed her lips, cheek, neck, and chest where her collar parted. He unfastened the buttons on her shirt, brushing her bare skin as each one opened. She wiggled out of the shirt, then tried to help him with his. Her fingers fumbled, the buttons feeling like a lock that needed to be picked.

"It's alright, I've got it. Just relax," Bradley said as he unbuttoned his shirt and removed it to bare his hairless, toned chest.

Her firm, rounded breasts filled a black lace bra. Bradley reached behind her and set them free. He tossed the lace aside.

Moving himself closer, he turned her on her back. Lying on top, he used his hands to position his legs to straddle her lower body. With his arms extended, he kept the bulk of his weight off her as he brushed his lips along her shoulder, nipples, and neck.

Her body tingled with each touch. She desperately wanted to stay in the present and enjoy every moment, but her mind convinced her it wasn't right.

I'm not worthy of all this attention, she thought.

Cassie pushed Bradley off her and rolled him on his back. His legs caught in an awkward tangle, and she reached down and straightened them.

"Cassie, wait," Bradley said before her mouth attacked his. In a frenzy, she moved down his body, her teeth nipping at his chest before reaching his groin. Her mouth engulfed him as she vigorously rolled her tongue and used the motion to elicit full erection.

"Cassie!" Bradley yelled, lifting her head.

Her eyes were those of a wild animal, a conqueror.

"Stop," he said.

"But I have . . ."

"No. You don't," Bradley whispered.

He gently rolled her off him and leaned beside her.

"This isn't going to be like the other times," he said, then ever so gently kissed her lips and cupped her breasts. "Lie back and relax."

Bradley straddled her once again, his mouth full of her freed right breast. His tongue twirled over her areola, and he could feel Cassie's back arch. He repeated the same on the left side with matching result.

Using his arms to guide him down Cassie's thin, sultry body, Bradley halted every few inches to tickle a rib, her stomach, and thigh with his tongue.

Finding her cleanly shaven, Bradley wondered if Cassie's abuser insisted on daily grooming.

The tip of his tongue titillated her clitoris, and she jumped.

"Are you alright?" Bradley asked, concerned she might be changing her mind.

"Yes," she simply said.

Bradley had no idea whether she enjoyed his playfulness. She didn't make a sound or move voluntarily. He could only hope she was pleased. Maybe, he thought, I need to ask her more often.

He had never been vocal in bed other than involuntary sounds when enjoying an orgasm.

His tongue graced her clitoris again and produced the faintest of yelps.

Bradley smiled.

Her body began to undulate as he moved back and forth, occasionally dipping into her moistening vagina. He went slowly, but her movements became chaotic. The faster she moved, the slower he proceeded until she relented and matched his unhurried tempo.

When he felt the moment right, he shifted himself up her body, and, holding himself above her, gently lowered himself into her slowly and just slightly at first. His arms directed his pace and depth. He penetrated a little more each time until she held his full self. He moved slowly and methodically.

Then, suddenly, he stopped and lifted himself off her. Capturing her glazed eyes with his, he rolled onto his back.

"Come here," he said, motioning for her to straddle him.

She did as he asked, sliding him inside her.

"You are in control, Cassie. Make it last," he whispered.

Cassie leaned her breasts into Bradley's chest and found his tongue with hers as their bodies moved as one. Cassie had never known such pleasure, and she hadn't yet reached her peak. Bradley cupped her rear and pulled her toward him to make each thrust more effective than the last. Her rhythm increased not in a brutal, frenzied fashion, but in the harmony of sexual passion and arousal.

Bradley could tell she was close, as was he. He held on as long as he could but nothing could contain the explosion that ensued. A high-pitched scream escaped Cassie as she sat atop Bradley with her back arched and herself fully latched to him. Her body shuddered, causing her breasts to bounce and her hair to fall onto her face. Bradley held her until she released and collapsed.

Her trembling body covered his.

He wrapped his arms around her and held her, then brushed hair from her face. Her copper eyes glistened above her rosy cheeks. She smiled down at him and he up at her.

Their heartbeats raced as they lay and gathered their breath.

With wonderment, Cassie said, "I never knew it could be like that."

"I hate to think what it's been like for you."

"I don't think my therapist is going to top this one," Cassie laughed as she rolled off Bradley.

"Well, I don't know how much of a compliment that is, but I'll take it," Bradley smiled.

"You have no idea, do you?"

"No idea of what?" Bradley asked.

"How amazing and unusual you are, Whitman."

"Unusual?"

"Unusually . . . nice," Cassie said.

"Ah, I think that's the sex talking," Bradley laughed.

"Oh, it definitely is!" Cassie snickered. "But, no, it's much more than that, Bradley. You are one in a million."

Bradley's jaw dropped. He tried to catch it before Cassie noticed but it was too late.

"What was that? What did I say?" Cassie asked.

Bradley decided to share the painful memory with Cassie.

"You never asked what put me in the wheelchair," Bradley said.

"I didn't figure it was my business."

"When I was six years old, I contracted an enterovirus that left my legs useless. The doctors told me it was one in a million odds. So, I guess you're right, Papadakis. I am one in a million."

Not used to complimenting people, Cassie couldn't help but finish the conversation with, "You may have lost your legs, Bradley, but you have a beautiful soul."

"That's it. All the blood that just rushed to your head has induced a relapse of the concussion. You don't know what you're saying," Bradley joked.

"That's not where my blood rushed to." Cassie smirked. "Hey, there's one more thing I'd like to do."

"What's that?"

"Let's go take a shower!"

Bradley and Rusty followed Cassie home after retrieving her Jeep from the impound yard.

"You didn't have to come all this way," she said while she stood at the driver's side window of Bradley's truck.

"You just had a concussion and probably too much strenuous activity for your condition," he smiled. "I wanted to make sure you made it home alright."

Cassie grinned. Then her expression saddened.

"When are you leaving for Washington?"

"In the morning, I think. I haven't talked to my new boss yet."

"I'm going to miss you, Whitman."

"Me, too, Papadakis."

Cassie leaned through the open window and kissed him.

"Take good care of him, Rusty," she said as she turned and walked the stairs to her Boston townhouse.

Cassie unlocked the door, turned, and waved. Her smile cast a net of warmth over Bradley.

He waved goodbye and drove away.

On the drive home, Bradley used his truck's hands-free device to dial Sam Houghton's office number.

"This is Bradley Whitman calling for Director Houghton," he said into the phone.

"One moment, please, Agent Whitman," the voice said.

In a moment, Sam answered. "Bradley, good to hear from you. I understand that your situation in Massachusetts is cleared up."

"Yes, it is. Agent Noor was of great assistance. Thank you for that."

"I'm happy she could help. What's your plan?" Sam asked.

Bradley liked the fact that Sam didn't waste time with banter.

"If all goes according to plan, I will leave tomorrow morning. I can be in DC by late afternoon. I assume Naila has filled you in."

"Yes. Come see me as soon as you get into town."

"I will do that. Thank you for this opportunity, Sam."

"Don't thank me. You earned it. See you tomorrow," Sam said, then hung up.

Bradley's next call was to Derek.

"Is everything alright?" Derek asked.

"I wish you would stop asking me that?" Bradley said.

"It's a hard habit to break," Derek chuckled. "What's up?"

"Zayt's in the clear. We got the guy yesterday. Sorry I didn't call sooner, but it's been a little hectic."

"That's great news. You mean you're coming to Washington?"

"Tomorrow. I know it's short notice, but can Rusty and I stay with you for a couple days? At least until I can get a hotel room?"

"Don't be stupid. Do you think Cate is going to let you go to a hotel? She's had your room ready since I told her you were taking the job."

"I really appreciate this, Derek. I'm going to look for a place when I get there. I promised my mother an in-law apartment," Bradley laughed.

"We have a great Realtor. We'll call her when you're ready. And I want to hear what happened with Zayt at dinner tomorrow night."

"I'll be getting in late afternoon and heading straight to Sam's office. I'll let you know when I arrive." After quick sign-off pleasantries, he and Derek hung up.

Bradley knew he needed to speak to Zayt. He hadn't talked to him about the new job, although he assumed his parents had spilled the news.

"Yeah?" Zayt answered.

"That never gets old, Zayt. Are you around?" Bradley asked.

"I'm in the office with Shea."

"I'll be there in five minutes. I need to talk to both of you."

"Yeah, I know," Zayt said, somberly.

"See you in five."

Bradley felt awful that Zayt didn't hear the news from him, but Bradley had never found the right time to tell him.

Zayt and Shea glared at him as he rolled through the door with Rusty.

"Come on! It all happened so fast! When should I have told you, Zayt? When they slapped the ankle monitor on you? And Shea? That would have been a fun conversation, right? 'Zayt's in jail, and oh, by the way, I'm moving.'"

"When are you leaving?" Zayt asked, stroking Rusty's head.

Bradley sighed, "The deal was I would leave once we got your murder charge dropped. Doyle took care of that yesterday. I leave in the morning."

"Tomorrow?" Shea screeched. "We didn't even have time for a welcome home party and now you're leaving again? So soon?"

"We could go to Zayt's cabin and have a beer," Bradley said, then asked Zayt, "How's Tasha doing?"

"The broken ribs are the worst of it. She can't move without it hurting. But I think she's going to be alright. I think she might be able to put all that behind her now."

"That's great," Bradley said.

"But I'm going to have a chat with Papadakis," Zayt said, angrily.

"Hey. They both made their choice. Just like you and I did back in the day. Besides, Cassie had her own reasons for doing what she did."

"Cassie, huh? Did you develop a soft spot for that . . ." Zayt caught himself, " . . . woman?"

"Let's just say I understand her much better. She's a good person, Zayt. And you kind of owe her."

"Owe her? She nearly got Tasha killed."

"Cassie tried to talk Tasha out of it. Don't you see? In this scenario, Cassie is you! How can you be angry with her?"

"He's right, you know," Shea said.

"Ah," Zayt swatted his hand toward Shea. "Who asked you?"

Bradley chuckled. "How about that beer now? I'd like to say goodbye to Tasha."

Soon after, while enjoying a beer, Bradley made arrangements for Zayt to take care of the house, telling him to use it whenever he wanted. Bradley even suggested that Zayt and Tasha move in there together. The idea did not seem unappealing to Zayt. Bradley promised to visit and extended an invitation to them to visit him in DC after he found a place of his own.

Tasha thanked him for his role in exonerating Zayt, Shea shed tears, and Zayt gave him a bear hug.

It was late afternoon by the time Bradley got home. He had one more phone call to make.

"Hey, Dad."

"Hi, Bradley. Is everything . . . I mean, how are you?"

Bradley smiled. "I'm great, Dad. But you and Mom left so quick this morning I didn't have a chance to tell you that I'm leaving in the morning."

"For Washington?"

"Yeah. There's a case I've been working. And now that everything is okay with Zayt, I need to get back to it."

"I understand, son. Let me get your mother."

Bradley could hear Doug telling Lynn that Bradley was on the phone.

"Bradley, how nice. Did you have a nice afternoon with Cassie?" Lynn asked.

"Yes, Mom, we had a very nice afternoon," Bradley answered. He could almost hear his mother smile.

Then he said, "Mom, I'm leaving for Washington in the morning. Rusty and I will be staying with Derek and Cate until I find a place. As soon as I do, I want you and Dad to come visit."

"Bradley, so soon." She paused. "Of course, we will. Honey, I'm very proud of you. I love you."

"I love you, too, Mom. I'll see you soon."

To the others—Holly, John, Mike, Olivia, Sheila, David, Nick, and Mara—Bradley sent a text message informing them of his new job and move. While packing that night, he received responses of a congratulatory nature from each of them. Mike made him vow to attend his wedding, whenever that might be.

Thinking he would return occasionally, Bradley decided to leave the house mostly intact. If not, Zayt could keep it all, he thought.

Lying in bed that night with Rusty, Bradley found himself feeling excited about his future both in his professional and private lives. He had thought he might have regrets about Cassie, but it proved the opposite. As he lay there, he could almost feel Laney smile down on him. She was happy to see him living again, and he was happy to oblige.

HIDDEN ANSWERS

Sunday, his first full day in the DC office, had him settling into a quiet, fifth-floor windowless corner cubicle large enough to accommodate Rusty. Only half of the twenty cubicles were occupied that day. Rusty lay quietly in his bed.

Other than a desk, landline telephone, desktop computer, filing cabinet, and chair, the one removed from behind his desk, the only other things in the office were a wastebasket, Rusty's bed, and water bowl. He already missed his computer system at home in Revere.

Ever since Naila returned to Washington, she headed a team to determine Ali al-Haqani's movements while in the United States in hopes of learning the intended target.

Trying to catch up, Bradley read the progress report on al-Haqani's activities. As he expected, the team had found evidence of al-Haqani at the Mall of America and in New York's Time Square. The closest they could place him to the USS *Midway* museum was an archived traffic camera video two blocks away showing the subject driving a rental car. His credit card statements revealed he visited Disney World in Orlando, Bourbon Street in Louisiana, and many Massachusetts venues while living in Hopkinton. If he went anywhere using cash, which was quite likely, there was no way of tracking those movements.

Bradley found himself rewatching the taped videos Ali al-Haqani had broadcast to date.

"I figured you would be here," Naila called from across the room.

Bradley looked up and smiled. "I'm getting settled in. What's your excuse?"

"I just wanted to get a little more research in. I'm getting ready to leave for the day."

Surprising him, Naila walked around the desk and gave Bradley a light hug. Rusty lifted his head to say hello.

"Ah, you're rewatching the videos. How many times have you seen them?" she asked.

"Too many."

They both watched the end of the first video as al-Haqani confidently and assertively spoke in Arabic while Bradley read aloud the translated text from the sheet in front of him.

"The western world has become a place of pretenders. A once mighty nation has loosened its grip on the globe, and it is time to destroy them. Praise Allah!" Bradley read.

"Is that what the translation says?" Naila asked.

"Yes, why?"

"Well, it's close. But the literal translation would be, 'A once mighty nation has dropped the ball, and it is time to destroy them.'"

Bradley scrunched his face and said, "Really? Why would he say that? Dropped the ball? Loosened its grip on the globe makes more sense in context," Bradley said.

"It's possible the translator thought that's what al-Haqani meant. Sometimes it's difficult to know exactly what the person is trying to say. Especially if they are not well versed in the English language," Naila said.

"You didn't translate this?" Bradley asked.

"No. I only translated the messages we intercepted about the White House attack."

"Dropped the ball. That's a western phrase. If that's what he said, he meant to say it." Bradley paused, then asked, "Naila? What are your plans for the rest of the day?"

Naila closed her eyes, sighed, and then opened her eyes and concentrated them on Bradley.

"I was going to go home, put some clothes in the washing machine, and put my feet up. But something tells me that's not going to happen."

"I will buy you dinner tonight if you check the translations of these videos for me," Bradley smiled.

"Alright, but I haven't eaten all day, and I'm starving. This is going to cost you," she grinned.

"I'm in."

"Actually, it won't take long. I've seen every one of these videos multiple times. I know where the possible mistranslations are. And I use the word mistranslations loosely."

"Naila, Ali al-Haqani doesn't say anything that he doesn't mean to say. He is fluent in the English language, and he writes his own speeches. You need to be as literal as possible with your translation."

As Bradley watched Naila tap the keys on his computer while listening to Ali speak, it became clear that al-Haqani had been playing with the FBI. It didn't surprise Bradley that he would, since Bradley had ascertained that al-Haqani thought of himself as a superior intellect.

"Are you seeing this?" Bradley asked Naila, as she typed the last words of the third video.

"Apparently not. What are you seeing?"

Bradley read the first re-translated video, "The western world has become a place of pretenders. A once mighty nation has dropped the ball, and it is time to destroy them."

Then he continued, "A place of pretenders. Broadway! Dropped the ball. Times Square!"

Bradley watched Naila's reaction.

"He told us his target? Why would he do that?"

"He didn't think we would figure it out, and he was right, we didn't. But now we know. And look. It's the last few lines in each speech where he reveals the target."

Bradley pointed to Naila's translation of the second video.

"I will crush their greed and vanity as a maul crushes the largest of stones. Their house of excess shall be obliterated. Praise Allah!"

"The word 'maul' was originally translated as hammer. It gave the message an entirely different meaning. The house of excess, greed, vanity, and maul point us to the target. In this case, maul would be replaced with mall, M-A-L-L. Mall of America, the largest shopping mall in the country, the house of excess," Bradley said, getting excited.

"Okay, I see it now. But that would have been a stretch to figure out before we knew the target," Naila said.

"Yes, but now we know what we're looking for. Next, we have 'They are weakened and soft and show off their once victorious ships as souvenirs of the past. But the great war is over. The greatest war is upon us, and we will prevail. Praise Allah!' You've replaced the word things with souvenirs. Do you see how it changes the meaning? It points to the USS *Midway* Museum."

"Alright," Naila said. "So the latest video, the fourth one, should tell us his next target."

"Yes. Unless I am clutching at straws, yes," Bradley replied. "Go right to the last few lines."

"I will attack where they most feel it: personally, financially, politically, and academically," Naila read. "Soon I will draw the United States into war, destroy the infidels, and establish a single Islamic state using all that was given me by my heart and mind. Praise Allah!"

"Wait! What?" Bradley asked.

Naila repeated the text.

"Are you sure he said heart and mind? The text says, heart and brain," Bradley said, a chill running up his spine as he waited for her answer.

"I'm positive. It says heart and mind. What does that mean?" she asked.

Bradley felt a sharp pain in his chest and, as he had seen Derek do many times before, tried to rub it away.

"It means I know his next target. You better call Sam."

"Are you sure?" Sam asked from the other end of the phone.

"As sure as we can be. We thought it would be a school or university in either Florida, Louisiana, or Massachusetts," Bradley said.

"Yes, but how do you know it's that one?" Sam asked.

"Because the motto of Hopkinton Engineering Institute is corde et animo, which translates from Latin to heart and mind. He used that phrase in his last message.

"He likes to keep things personal. I've spoken there many times, Sam. I know the layout of the place like nobody else. I think I could help if I were there."

"You're an analyst, Bradley. You did your job. And you're going to continue to do your job . . . from here."

Bradley lowered his head and rubbed the side of his neck, finally resting his palm under his chin and placing the full weight of his head in his hand.

"Alright, Sam. I understand," Bradley said. "Are you going to inform the Chelsea, Massachusetts, headquarters about the situation?"

"I've got to run it up the ladder. We'll talk in the morning," Sam said. "And Bradley, great work. I knew this was the place for you."

"Thank you, Sam. But I couldn't have done it without Agent Noor."

"It seems the two of you make a good team," Sam said before he hung up.

Bradley put the phone down.

"Thanks for putting in a good word for me," Naila said.

"Well, it's true. If you hadn't noticed the translation discrepancies, we wouldn't have gotten anywhere. Now we need to figure out how and exactly where he'll place the device or devices. He used two on the USS *Midway*, right?"

"Yes. But that was the only time he did," she replied.

"Naila? Would you mind if we ordered dinner in?" Bradley grimaced.

Naila shook her head. "Okay. But you still owe me a decent meal out."

They occupied the fifth-floor conference room off the main hallway. At the head of the table sat Sam and Derek's boss, Deputy Director Michael Mendez.

Sam sat on the director's right. Derek sat on his left. Members of the FBI task force team lined each side of the table. Bradley and Naila sat at the far end of the table. It was barely eight o'clock on Monday morning.

"Where's the dog?" Naila asked.

"Cate has him for the day," Bradley replied.

Naila pouted.

Sam laid out a simplified version of evidence pointing to HEI as the next target.

"And how can we be sure?" Mendez asked.

"We can't be. But it makes the most sense. Al-Haqani has been including intimations in his speeches. They hadn't become clear until now. But we've got the upper hand. He doesn't know that we know," Sam said.

"Do we know when?" Mendez asked.

"Our best guess is within the next two weeks, once school is in full session," Sam replied.

"HEI's a big place, isn't it? Has he intimated where on campus he may place a bomb?" Mendez asked sarcastically, unhappy that al-Haqani had been leaving clues all along and no one had previously picked up on them.

Sam glanced toward Bradley.

"Anything?" Sam asked.

"It's possible he could focus on the clock tower building. It's the center of HEI's campus and one of the original buildings. It would be a sentimental target. But I think Building 7 is the most obvious target. It's the chemical engineering department where he spent most of his time while in school," Bradley replied. "But sir?"

Mendez looked at the unknown man at the end of the table.

"Yes?" he asked.

"I don't think he will use a conventional bomb this time," Bradley blurted.

Because they hadn't talked to Sam about the prospect yet, Naila put her hand on Bradley's leg and squeezed to try to stop him from going further. But Bradley couldn't feel her attempt.

Everyone in the room sat straight in their chair and leaned in. Sam's eyes bulged as he looked toward Derek, who shrugged his shoulders.

"What makes you say that?" Mendez asked.

"It's the phrase he used in the last message. He said he would use all that was given him by his heart and mind. The term heart and mind refer to HEI. All that was given him by HEI was a degree in chemical engineering. I think it's possible he'll use a chemical weapon this time, sir."

"Um, Mike," Sam jumped in, "we have no indication that chemical weapons have been brought into the country."

"Well, it looks like you better find out, Sam," Mike Mendez said before he stood to leave.

Sam and Derek both stood and walked behind Deputy Director Mendez, who headed toward Bradley.

"I don't know you. What's your name?" Mendez asked Bradley.

"Agent Bradley Whitman, sir."

Bradley held out his hand and they shook.

Mendez smiled and turned to Derek.

"This is the kid from the cruise?" he chuckled.

Derek smiled in return. "One and the same," Derek replied.

"Good to have you on board, Agent Whitman," Mendez said, then left the room with Sam and Derek behind him.

Bradley was stunned that Derek had told the deputy director about him, especially about meeting him when he was twelve. His wonder soon turned to panic when Naila asked, "What were you thinking?"

"About what?"

"You don't say stuff like that without talking to Director Houghton first. You just threw him under the bus," Naila said.

"Shit. I didn't think about that. Derek was always fine with me voicing my hunches. Dammit!" Bradley spat.

Bradley's text alert sounded.

Then so did Naila's.

Come to my office.

It was from Sam.

"Sam, I'm sorry. I should have talked to you first. It's just that he asked . . . " Bradley started as soon as he got through the door.

But Sam interrupted him. "Bradley, relax. We have more important things to talk about than that."

Bradley sighed in relief. Derek was in Sam's office, and Bradley caught him smirking at Bradley's nervous entrance.

"Naila, have a seat," Sam said.

Sam sat behind his desk, Derek on the couch, Naila in a chair in front of the desk, and Bradley in his chair beside her.

"Explain again the chemical bomb theory," Sam said.

Bradley did.

Sam glanced at Derek, who nodded.

"But he may not need to bring any chemicals into the country to achieve this," Bradley added.

"Where would he get them?" Derek asked.

"Depending on what they are working on, he could get them from the biology department building right next to the chemical engineering building. They are attached by a walkway," Bradley said.

"Do they routinely keep dangerous materials there?" Sam asked.

"I'm not sure what they keep there. But even household chemicals can do damage if used with malicious intent. I would think Buildings 7 and 9 would be his prime targets."

"That makes perfect sense, Sam," Derek added.

"Alright, bring the Chelsea office into the loop. Bradley, go with Derek so you can answer any questions they may have. I'm setting up a meeting with the task force and response team for 1 p.m. in the command center. I'll see you two there. Naila, you're going back to Boston. Leave as soon as you can. You are our advance coordinator. Stay in touch with Bradley for updates."

"Yes, Sam. I'll leave right away," Naila said.

"Here," Bradley said as he pulled something from his pocket. "I'll call Zayt. Stay at my place."

He handed her his house key.

Derek and Bradley made their way to the elevator.

"Jesus, Bradley. You don't waste any time, do you? You've already got Sam playing catch-up," Derek grinned.

"I didn't mean to jump the gun, Derek. I just did what I always do. I answered the question as thoroughly as I could. You never seemed to mind."

"Yeah, I guess I got used to being a step behind you," Derek said.

"You were never behind, Derek. Maybe just a little left of center," Bradley chuckled. "And why would you tell the deputy director of the FBI about our cruise twenty-two years ago?"

"I didn't tell him," Derek smirked.

"Well, how did he know?"

"Mike Mendez used to work for a guy named James Harrison. Does that name ring a bell?" Derek asked.

"Yes, but why? Why do I know that name?"

"Probably because you've looked at it almost every day of your life. Director James Harrison of the FBI. He gave you . . ."

"My commendation! It's signed Director James Harrison," Bradley smiled.

"I didn't tell Mike about you. Jim did. When Jim took the deputy director job ten years later, he was still talking about the smartass kid who helped take down Benny White and Frankie Piscelli. He followed you all through MIT and your career in Chelsea."

"No kidding. Where is he now? Retired?" Bradley asked.

Derek's bright expression dulled.

"He died of a heart attack five years ago," Derek said.

Bradley fell silent.

The elevator doors opened on the sixth floor, and Bradley and Derek went directly to Derek's office.

"Bradley, it's nice to see you again," Derek's assistant Madelyn Cross said.

"Madelyn, could you get Nick Gaston on a secure line for me, please," Derek asked.

"Certainly."

Derek put the phone on speaker.

"Hey, Nick. I've got Bradley here with me," Derek said.

"Hey, Derek. Hey, traitor," Nick said.

Bradley shook his head and glanced at Derek.

"I wanted to tell you, Nick. I really did," Bradley said.

"Yeah. And thanks for the group text message saying goodbye."

"Things happened faster than I expected," Bradley said.

Derek jumped in, "Alright, we're not doing this right now! Nick, the NSB has information you need to know. Bradley is going to lay it out for you."

Sam had decided not to include the previous attacks in the briefing with the Chelsea office. He said they could revisit that if need be.

"We have credible information of a terrorist attack attempt at Hopkinton Engineering Institute in the next one to three weeks," Bradley began. "Our best guess is he will target Buildings 7 and 9 on the main campus. Those are the chemical engineering department and the biology department, respectively."

"What kind of information?" Nick asked.

"Classified," Bradley said. "I can't share it at this time."

"What the fuck am I . . . ?"

Derek interrupted him.

"Nick, we're sending you a team. The advance coordinator will be there tomorrow. Her name is Agent Naila Noor. We're going to give you as much help as we can. Agent Noor will be able to answer some of your questions, but this is a highly classified situation. You'll need to put every available agent on this while giving away as little information as possible," Derek said.

"I'll start clearing schedules," Nick replied. "Can you tell me what kind of attack we might be expecting?"

"For your ears only, Nick," Bradley said. "Best case we are looking at a large conventional bomb. Worst case we can expect some sort of chemical device."

"Jesus," Nick paused. "How reliable is this information?"

Derek and Bradley shared a look.

"Let's just say it's more than one of Bradley's hunches," Derek said.

"Shit," Nick replied.

"You can bring the campus police in, but you can't give them much information, Nick. You know the drill. An unknown threat from an unknown source," Derek said.

"Bradley, are you coming?" Nick asked.

Bradley closed his eyes and dropped his head. "No, Nick, I can't. I've got to work it from here." Bradley's voice echoed his disappointment.

"Do your magic, buddy. It's been a little windy here in Boston. We don't need chemicals flying around out there," Nick said with slight fear in his voice.

"I've got your back, Nick."

"I know."

Nick hung up. Bradley looked at Derek and said, "The baby."

Bradley knew Nick was thinking about the proximity of the institute to Chelsea FBI headquarters. And the wind always came from the west. Even if he kept Mara inside, there would be no guarantee she wouldn't be affected.

"Let's get to it," Derek said.

PREGNANT PAUSE

The command center was housed on one of the three underground levels of the J. Edgar Hoover building. Large monitors covered the east wall, and multiple computer stations sat below. Black leather chairs embossed with the FBI logo made up stadium seating facing the monitors. Between the two, a long table ran the width of the room lined with black leather swivel chairs, each chair sat facing the stadium seats.

Bradley followed Sam and Senior Agent Jonathan Williams into the room, and Sam motioned him to position himself behind the long table. The room was full, and Bradley noticed Derek sitting in the front row of stadium seats.

One of the monitors behind them displayed a map of the Hopkinton Engineering Institute campus. Another monitor zoomed in on the main campus that included Building 7, the chemical engineering building, and Building 9, the biology building.

Another monitor showed the clearest pictures the FBI had of each man who carried out bombings in New York, Minnesota, and California. The fourth screen displayed a still picture of Ali al-Haqani taken from one of the videos.

When Sam stood, chatter in the room stopped.

Without preamble, he began.

"We believe we have identified Ali al-Haqani's next target as the Hopkinton Engineering Institute in Massachusetts. That's where al-Haqani graduated nine years ago with a chemical engineering degree. Although he has used conventional explosives to date, we believe al-Haqani may incorporate a chemical weapon in this next attack. We are considering the entire nineteen-acre campus as the target. However, there are a couple of areas we will pay particular attention to. Agent Bradley Whitman will walk you through those areas."

"Good afternoon," Bradley began. "Before we talk about the specific buildings that we think will be targeted, it is important for you to know how to get around the institute. There are five sections that make up HEI. You've got the main campus," Bradley said as he turned his chair and pushed one of the keys on the computer station behind him.

On the monitor's map, the encompassing main campus instantly highlighted in red. He pushed another key for each section as he spoke, each highlighted in a different color.

"This is the east campus, west, north, and northwest. Almost all the buildings are referred to by number with a few exceptions. East campus building numbers start with the letter E, west campus with W, north with N, and northwest with NW. Main campus numbers do not use a letter.

"Room locations can be identified by their room number. For instance, let's look at room number 1-390. The number before the dash denotes the building number. The number immediately after the dash is the floor number, and the number following that is the room number within that building on that floor. So, Room 1-390 is in building number one on the main campus because there is no letter in front of it, third floor, Room Number 90.

"So, if you get a call on your radio to report to E23-245, you will go to the east campus, Building Number 23, second floor,

Room 45. I've got paper maps available, or you can find the map using your cellphones."

Bradley took a deep breath, then continued.

"As for the specific areas of concern, main campus Building Number 7 houses the chemical engineering department where al-Haqani spent most of his time. We can assume he is familiar with every inch of it. That building is connected by a walkway to Building Number 9 which is home to the biology department. We believe he is well acquainted with the layout of this building as well, which makes these two his best option for success. We also think he intends to use both to his greatest advantage."

Bradley backed away from the computer terminal and positioned himself back at the table.

Agent Jonathan Williams stood to address the group. Bradley had first met him when he arrived in Washington from India. Williams headed the al-Haqani task force and although they had been in the same room multiple times, Bradley didn't know much about the man.

"We will be working with the local FBI field office in Chelsea, Massachusetts, located several miles from HEI. Agent Noor has gone ahead to coordinate with Supervisory Special Agent Nick Gaston. These agents know the area and have contacts. We will pair each of you with someone from their team," Williams said.

"He's already hit us hard three times," he continued. "His foot soldiers used two bombs on the USS *Midway*, and they could be planning to do the same here. This is our best chance to date to stop al-Haqani. We need these terrorists alive if possible. They are our only link to finding him."

Williams sat and Sam stood.

"Call your families," Sam said. "Let them know you will be away for a while. You leave in the morning."

The room began to empty. Williams approached Bradley and asked him to stay behind.

"I understand you came from the Chelsea office," Jonathan said.

"That's right," Bradley replied.

"Who is their best field agent?" Jonathan asked.

Without thinking, Bradley answered, "Mara Thompkins—I'm sorry, it's Mara Gaston now. She's junior to a lot of others, but she is sharp, analytical, and tenacious. And she's excellent at reading a situation."

"Gaston?" Jonathan asked.

Bradley nodded. "Yes, Nick Gaston's wife. But there is something you should probably know."

"What's that?"

"She's seven months pregnant," Bradley responded.

"Is she still on field duty?"

"Yes, as far as I know," Bradley replied as he wondered if he should have given him Tony Morrison's name instead of Mara's.

"Then she's the one I want," Williams said.

Shit, Bradley thought as he rolled out of the room.

Derek stood waiting for him in the hallway.

"Hey," Derek said.

"Hey."

"How are you holding up?"

"I'm alright. Why do you ask?"

"I just want to make sure you're not planning to jump in that truck of yours and head to Massachusetts."

Bradley's first reaction was to be angry that Derek would think that. But he would have been lying if he said he hadn't thought about it.

Instead, he grinned and said, "I guess I'm finally growing up. Maybe I've found my balance."

Derek smiled and said, "That's good to hear."

"I think Nick is going to kill me though."

"Why?"

"Agent Williams asked me who the best field agent in Chelsea was. I would have said Nick if he were still a field agent and not the boss now."

"Who did you say?"

"Mara."

"I'd have to agree with you. What's the problem?"

"Her condition, Derek. She's about to have a baby, and I may have just put them both in a dangerous position."

"That's not your call. He asked you a question. You answered it. Besides, think how mad Mara would feel if she found out you intentionally left her out."

"True," Bradley said. "I think I'd rather face an angry Nick than an angry Mara." He grinned.

Derek put his hand on Bradley's shoulder. "And that, my friend, is how this job works. You assess honestly, voice your concerns, share your opinions, and leave the dirty work to others. It's never easy, but if we can make their dirty work less messy, we've done our jobs well."

Bradley's face softened, and the corners of his mouth lifted slightly. Derek had always been able to ground Bradley. He had had a lot of practice.

"I've really missed your pep talks, Derek."

"I've missed giving them," Derek smiled.

"Professor Forsythe," Bradley spoke into his phone, "this is Bradley Whitman."

"Ah, Maestro Whitman. How are you?"

"I am doing well, Professor, and you?"

"I am still trying to teach our future generation, Maestro, but I haven't had a student with your symphonic flair since you graced my classroom."

Professor Andrew Forsythe formerly headed the chemical engineering department at MIT. He left to become president of Hopkinton Engineering Institute after Bradley graduated. Bradley had spent many hours with the short, plump man with a round, cheerful face and perpetual cowlick that gave him a youthful quality. At the professor's invitation, Bradley spoke to several of the institute's graduating classes. The professor gave Bradley the nickname Maestro because he thought Bradley's research papers read like a symphony.

"Professor, this is an official FBI inquiry. I'd like to ask you about another student you had at HEI roughly nine years ago. I'm hoping you will remember something about him that can help me. His name is Ali al-Haqani. I know it was a long time ago, but I . . ."

The professor interrupted, and said, "Of course I remember him. It's funny that you, of all people, would ask about Ali."

"Why do you say that, Professor?"

"Maestro, I have often spoken of you as the student who could turn chaos into cohesion."

"Yes," Bradley acknowledged. "I recall you telling me that also."

"Well, where you excelled at turning chaos into cohesion, Ali excelled at turning cohesion into chaos. You and Ali would match wits perfectly. I would love to watch a debate between you," Forsythe said with a childish giggle. "He is the static to your concerto."

The professor's comment sent a chill down Bradley's spine.

"What, exactly, do you mean by that?" Bradley asked.

"Ali is highly intelligent and his curiosity insatiable. He tended to approach a situation from back to front, so to speak. Or maybe it's best described as end to beginning, focusing on everything that could go wrong instead of the things that could go right. He lived in the chaos. His work was impeccable."

"Did he have a particular field of interest?"

"Maestro? What is this about?" the professor asked.

"I'm just collecting background information, Professor. Nothing of concern," Bradley lied. He hated to keep the professor in the dark.

"Well, I would have to say his interests lie in biomaterial, specifically engineered tissue. Chemical engineering overlaps considerably with biomedical science."

"And what exactly is engineered tissue? Does it have to do with genetics?" Bradley asked.

"No, although some of the research could be used in both fields of study. Tissue engineering concentrates on the use of chemical stimulation in a biological organism to achieve a desired response. It is the science of restoring, maintaining, and improving organ function."

"And you say Ali would work from end to beginning. So, does that mean he would study what chemical stimulation might destroy or obstruct organ function?" Bradley asked.

The professor paused before answering.

"Well, yes. But only to ensure that precautions were taken to avoid those mishaps."

"Of course, Professor. I understand," Bradley said. "Tell me, did he write many papers on the subject?"

"As I recall, he wrote several."

"Did you happen to keep copies of any of them?"

"Yes. I tend to keep files for my top students. I sometimes share the work with other promising students. Your file is rather thick."

"Professor, would you mind sending me Ali's file?" Bradley asked.

Forsythe's tone had become increasingly suspicious. "You say this is official FBI business?"

"Yes."

"Of course, Maestro. I'll send you what I have."

"One more thing, Professor. Do you recall if Ali had a favorite place on campus? A place that interested him more than any other. I know, for me, it was the MIT library."

"Yes, I remember that about you. I recall Ali spending a lot of time in the biology building. But that made sense because of his interests," the professor said.

"Yes, I suppose it would. Thank you for your help, Professor. I appreciate you taking the time."

"Don't forget, Maestro. You promised to be one of my guest lecturers this year. These youngsters could use some serenading."

Bradley envisioned Professor Forsythe grinning with his words.

"I haven't forgotten. Goodbye, Professor."

Professor Forsythe substantiated everything Bradley feared. Building 9, the biology building, would certainly factor into Ali's planning, Bradley had no doubt.

He placed his next call to Professor Patricia Lyndstrom, the woman in charge of the biology laboratories.

Due to the professor attending an out-of-state conference, it took several hours before Bradley was able to speak with her by telephone. Once he had her on the line he wasted little time with pleasantries.

"Professor Lyndstrom, could you to send me the current inventory of chemicals you have stored in Building 9?" Bradley asked.

"Yes, Agent Whitman, I have been instructed to give you anything you need. May I ask why you need it?"

"I'm sorry, Professor, but I'm not at liberty to discuss that. I will also need the location in the building where each chemical is kept. I appreciate your thoroughness," Bradley replied.

"I will have my assistant email it to the address you provided. It shouldn't take too long to put together as I have my students perform inventory at the end of each week. We keep tight rein on our hazardous materials, Agent Whitman."

Bradley surmised the professor felt defensive and wondered if the investigation had anything to do with missing chemicals. He wished to ease her mind.

"I appreciate that, Professor. I assure you our investigation is more about prevention than any mishaps or wrongdoing. Thank you for your cooperation."

Several hours later, Bradley received Professor Forsythe's file of Ali's papers and Professor Lyndstrom's inventory and storage information for the biology laboratory.

Bradley began with one of Ali's studies on the effects on organ tissue of specified chemicals when inhaled, taken orally, or in direct contact with the chemicals for a duration of fifteen minutes or more. Although most of the information had already been catalogued, Ali experimented with unusual delivery systems and occurrences of how each could be accidentally dispersed.

Professor Forsythe had been correct, Bradley thought. Ali al-Haqani was imaginative, thorough, and detailed in his experiments. Not to attract attention, in each scenario Al-Haqani provided directives on how to avoid such occurrences.

Turning his attention to the list of chemicals, Bradley appreciated that Professor Lyndstrom included the safety data sheet for each. The long list included an array of acids, notably hydrochloric, hydrofluoric, nitric, and sulphuric. Others on the lengthy list included, sodium hydroxide, potassium hydroxide, iodine, methanol, Decon 90, acetonitrile, chloroform, and more than fifty others, including many cleaning supplies.

The biology department stored the highly flammable chemicals in a locked, fireproof room while the cleaning solutions sat in a locked closet. Professor Lyndstrom made a note that small amounts of cleaning solutions were kept handy in the labs.

Of the many chemicals listed, acetonitrile caught Bradley's eye. From his chemistry days at MIT, he recalled the chemical converts to cyanide once inhaled, ingested, or absorbed through the skin.

And then there was chloroform that converts to highly toxic phosgene, used in World War I as a chemical weapon.

And that's only two. Bradley shuddered as the potential hazards ran through his mind.

The thought of what could happen to those exposed to the full list of hazardous materials raised Bradley's anxiety level. And more so, the possibility of Mara getting exposed terrified him.

Bradley sank himself into al-Haqani's mindset. He thought, I imagine al-Haqani would ask himself, "How do I create the most destruction using what's available to me?"

A plan began to formulate. The more he thought about it, the more it made sense, but he needed to talk it through with someone. Usually that someone would be Derek, but present protocol told him he must talk to Sam.

"I think I have an idea how he plans to attack," Bradley told Sam.

"Let's hear it," Sam replied.

"Al-Haqani has established the use of diversion tactics. I think he will do the same here. He may use at least two bombs, two terrorists. Maybe even two of the same from the previous attacks.

"The first foot soldier will be responsible for planting a bomb that will call attention away from the prime target. I believe that will happen in Building 7, the chemical engineering department. I also think the device will be placed in the far end of the structure, away from the walkover that attaches to Building 9, the biology building."

"And your reasoning?" Sam asked.

"It's the chemicals. They are stored in a fortified, fireproof room. If he simply detonates an incendiary device, most effects of the chemicals will be absorbed by the room and the automatic extinguishing system. They need to get the chemicals out in the open for maximum damage. They may even plan to mix a few together to create a more toxic poison, something al-Haqani wrote about in one of his college papers. They will do this while the response team is handling the first explosion and the surrounding buildings are being evacuated."

The contortion on Sam's face suggested a problem. "So, in your scenario, if the diversion bomb does not detonate, the second will never happen, and the terrorists simply blend into the crowd and disappear or decide to detonate the bomb in the crowd."

Bradley eyes widened. "I have an idea about that, too," he said.

He explained his plan in great detail while Sam's facial muscles scrunched and winced with surprise and doubt.

"That's the craziest thing I've ever heard," Sam said once Bradley had finished.

"We've done it before successfully," Bradley stated.

Sam's eyebrows lifted.

Bradley continued, "Look, Sam, if all goes well, it won't get that far. If we can somehow anticipate their moves before they get into the buildings and before they have a chance to detonate the initial bomb, we might be able to avoid the rest. But if even one gets away from us, they won't let their bombs go to waste."

"Let's assume for a moment that you are right about how they plan to attack. Why not just lock down the buildings to prevent it?" Sam asked.

"Because they will find another target. And if we tip our hand that we were one step ahead of them, the next time al-Haqani won't provide a video to reveal his plan. Not to mention the panic that would undoubtedly ensue if we shut things down without explanation. Imagine the questions from college officials and the public.

"Sam, once we have his men," Bradley continued, "maybe we get Ali al-Haqani's location. Until we have him in custody, he's not going to stop."

"That much I know," said Sam. "Give me some time to think about this."

Sam walked through Derek's door.

"Uh, oh. I know that look. You've been talking to Bradley," Derek said.

"I don't know what to make of it, Derek. I need to run something by you," Sam said.

Sam detailed everything Bradley had told him, including his plan for the capture of al-Haqani's men.

Derek sat quiet after Sam finished and tried to decide how to quantify his reply.

"I've been in your position more times than I can count, Sam. The truth is, as crazy and far-fetched as some of Bradley's ideas can be, he is usually right. I would put his hunches up against any other so-called expert's. So if he says this is what's likely to happen, I'm inclined to think he's probably right," Derek said.

Sam shook his head as in reluctance even to think about the next suggestion.

"What about his idea to allow the scenario to play out?" Sam asked.

"He's right. It's worked before on a much larger scale. But it played out just like we hoped it would. And no one was the wiser."

"Damn, Derek. I'd hoped you would talk me out of it."

"I know exactly how you feel, Sam," Derek smirked.

BARNDOMINIUM

With each passing day, Bradley grew more restless. He stayed in contact with Naila and Nick, and Sam briefed him daily. The FBI task force, along with the agents from the Chelsea office had embedded themselves into the HEI landscape.

The first night they arrived, they dressed as campus police and swept Building 9 using bomb sniffing dogs to determine that no devices had been previously planted. Onlookers were told the institute was conducting a training operation. Bradley felt positive they had uncovered al-Haqani's plan before he began to implement it.

Posing as chemistry and biology professors, Agent Jonathan Williams had teamed with Mara. Naila looked like she belonged and fit right in with the students. She spent most of her time in the biology building. Tony Morrison had teamed with a Washington agent and impersonated maintenance workers. Other agents monitored entrances, parking lots, and courtyards watching for the familiar faces of al-Haqani's men as well as anyone who fit details of Bradley's profile. In case Bradley had been wrong about the true target, agents also scattered and covered as many campus areas as possible.

Each night, Cate noticed Bradley becoming more and more irritable. When she questioned Derek about him, Derek simply told her Bradley missed Massachusetts.

While they ate dinner Thursday night, Cate said, "Bradley, I think I may have found the perfect house for you."

"You've been looking at houses? For me?" Bradley asked, surprised.

"Yes. Rusty and I have seen a few houses and condominiums," Cate said. "But Rusty doesn't like the condominiums."

"Rusty likes a yard," Bradley replied.

"This place has a beautiful yard," she replied.

"Where is it?"

"East Riverdale, Maryland, which is twenty minutes from here and thirty minutes from the J. Edgar Hoover building. As soon as I saw it, I knew it would be perfect for you."

"Does it have an in-law apartment?" Bradley asked.

"No, but it's on five acres of land, and you could build one if you want. The house has three bedrooms, two and a half bathrooms, and a beautiful covered back porch. It's a metal building, just like you have in Massachusetts, only this one is prettier on the outside and the rooms have walls. It's got an open concept kitchen and living room area with a stone fireplace. The front porch would need a ramp, and the garage entrance into the house would need one also. The kitchen might need a little customizing, but I'm sure you could do that over time. It's simply perfect."

"Are you trying to get rid of us, Cate?" Bradley smiled.

"You know I would keep you here forever if I thought you would stay. No, Bradley, I just think once you see this place, you are going to fall in love with it," Cate said sadly. "And Lynn will love it, too."

"When can I see it?" Bradley asked.

"I have pictures. Do you want to see them?"

"Yes! Why didn't you say so sooner?"

"Because I'm going to be sad when you leave. Even if it is only twenty minutes away."

Bradley swiped through the pictures on Cate's cellphone. When he first saw the outside of the home, he didn't believe that it was constructed of metal.

"They call the style barndominium. Don't you just love that?" Cate smiled.

"This is perfect, Cate. How did you find it?"

"I have a great Realtor," Cate replied.

"When can I see it?"

"How about Saturday?" she asked.

Bradley glanced at Derek, who shrugged his shoulders.

"Okay, Saturday," Bradley answered.

Friday morning, the campus bustled with students who waited until the last opportunity to move into their dorms. Moving trucks, vans, pickups, and overstuffed cars lined the campus streets. Vendor vehicles backed into loading docks, and postal delivery vehicles darted through the complex.

Although some classes had already begun their fall semester, most would not commence until the following Monday. A full schedule of campus activities would take place over the weekend to welcome new and returning students to school.

Mara sat on a bench in the first-floor hallway of the chemical engineering building, a briefcase on the floor by her feet. The building was quiet with few students roaming the halls. Intermittent chatter drifted through the listening device hidden in her left ear, most of it having to do with items agents watched students carry into their dorms.

One male student proudly carried a blown-up doll that, Mara heard, looked suspiciously like Marilyn Monroe. Another student walked toward the art center dressed as a zombie and carrying what looked like a gravestone. Multiple beer kegs were reported, each time with an added comment about stopping by that dorm at the end of the day.

Mara's feet were swollen and her back sore. She felt as if the baby were doing the cha-cha on her bladder. She was about to return to the bathroom when the first report came in.

"I've got one," a voice came over the radio. "It's the guy from Times Square. He's walking. Just took a right onto Ames Street from Amherst. He's wearing a blue Red Sox baseball cap, light blue polo shirt, tan khakis, sneakers, and carrying a large navy backpack. It looks heavy."

Mara's heartbeat quickened.

The voice continued, "He's heading toward 7."

"USS *Midway* bomber just exited a van on Main Street at E38. He's walking west toward the main campus. He's also wearing a blue Red Sox hat, blue jeans, white t-shirt with a colorful graphic, sneakers, and a big black backpack. He's heading toward a large group of students. I'm on his tail."

"Times Square just took a seat on a bench outside 7, I repeat, Times Square is no longer on the move. I've got to hand him off."

There was a short pause.

Then, "I passed him. Who's got him?" the first voice asked.

"I've got Times Square," a different voice said.

Mara pictured the first agent strolling by the suspect without a glance.

"*Midway* stopped near a group of students. He's scanning the area. Someone pick him up, I'm moving on," the agent said.

"I've got Midway," a fourth voice came. To Mara, it sounded like Tony Morrison.

Bradley's text tone sounded.

command center now

The message came from Sam.

Bradley rolled through the door and saw Sam, Derek, Director Mendez, and several other people Bradley did not know sitting in the stadium seating chairs.

Several people worked on the computers at the front of the room, and the monitors showed views from strategically placed cameras at HEI. One of them concentrated on the room full of hazardous materials.

A loud voice came over the speakers.

"Midway stopped near a group of students. He's scanning the area. Someone pick him up, I'm moving past him," the voice said. Followed by "I've got Midway." Bradley recognized the speaker as Tony Morrison.

Here we go, Bradley thought. Much like the wringing of a wet towel, his stomach began to cramp. He started second guessing everything that had seemed so obvious to him to that point.

"We've got a third player," Morrison said. "Midway is leaving the group with an unknown suspect. Wearing a blue Red Sox cap, black t-shirt, jeans, sneakers, and brown backpack."

Derek glanced at Bradley. Bradley shrugged.

"Midway and friend just took a left onto Ames Street. They're heading toward 9. I'm holding back," Morrison said.

"Times Square hasn't moved. He keeps checking his watch." Another voice came over the speaker.

"Midway suspects are entering 9 from the north side," Tony said.

Hearing that, Mara got ready to act. She heard the footsteps but didn't look back. Using the arm of the seat to help her stand, she struggled to get herself off the bench. She rested her hand on her bulging belly, and her cheeks puffed as she let out a large breath. Releasing a wince she slowly bent down for her briefcase.

The suspects walked past her without offering to help.

She shuffled slowly, following them down the hallway, staying roughly twenty paces behind. They stopped at the elevator, and Mara ambled by them. She glanced back when she heard the elevator doors open and watched them step in. Once the doors closed, Mara moved quickly back to the elevator and watched the light on the wall above it to see which floor it stopped on.

"Third floor, Jonathan," Mara said. "Midway and friend at 9-3."

Bradley turned to Derek and Sam and said, "The hazardous materials are on the second floor, not third."

"Is there another way into that room?" Sam asked. "Maybe from above?"

"Not that we've been told. The only way into that room is through the door from the hallway on the second floor," Bradley said.

"They're just waiting to see if they are followed, then," Sam said.

"Maybe," Bradley said. He kept his eyes on the monitor with a view of the room housing the chemicals.

The radios went silent. After a full two minutes, Sam said, "Jonathan, what's happening?"

"We don't know, Sam. We are holding our positions on the second floor but there's no movement. I'm going to send someone upstairs," Jonathan answered.

Bradley had not realized Sam was in direct contact with the agents.

The next words he heard turned Bradley cold. "Agent Gaston, check the third floor."

Bradley glared at Derek who shook his head.

Bradley tried to remain silent but couldn't.

"Jesus, Sam. She's seven months pregnant. Have him send someone else."

Sam gazed at Bradley and said, "It's the job. She knows that."

"Times Square is on the move," the agent said. "We may have a problem. He is turning away from 7 and heading the opposite way."

Sam glanced at Derek, then Bradley.

"That's toward the clock tower building, if I'm not mistaken," Sam said.

Bradley nodded.

Another minute passed before they heard, "Times Square just entered Building 14."

"What does that mean?" Sam asked Bradley.

"It means he could be going to either building. But I think he will double back, pass through Building 5, then use the walkway to get into 7. The tower means nothing to him," Bradley said as he looked directly into Sam's eyes.

Sam turned to Derek, who didn't say a word. Bradley could see Sam contemplating his next move.

Finally, Sam said, "Hold your positions. He's going to double back."

Mara's voice came over the speaker.

"The third floor is clear. They're not up here," Mara said.

"Son of a bitch! What the hell is going on?" Sam yelled.

Bradley went over the building's blueprints in his head. There was nothing in them that indicated a way to get into the chemical room. It was purposely built that way.

Sam stood and began to pace.

"Times Square is doubling back," the voice came.

Sam stood still, lowered his head, and exhaled loudly.

"Take him as soon as he reaches into that backpack," Sam spit. then asked, "Is the critical incident response group in place?"

"Yes, sir, CIRG is standing by," Jonathan said.

"Start clearing the building."

"Yes, sir."

"Times Square is moving on 5-2. I can't follow. He's moving toward the 7 walkway. Someone pick him up at 7-2," the voice said.

"He's mine. I've got Times Square," Naila's familiar voice sounded.

"I'm checking 9-4. Nothing yet." Mara said.

Bradley rocked back and forth in his chair. He didn't know which was worse—listening to what transpired or not knowing. He only knew that if anything happened to Mara, he would never be able to forgive himself. His concern for Naila and the rest of the team escalated as well. He rocked.

Sam continued to pace. "What the hell is happening? It's too quiet."

"Advance to 7-232, 7-232 now!" Naila yelled into the radio.

Sam stopped pacing, Derek shot out of his chair, and Bradley stopped rocking. The radios went silent.

Bradley eyed his watch. A minute had passed. Then two. Five minutes passed, and Bradley's body filled with dread. Ten minutes went by.

"Goddamn it, what the hell is happening?" Sam screamed. Bradley didn't know whether Sam spoke into the radio or was just letting out his frustration on the room.

"Sam, we've got an explosion from next door. It sounds big. What can you tell me?" Jonathan asked over the radio.

"Nothing, Jonathan. I don't know what happened," Sam said, shaking his head. "Stay the course."

"What's happening with the feed from 7?" Sam asked the workers at the computers. When he received nothing but shrugs, Sam stormed to the front of the room.

Derek sat back in his chair with his elbows on his knees and his head in his hands.

Bradley watched the monitors. Something caught his attention.

"Sam, Derek, look at the door," Bradley said.

Derek and Sam turned to the monitor.

"Watch the chemical room door," Bradley repeated.

Slowly, the door to the fireproof room opened from the inside and the man they called Midway stuck his head into the hallway.

"How the hell? Jonathan, are you seeing this?" Sam asked.

"Got it, Sam," Jonathan replied. "CIRG, get ready to move."

From the speaker came Naila's voice. "We have Times Square in custody. Repeat, Times Square is in custody. Diversion complete."

With the door wide open, Midway and his accomplice began to move containers into the hallway. Sirens could be heard in the distance.

"Whenever you're ready, Jonathan," Sam said.

When both men returned to the storage room, Jonathan said, "Move in."

On the monitor, those in the command center observed as CIRG team members poured with guns drawn into the hallway from adjourning rooms and each end of the corridor.

When the suspects saw what was happening, they dropped what they held and ran back into the storage room. As Midway picked up his backpack, he suddenly went rigid. His muscles spasmed, his pack slipped out of his hand, and he fell to the floor. In the seconds it took suspect number two to realize Midway had just been tased, Mara already had her gun leveled at his head through the hole in the storage room ceiling—his only means of escape.

A member of the CIRG team rushed into the storage room and seized the suspect, allowing Mara to sit back on the third floor and calm herself.

Midway could do nothing but groan as another agent cuffed him and dragged him away from the backpacks and hazardous materials.

Still unsure exactly what happened, Sam asked, "Was that our explosion or theirs?"

"It was ours," Naila responded. "Nothing like the sounds of a well-timed explosion to get your blood pumping, Sam."

"Jonathan, situation?" Sam asked.

"Contained, Sam. We've got some cleanup to do but the situation is fully contained," Jonathan said.

Sam plopped into the nearest chair and sunk his head in his hands.

Bradley and Derek shared a hearty handshake and a relieved chuckle.

Director Mendez, who hadn't said a word since Bradley rolled into the room, stood, walked over to Bradley, and said, "A goddamn Hollywood movie explosion soundtrack. Fucking brilliant!"

"I was hoping we wouldn't need to go that far, but I always like to have a backup plan just in case," Bradley replied, shaking Mendez's hand.

"What I wouldn't give to see Jim Harrison's face right now," Mendez said to Derek as they shook hands. "Sam, great work. Come see me in my office as soon as you wrap things up."

"Will do, Mike," Sam said, sounding exhausted. Sam struggled to get out of his chair. He had seemed so much in control that Bradley was shaken to see the toll the operation had taken on him. Bradley realized then the amount of pressure Sam and Derek lived with each day.

Sam walked over to Bradley with an outstretched hand and said, "Welcome to the NSB, Bradley. I have a feeling it's going to be one hell of a ride." Sam inhaled deeply, straightened himself, brushed his hair with his hand, and left the room.

"Now the real work begins," Derek said.

Bradley gazed up from his chair and asked, "What do you mean?"

"We took them alive. Now we need to get information out of them. Ali al-Haqani is still out there. And we just stuck a thorn in his ass."

Jonathan helped Mara off the floor.

"That was great work, finding this closet. How did you know?" Jonathan asked.

"I didn't," Mara replied. "But I asked myself what my friend Bradley would do. He would solve the puzzle. When I found no one on the fourth floor, I determined where the chemical room was below and found the third-floor closet. That's when I saw the hole in the floor. Look at the construction of the trap door," Mara said, pointing to the hinged square lying open and revealing the room below. "It's old. I'll bet it's been hidden under that shelf for at least nine years," she said, staring at the wire rack shelf that had been moved.

Jonathan cringed. "Which means this room hasn't been truly fireproof for that long. It's a damn good thing nothing happened."

"Al-Haqani would not have gone through all that trouble just to someday in the future implement a plan. I'd be willing to bet the university's records reveal missing chemicals from eight or nine years ago," Mara said.

"I'd say it's a good bet," Jonathan replied.

"I'll get on it."

ALL IN

A gentle breeze gave Bradley and Rusty relief from the beating sun as they headed toward the shade provided by the hundred-foot American walnut tree standing alone in the open countryside. The rich brown bark indicated the beauty of the contents within—the much sought-after planks to adorn homes and barns or create elegant furniture and fencing. But that would be a shame, Bradley thought.

Once protected by its shade, Bradley examined the fruits of the grand structure. Spherical in nature, husks of the walnuts varied in color from green to yellow, some showing signs of invading worms, but most unblemished and healthy. Bradley knew the fruit would soon drop from its branches and, not surprisingly, his thoughts went to the kitchen.

He imagined himself harvesting the meats of the husks and creating culinary treats such as raisin-walnut pie, walnut-crusted honey-glazed chicken, or a simple roasted walnut pesto sauce.

Beside him, Rusty yawned and sprawled on the cool, lush grass. Bradley looked back toward the house. Cate, Derek, and their real estate friend, Brenda, sat on the barndominium's screened back porch sipping iced tea.

The deep red house exterior expertly disguised the underlying metal construction, and with white trim accents mimicked a horse barn possibly found on a grand Kentucky estate. For Bradley, it was love at first sight.

Wheeling back toward his friends, Bradley had already formed a plan for renovations. With the portable ramp set at the front stairs, Bradley and Rusty rounded the front of the house, rolled up the ramp into the tiled foyer of the cathedral-ceilinged center of the home, then onto the hardwood floor of the living room and straight out to the back porch.

"I'll take it," Bradley said to Brenda. "When can I move in?"

Brenda's eyes sparkled with joy as her cheeks flushed. Before she could respond, Cate asked, "Bradley, are you sure? You haven't even looked at anything else."

"No, but you have, Cate. And you found the perfect place. Rusty and I will be happy here," Bradley confirmed.

"We can start the paperwork today," Brenda said.

Bradley poured himself a glass of iced tea, and the four toasted to his new home.

Conversation became animated on the ride back to Derek and Cate's. Cate suggested names of decorators and styling options. Bradley revealed his thoughts on changes to the kitchen for easier use from his chair and renovations to the master bathroom.

"The first thing I need to do is get my mother down here to look at it," Bradley said. "I won't hear the end of it if I don't let her help me decorate this time. She's been on me about the house in Revere since I moved in."

"Call them. Call your parents and make plans for them to come and stay with us. We have plenty of room, and I would love to have a house full of people for a change," Cate said. "Then Lynn and I can start shopping for furniture."

Derek chuckled. "That's it, Bradley. You do realize that you will have little influence on the furnishings of your new home. Cate, please, at least let him set up his own office."

"As long as it doesn't clash with the rest of the house, Derek," Cate smiled.

When they returned to Derek and Cate's, Bradley called his parents. He sent pictures to his father's cellphone because his mother could not figure out how to use her phone. Bradley relayed Cate's invitation, and they made plans to visit once Bradley closed the deal on the house.

As he sat on the guest room bed, an unusual feeling of excitement emerged. A new job, a new house, and a new beginning provided optimism and hope for a life of balance.

The thoughts led him to think of Cassie. He hoped she too had felt liberated of her past. He hadn't realized it before, but as he thought about her, it struck him how much alike they were. How similar her path had been, he considered, a reflection of his feelings of inadequacy and a heightened sense of obligation.

He dialed her number.

"Whitman, I didn't expect to hear from you," said Cassie.

"Papadakis, I didn't expect to call," he replied.

"How is DC?"

"Extreme. How's Boston?"

"In progress."

"I bought a house today," Bradley blurted.

"A real house? Or an old silo or bunker?" she chuckled.

Bradley smiled.

"It has a nut tree. It made me think of you," Bradley said.

"I hope that wasn't some kind of metaphor, Whitman."

Bradley howled as he hadn't in some time. His unexpected cackle took him by surprise as he could not remember the last time it occurred so naturally.

When he caught his breath, he replied, "Papadakis, besides me, you are the darkest person I know. But your wit and smile are full of light."

"And you are full of . . . ," Cassie did not finish. Instead, she sighed.

"Come visit me," Bradley said. "As soon as I get the house in order."

"I've got work," she replied.

"I know. But when did you take your last vacation?"

"I . . . ah . . . never."

"I figured as much. Come to DC. Rusty misses you. And I am in much need of a therapy session."

"Well, I suppose if it is a matter of mental health, I could take some time off—for the sake of national security."

Bradley could sense the smile that graced Cassie's lips.

She continued, "But I have to warn you. I'm not the same person I was when you left."

"How do you mean?" Bradley's face morphed to concern.

Cassie cleared her throat, then said, "I seem to have gained a few pounds."

Bradley beamed as he lifted his head toward the ceiling and exhaled a deep breath.

"Cassie, I'm so happy for you—and proud. Congratulations. I can't wait to see you."

"And you will. All of me." And then Cassie giggled, a sound that spoke volumes.

Six days had passed since the attempt on HEI, and multiple reports had circulated behind closed doors. With Derek in charge of CIRG, it did not seem odd to Bradley when Derek summoned him to his office. Bradley assumed they would receive an account of CIRG's findings.

Derek sat behind his desk with Jonathan seated by his left. Both men placed their full attention on Derek's desktop computer.

"Bradley, come in. Come around the desk. We have Mara and Nick on an online conference call," Derek said.

Bradley pushed the throttle then parked his chair to Derek's right.

Seeing Mara and Nick onscreen, Bradley smiled.

"You look radiant, Mara. Nick, you look like . . ."

Derek cut Bradley off.

"No banter this morning, guys. Alright, Mara. Start from the beginning," Derek said.

"When the investigation confirmed the materials that made up the trap door on the third floor leading into the chemical storage room were ten years old, I dove into the records. Ali al-Haqani would have been in his third year at HEI. That school year, the chemistry department recorded shortages of chemicals each month, prompting the professors to call for weekly inventory reports. The shortages continued despite every effort to control the inventory."

"What did the school do about it?" Derek asked.

"The only explanation they came up with was faulty reporting. And because the amounts were considered minimal, no action was taken. The trend continued the following year with, again, no substantial action taken. Ali al-Haqani graduated, and the following school year there were no reports of shortages."

"So evidently al-Haqani consistently stole small amounts of chemicals from the school. The question is, what did he do with them?" Derek asked.

"I think I can answer that," Mara said. "I searched old records for anything including hazardous materials or toxic fumes and found something interesting. During al-Haqani's senior year, there were seven unsolved events that could fit the criteria. Three of them occurred at HEI and four in the area surrounding the school."

Bradley said, "Jesus, I remember that. There were wild speculations about a curse of some kind. The students called it the diabolus pestis, the devil's curse."

"It took time," Mara continued, but authorities found the first incident that sent two female students into respiratory failure was caused by toxins in their dorm room rug. The students eventually recovered but have had lasting medical issues.

"I have each incident listed separately in my report but for the sake of time . . . " Mara cleared her throat and continued, "Toxic paint was the cause of two more hospitalizations, and one student died of cyanide poisoning. The origin of the poison was never discovered. Outside HEI there were unexplained instances of asphyxiation, tissue deterioration, and multiple respiratory maladies. The only explainable cause found was one instance of bacterially contaminated soil."

Derek sighed. "He was experimenting on his classmates and neighbors."

Bradley's gut wrenched. More than ten years, he thought. Something isn't right. If he's been planning this for that long, why would he bother with the targets he chose? And the methods he used?

Bradley felt the black sludge of darkness envelope his body, as if al-Haqani himself stood, pouring it over him.

"Derek, it's possible I may have grossly underestimated Ali al-Haqani's intentions," Bradley said.

"After what you just heard, how could you say that? His intention is to kill us," Derek said.

"Exactly," Bradley replied. "But he's been planning this for more than ten years. I didn't take that into consideration. He is in this for the win, not just a few small triumphs. I think he's still experimenting."

"Experimenting? For what?" Derek asked.

"Annihilation. He's studying our every move: our analysis, our response, our tactics, our strengths, and our weaknesses. He has no interest in killing a few thousand people. He wants to kill millions. And if I'm right, he's already got his weapon. I think he may be experimenting on how to deliver it."

Derek's eyes blinked rapidly. "What are you saying?"

Bradley replied, "I'm saying he's all in. He's playing Texas Hold 'em, and we've been showing him the flop, turn, and river."

"I don't know Texas Hold 'em. What does that mean?" Mara asked.

"We're showing him all the cards, Mara. He creates the situation and watches how we react."

"But we have no choice but to react," said Mara.

"Exactly," Bradley replied.

"So, where does that leave us?" Derek asked.

Bradley sighed, "Like Mara said, with no choice. We wait until he deals the next round."

I AM WHO I AM

A week later, Bradley sat with Rusty on his new back porch sipping bourbon and watching the sunset. It's a strange life I've chosen, Bradley thought. I could be sitting in the Himalayan Mountains, becoming one with my surroundings, without a care in the world. But at what cost? The cost of denying who I am and who I could become.

Bradley set his glass on the table and, with palms turned up, rested his arms on his wheelchair. He formed a circle with each index finger and thumb.

Concentrating only on his breathing, Bradley fell into a state of blissful peace. In his meditation, he stood on a hot sandy beach, the heat from the sand sending electrical charges up his legs, through his body, and out the top of his head. She rose from the water in a white flowing dress, her auburn hair blowing in the breeze. She smiled, then blew him a kiss before turning and merging back with the crystal-clear water.

Bradley spoke a mantra he had learned from an author he met while on his travels, a mantra that helped to ground him, soothe him, and prepare him for things to come. "I am who I am, I am who I'm going to be, I'm going to be who I am."

When Bradley opened his eyes, he was smiling. He lifted his drink and took the last sip as the sun disappeared over the horizon. He heard a shuffle behind him.

"Did you miss me?" Cassie bent and whispered into his ear.

"More than watching the sun rise from the mountaintops."

ACKNOWLEDGMENTS

I continue to be humbled by the incredible support and encouragement I receive from friends, family, and devoted readers. I hope this story will resonate with those who have loved, lost, and found a way to live with that loss. But this is also a story of resilience—rising from the darkness into light. May you always live in the light!

Thank you, Debra Ellis, for your expert copy editing of the manuscript. I appreciate your care, thoughtfulness, and attention to detail.

To my good friend, Brenda Anderson—your keen eye and love for Bradley contributed greatly to this book and I am forever grateful.

Fellow author Paula Francis is not only my sister, but she is also my stabilizer, soundboard, wordsmith, and cheerleader. Her insights have been invaluable and her love and support incalculable.

To my editor, publisher, and very good friend Marcia Gagliardi of Haley's Publishing—none of this would have been possible without you. Many thanks for continuing to nurture my fictional family and your encouragement.

ABOUT the AUTHOR

You can't always plan where life will take you.

That certainly proved true for Christine Noyes. Growing up a tomboy in Shrewsbury, Massachusetts, she spent her youth building forts, playing sports, and enjoying the perceived innocence of the 1960s.

Without a clear vision of what her life should be, she went where she felt most comfortable: to the kitchen. At the age of eleven, she began her work life as a dishwasher in her grandfather's restaurant. She spent the next several decades reinventing herself, becoming an accomplished chef and then a sales representative, an entrepreneur, and eventually a writer and illustrator.

Chris never chose her professions. They chose her.

When not at her keyboard, she can be found in her kitchen: back to her roots and love of cooking.

from the next Bradley Whitman novel
by Christine Noyes

MAESTRO'S MOVE
DUST TO DUST

He placed his dinner dish in the kitchen sink, kissed his wife on the cheek, and shuffled out the door. A red paisley handkerchief hung from the back pocket of his worn farmer's jeans, and the soles of his boots were thin as cloth.

The sun had just begun to sink into the horizon as the elderly farmer reached his fields. While walking among his crops, he held his hand over the top of wheat stalks as if willing them to reach for his palm. With bones creaking and expelling an involuntary grunt, the farmer knelt. He dug into the earth with his wrinkled and calloused hand, then watched the dry dirt slip back to the ground through his thick fingers. With much effort, he stood and wiped the dirt onto his chambray shirt.

He continued his walk among the rows and inspected the stalks. With rain scarce the previous fall, crops were well behind schedule in growing tillers on the main stems critical to the yield of plants. However, he knew better than to worry. It took too much energy and never provided a solution. Instead, as always, he chose to have faith.

"Be nice to me now," he spoke to his stunted crops. "I don't know how much time we have left together."

He reached for his cap, pulled it off his head, and revealed a thick crop of bright white hair. Wiping sweat from his brow, he dragged his sleeve across his forehead, then glanced at the setting sun. With its final rays, the sun seemed to concentrate all its energy on the old man. Had anyone been there to witness the moment, the sparkle from the farmer's brilliant blue eyes would have been a sight to see.

A thin smile creased his lips as he once again wiped sweat from his brow, an increasingly common occurrence. Perspiration had accompanied a slight headache, and he'd been having difficulty swallowing. Not wishing to worry her, he hadn't mentioned to his wife the discomfort he had felt the previous twenty-four hours, but something told him he was beginning his final countdown. He just hadn't expected it so quickly.

He scuffed his worn leather boots in the dirt before turning toward the farmhouse. It took only five steps before his throat swelled and reduced his air intake to almost nothing. Puss-filled blisters formed where perspiration had been, and his royal blue eyes turned black.

He collapsed to the ground with his arms by his side staring toward the heavens but seeing only darkness. He once again dug his hands into the earth, clinging to his lifelong mistress, one of the few things in his grueling life he could always depend on.

THE DEVIL'S CURSE

Bradley Whitman slumped in his wheelchair as the gravity of his thoughts sunk his chin to his chest. The computer screen he studied displayed an archived Hopkinton Engineering Institute's newsletter dated ten years earlier. The headline read, *Diabolus Pestis Strikes Again.*

Diabolus Pestis, the devil's curse, Bradley translated. He remembered the mysterious string of events chronicled in the newsletter from the nearby institute. At the time, he had been with the Chelsea, Massachusetts, division of the Federal Bureau of Investigation for only two years. Fresh from graduation from MIT, Bradley's old friend, then Supervisory Special Agent Derek Richards, had hired him as an analyst.

It was no surprise that Bradley ended up working with Derek. Each had done his best to make it happen. But life, as usual, is ever-changing. Derek accepted a promotion to executive assistant director of criminal, cyber, response, and services that moved him to headquarters in Washington. Nearly nineteen months later, Bradley's new position with the National Security Branch brought him there as well. Although Bradley no longer worked directly for Derek, they occasionally worked the same cases.

Bradley tried to recall circumstances around unsolved, life-threatening incidents attributed to the satanic spell that occurred at the prestigious Hopkinton Engineering Institute but remembered little. As he read through old issues of *HEI*

Weekly, he couldn't help but recall the underlying feeling of helplessness he refused to show in those days.

In everything other than his physical being, Bradley had always had the confidence of a mountain lion doing battle with a mouse. But as a young man, the inability to use his legs caused him to feel inadequate. The one-in-a-million enterovirus he contracted at the age of six had cost him his original dream of becoming a marine like his father.

At twelve after a chance encounter with Derek during an FBI investigation, he made up his mind to join the FBI. He had hoped to be a field agent, but once again, his physical limitations held him to an analyst position with the bureau. Even so, he had worked hard over the years to conquer his psychological flaws, the most prominent of which was his savior complex.

But then, sitting shirtless in his wheelchair in front of his computer, Bradley delved into the actions of the man who had since been identified as responsible for the atrocities at HEI. The same man he had grossly underestimated just eight months earlier when he attacked Bradley's own beloved alma mater remained a threat. And with that thought, Bradley felt the scrutiny of a sword-wielding mouse slash at his lion's confidence.

"You said you were going to the bathroom," a voice said from behind.

Bradley straightened in his chair, then turned it around to face her.

Wearing nothing but his blue oxford shirt, Cassie rigidly stood with hands on hips. Her short black hair sprouted in every direction, and her five-foot, five-inch frame loomed larger than it was due to the menacing glare from her deep brown eyes. With that gaze, Bradley knew she could instill fear into most everyone with whom she came in contact. She had an unpredictable aura about her. The only evident softness to Cassie Papadakis was her smooth, caramel skin. Bradley allowed his eyes to travel from her accusing glare down to her bare feet.

Her defiant stance made him grin.

"What are you smiling about?" she barked.

"Am I smiling? Sorry. I know how you hate it when people seem happy," Bradley said.

"What the hell, Bradley. You're out here working again? It's Sunday. I've got to leave today. It's hardly worth me coming all this way if you're not going to pay attention to me."

Rusty, Bradley's black-and-rust-colored Doberman Pinscher pranced into the room and sat next to Cassie.

Cassie continued. "I get more attention from Rusty than from you."

"I couldn't sleep." Bradley replied.

"I hadn't planned on going back to sleep, numbnuts. I thought you were coming right back to bed."

"That was two hours ago, Cassie."

"Yeah, well, I fell back to sleep. But that's not the point. I thought we could go another round, but if you'd rather sit in front of your computer, then fine, I'll just pack and go home." She finished with a deep huff.

"Are you done?" Bradley asked.

Cassie began to open her mouth, but Bradley held up his hands in defeat.

"I'm sorry, you're right. I've been preoccupied, and that's not fair to you. Look," Bradley said as he turned back around, "I'm shutting down the computer."

For a moment, neither said a word.

"I'm really sorry," Bradley told her as he inched his way toward her.

"No, I'm sorry. That was stupid. It's just that . . ."

"What?" he asked as he reached for her hands.

"Sometimes I wonder if this is a bad idea."

"Why would you think that?"

"Because I live in Boston, and you live in DC. And it's not like we're a couple or anything. I mean, don't you think our relationship is a little weird?"

"Maybe unconventional, but not weird. I like you, Cassie. I like how we spend time together without having to worry about the whole relationship thing." Bradley paused, then continued. "Unless you're changing your mind about that."

"No. I'm still not ready for a relationship. I'm not sure I ever will be."

"I told you before. I think you're more than ready. And you don't need to worry about hurting my feelings. I'd be really happy for you if you found someone special. I want that for you."

Cassie moved to the couch. Bradley followed and parked his chair in front of her. Rusty jumped on the couch and cuddled beside her.

She sighed, then said, "I'm going on a date."

He didn't expect it. A boot to the gut. A totally irrational response to Cassie's news. But he wouldn't let it show.

"That's great! Who is he?"

"A guy I met in court."

"A petty thief?" Bradley teased.

"A lawyer. He was assigned to a case that I investigated for Damien. He's been after me for a month to go to dinner with him. He finally caught me at a weak moment."

"A weak moment? What does one of those look like on you?"

"Stop, Bradley. I'm serious. What am I going to do?"

"Is he a good guy?" Bradley asked.

"Damien says he is."

One of the best lawyers in Boston, Damien Sullivan, had helped Bradley prove his friend, Zayt, a Navy Seal who served three tours in Afghanistan, innocent when he was framed for murder. Bradley and Cassie met when Damien hired her as the private investigator on Zayt's case. She was largely responsible for Zayt being exonerated. Bradley and Cassie had worked on the case together but not without personal clashes. They eventually found mutual ground and ultimately a mutual bed.

"Well, I trust Damien's judgement, don't you?" Bradley asked.

"Yes, that's not the problem."

"Then what is?"

She flashed him the "You-know-what-the-problem-is" glare.

Bradley knew the look. Before they met, Cassie was in a long-term abusive relationship. After she extricated herself from it, she found it nearly impossible to trust men. Bradley understood that brandishing an intimidating personality was Cassie's way of protecting herself.

Bradley grasped her hand and said, "You trust me, right?"

"Most of the time."

"Come on, Cassie."

"Yes, I trust you. But you're you! An FBI nerd in a . . ."

"Wheelchair?" Bradley interrupted.

"I was going to say a dorky oxford shirt, but now that you mention it, if I'm being brutally honest, the wheelchair did make it easier. Sorry."

"Really? You didn't seem to cut me any slack when we met," Bradley laughed, hoping to lighten the mood.

"Seriously. What am I going to do about Tom?"

"Tom?" Bradley felt a twinge of jealousy, a useless emotion since he decided he would never again allow himself to fall in love. "You're going to dress in your best baggy cargo pants, do something with that electromagnetic mop on your head, and go have a nice dinner with Tom."

"I don't know if I can."

"You can. You're ready."

Rusty lay his head on Cassie's lap and gazed into her eyes.

"See? Rusty agrees. Now, are you going to pack? Or are we going to—how did you so eloquently put it?—go another round!"

The corners of Cassie's mouth curled, but only slightly. "Lead on, Maestro."

Bradley laughed at the use of the nickname his college chemistry professor had given him. "I never should have told you about that. I don't know why I did. I never even told Derek about it, and he's my best friend."

"But the name fits you so well," Cassie smiled. With Bradley's hand still in hers, she stood, and they made their way to the bedroom.

Three hours later, Bradley booted his computer. While the desktop updated, he thought of Cassie on her way to the airport. The simple, uncomplicated relationship they had had seemed anything but at that moment.

He felt uneasy about his involuntary reaction to her news of dating. Not because he was in love with her. He knew he would never fall in love again. And he knew she didn't love him. They were two broken people who each used the other to try to make themselves feel whole. And it had worked until that morning. Bradley knew he had no right to feel betrayed, but illogically, he did.

"You're a selfish bastard, Bradley Whitman."

Lying by his feet, Rusty looked up.

"What are you looking at?"

Bradley reached down to pet him, and Rusty gladly accepted the affection.

Once the desktop came to life, his research captured his full attention. He didn't take his eyes off the screen for the next four and a half hours.

The focus of his research was a man named Ali al-Haqani.

COLOPHON

MVB Verdigris is a Garalde text family for the digital age. Inspired by work of sixteenth-century punchcutters Robert Granjon, Hendrik van den Keere, and Pierre Haultin, MVB Verdigris celebrates tradition but is not beholden to it. Created to deliver good typographic color as text, Mark van Bronkhorst's design meets the needs of today's designer using today's paper and press. A full-featured OpenType release with an added titling companion, it's optimized for the latest typesetting technologies, too.

Garalde: the word itself sounds antique and arcane to anyone who isn't fresh out of design school, but the sort of typeface it describes is actually quite familiar to all of us. Despite its age—born fairly early in printing's history—the style has fared well. Garaldes are the typefaces of choice for books and other long reading.

www.ingramcontent.com/pod-product-compliance
Lightning Source LLC
Chambersburg PA
CBHW050206030726

47505CB00005B/1541